About the Author

Valerie Maple, born in Wareham, Dorset in 1950. Married with grown children, she travels to many places around the globe. Her inspiration came from the Canadian Rockies and subsequent cruise to Alaska. Valerie enjoys time with her family, travel, quilting and reading. Living on the south coast, she enjoys being beside the sea.

For my family, with love.

Valerie Maple

THE GIRL IN THE TURQUOISE DRESS

AUSTIN MACAULEY
PUBLISHERS LTD.

A CIP catalogue record for this title is available from the British Library.

ISBN 9781785546761 (Paperback)
ISBN 9781785546778 (Hardback)

www.austinmacauley.com

First Published (2015)
Austin Macauley Publishers Ltd.
25 Canada Square
Canary Wharf
London
E14 5LQ

Printed and bound in Great Britain

A very big thank you to my family; Eric, Dawn, Geoff, Carolyn, Jack, Charlotte and Noah for the help patience and encouragement they gave me with this, my first novel. Thank you, Carolyn for designing the wonderful cover. Thank you Nora, for your help.

PROLOGUE

Dorset summer 1899

Daisy was crying. Keeping a secret was a painful business. Deep, heart-wrenching sobs racked her body as she curled up in the faded armchair in the old railway carriage. Her surroundings reminded her of her dear granny and grandpa, now dead, but who once lived in there. The aroma of the violet toilet water granny used still clung to the cushions and curtains. The carriage sat at the bottom of the garden, surrounded by the chickens that pecked and scratched the bare earth. She felt that she couldn't take any more. Nobody was around to hear her despair, except for the chickens.

Slowly rising from the chair, Daisy stepped off the doorstep, leaving the door open allowing the hens to peck around inside. She noticed nothing as she made her way past the washing hanging on the line and the pigsty, through the back door, across the scullery and up the narrow stairs to her bedroom. Bending down, she pulled out the cardboard box from under her bed and blew the dust off the top. Taking off the lid, she released the turquoise dress from its covering of tissue paper. 'This is beautiful' she whispered as she held it to her face. The silk caressed her cheek and she noticed that it still smelled of honeysuckle. She'd expected it to smell musty; the dried flowers in amongst the tissue paper ensured the dress retained a pleasant aroma. Holding the garment in her hands, she now knew what she had to do. Having decided she quickly took off the fustian garment they forced her to wear and stepped into the silk dress. It took her a while to fasten the tiny pearl buttons on the front of the bodice. The dress still fitted her perfectly. The fabric whispered as it flowed around her legs. It curved into the small of her back like a second skin, flaring out over her hips.

Keeping the canvas shoes on her feet, Daisy flew down the stairs, out of the front door, through the gate and onto the road verge. She knew the times of the trains and realised there wasn't much time before the London train reached the halt. She ran like the wind. She was going to meet Tom, she'd promised to wave to him from the crossing gates. She'd go one better than wave.

Stan and Ada's house was situated right next to the platform at Thorpe Matravers' halt. Stan, the crossing keeper was just closing the gates to traffic, prior to the London to Wareham train speeding through. He then turned around and slowly ambled back to the tiny ticket office. As soon as the train was through, he would go back and open the gates again. Not much passed along the lane that the railway tracks crossed; just a few farm carts and the carriages belonging to the gentry at the big house.

'A cup of tea is just what I need,' mumbled Stan to himself.

Standing in her kitchen and looking out of her window, Ada saw a flash of turquoise dash past at speed. 'Funny' she mumbled to herself. 'That looked just like Daisy Evans. She should slow down 'afore she 'as an accident.'

CHAPTER ONE

Dorset September 1897

The sun drenched gardens looked beautiful, the borders and rockeries ablaze with colour; chrysanthemums, asters, dahlias and phlox in vivid red, orange and white glowed in the late summer sun. On either side of the path stretched finely mowed lawns, their broad sweep broken here and there by sturdy oaks that cast long shadows over the gravel paths. In the near distance, in contrast to the green of the grass, the stubble of the newly harvested hay fields gleamed tan and gold in the late sunshine; haystacks rising in the middle of the fields like watching sentinels. Looking stately in her russet coloured velvet dress, and buttoned black boots, Matilda, Lady Thorpe strode from her house, down the Lady's Walk towards the Big Lawn and the marquee where the annual village harvest supper was to be held, as was the custom, every September. This year, the evening was warm and fine. The winds of the previous day had quite abated allowing the flaps of the marquee pegged on the largest lawn, to be tied back and ripple in the gentle breeze. Last year the rain poured incessantly, destroying the decorations, followed by a thunderstorm which completely spoiled the evening. Matilda's dressed hair was hidden by her wide brimmed hat that kept the sun from her pale skin, and hid the fine oval bone structure of her face and her big hazel eyes. In one hand she held a rolled parasol and in the other a small bag. A warm fringed shawl was wrapped loosely around her shoulders and the scent of the lavender water she used wafted on the breeze. Her lady's maid, Jane Evans, followed reverently a few steps behind, her black bombazine dress and cotton petticoats rustling as she moved.

Waiting on the lawn smoking a large cigar hoping to ward off midges, was her husband, Harry, Lord Thorpe, landowner, philanthropist, squire of Thorpe Matravers village and Justice of the Peace. His broad-shouldered figure was immaculately dressed in a lightweight dark coloured suit, cravat, and white high collar shirt. He held a soft felt hat in his hand, occasionally flapping it around the flying insects that pestered him. As he waited, Harry's thoughts were of last year's harvest supper. His eldest son and heir, William had been here, but now he had left Thorpe and travelled to Alaska to join the gold rush. He was a budding journalist and artist. As part of his craving for something exciting to do, he embarked on a mission to explore and report back first-hand how it was to be part of this exciting but dangerous event. Will sent back items and drawings describing his travels via Liverpool, New York, Ottawa and Vancouver. Many of these articles having been printed in several publications of note such as '*Travel News Monthly*' and *The Dorset Traveller;* it was known that a loyal fan base was expectantly reading his exploits. The family also avidly read the few letters he wrote home, which detailed more personal news, such as his health and finances, giving them a clearer picture of his experiences, alongside some personal illustrations.

Harry and Matilda's second son, Tom, was restless as well. He expended some of his energy in turning a corner of the estate into a folly park. After visiting a similar park in Shropshire he decided to build one at Thorpe Park.

Two miles from the house and park was situated the Thorpe Matravers Pottery, whose one hundred and fifty foot chimney could be seen for many miles around. Managed by Tom, Harry built it as a place of employment for the labourers in the village and surrounding areas, as due to the collapse of the button making industry in the area, unemployment had taken a dreadful toll. Attached to the pottery was a small railway that also employed workers. The pottery and railway was Thomas's domain and Harry rarely intervened in the business.

'My dear,' said Matilda cheerfully. 'The farm cart will be here any moment and you seem very pensive. What is on your mind?'

'There you are, my dear. I was thinking of Will and Tom. We haven't had a letter from Will for a while, I do hope all is well,' said Harry, as he put his arm around her shoulders. He looked at his beautiful wife; he was so lucky to be married to such a woman; elegant, kind, compassionate. The improvements she had made to the village pleased him immensely, in particularly the church school full of children, many of whom had never been taught before. The villagers in the past had struggled for so long with poverty and lack of employment. Now, their work together, building the pottery and church school improved the lot of many of the village people, as had the home farm and surrounding farms owned by the Thorpe Matravers estate. He was, quite rightly, proud to have her by his side. The villagers were pleased to be able to celebrate this festival with their employer and family; who were remarkable people and landlords.

'Here they are, now we can get on with the festivities.'

As Harry spoke a farm cart appeared. It was highly decorated with wild and cultivated flowers, greenery and stalks of corn. Being Her Majesty Queen Victoria's Diamond Jubilee year, red, white and blue bunting was strategically placed all around the festivity areas. The proud farm horse was also decorated with a garland of flowers around his neck. Harry and Matilda smiled at hearing the young village girls squealing with laughter as the young men gallantly helped them down off the cart. Amongst the girls were Daisy and her sister, Ivy, the daughters of Jane and Bert Evans; Bert being the foreman of the pottery, and Jane, Matilda's maid. Davey, a furnace stoker at the pottery, was fond of Ivy. 'Yer we be, then Ivy my love' he chuckled as he helped her off the cart. At seventeen, he was two years older than Ivy and was trying to gain her affection by pinching her firm, young buttocks, believing she liked it.

'Stop it, Davey!' shrieked Ivy, feigning disapproval but pleased nonetheless at the attention.

'Dance wi' me, tonight, Ivy,' he pleaded. 'Then I'll walk yer 'ome, make sure you get in safe.'

'Why would I want to dance with you, Davey Barnes? I want to dance with someone 'and some.'

'andsome is as 'ansome does, Ivy. I could do you 'ansome anytime.'

'Ya 'aint getting the chance. Can ya hear 'im, Jessie?'

'Just ignore him.'

'But he keeps pinchin' me bum.'

'Then clout 'im round his earole.'

Momentarily giving up on Ivy, Davey joined his mates who were heading for a barrel of ale and the girls ran giggling into the marquee. There was much laughter, too, from the village folk walking to the event behind the cart. This way of travelling to the supper was a Thorpe family tradition, having been started by Harry's grandfather who had originally built Thorpe House. Harry and Matilda were keen to uphold the traditions.

The men had put up the marquee and placed bales of straw around the inside edges. The marquee was also decorated with garlands of wild flowers, crowns of wheat and sheaves of corn. Candles, set in greenery, were placed around the tables, and oil lamps hung from poles set firmly in the ground. A trestle table and chairs were set up on a rostrum for the Thorpe family, alongside two trestles covered with white damask cloths set ready for the food. The staff in the big house spent days cooking meat, bread, pickles and suchlike, and baking bread and pies, sweet and savoury. The two dairymaids, Jessie and Annie produced the cheese and cream, which they made daily in the dairy shed. The ale had been delivered by dray from the brewery in Wareham. Six of the village women had decorated the cart and horse that morning. At five in the evening, the cart was led around the village collecting the girls, young men and those too elderly or infirm to walk and make its way slowly to Thorpe estate. All the villagers wore their Sunday best: the girls very pretty in cotton or muslin sprigged dresses and bonnets decorated with flowers; the men feeling uncomfortable in their suits with highly polished boots: the women's shawls draped elegantly around their shoulders. This all combined to produce a very pretty picture, thought Matilda as she looked around her. Also, this year, Lord Thorpe had hired a photographer from Poole to produce memorable pictures of the occasion. Harry had agreed to Mr Martin Kimber's request to include some of the pictures he produced in a pamphlet he was creating to celebrate the Jubilee. Will would enjoy seeing them upon his return. These pamphlets would be sent as far away as London.

'Photographs are a wonderful record, Lord Thorpe,' said Mr Kimber expansively. 'Wonderful to pore over in years to come, especially as cold winter nights will soon be upon us.'

'I'm looking forward to seeing them,' replied Harry. 'I wish we could have had more photographs taken of the children. Maybe grandchildren will come along soon to have photographs taken. We will invite you to take them, Mr Kimber. Now, we must get on with the festivities. Feel free to take any photographs you care to. Make sure you have a drink and plenty to eat,' said the genial host.

As folk sauntered into the marquee and seated themselves comfortably, Harry noticed Tom amongst the group of young men gathered around the village girls. Educated privately, Tom was allowed all the advantages his father's money could afford. He was six feet tall, had dark hair cut short, brown eyes, heavy brows and a muscular build due to the hauling of the sandstone rocks as he helped build the follies. His skin was tanned and he was aware that women found him attractive.

'Tom needs a wife, Matilda. We should look again amongst our friends and acquaintances for a suitable match. He's too familiar with those wenches,' said Harry, pensively. 'What became of Colonel Harris's daughter, Victoria? I thought she and Tom hit it off really well. Haven't seen her around lately.'

'She married Digby, Marquess of Seabourne. It appears to be a love match. Georgina Mellor is coming to lunch tomorrow. Tom has said he will join us. She is a lovely girl, if a bit scatty.'

Harry strode into the marquee with Matilda on his arm.

'I think there's plenty of time for that, my dear.' Matilda replied, casting a glance at her husband. 'He's enjoying himself. Anyway, Will is the eldest; he should be the first son to marry.'

Harry stopped suddenly, Matilda nearly tripping but still holding on to his arm. Turning towards her, with a pensive look he added quietly 'We'll enjoy this evening, my dear. It all looks very jolly in here.'

The family took their places at the top table. Harry and Matilda's only daughter, Amy and her husband Eddy Harris-Fletcher, were already seated; Florence, Amy's King Charles Cavalier spaniel, lying under the table hopeful for dropped food scraps. Amy had a lovely oval face, with high cheekbones. Her brown eyes were big and bright with long lashes, the same as her brother Tom. She had inherited her mother's slenderness and grace and was a beautiful woman, with smooth, flawless skin. Eddy was considerably older than his wife with a tendency to overeating and therefore was overweight. He also drank heavily. His shifty eyes wandered occasionally to the giggling girls sitting together on the other side of the marquee. Amy was aware of her husband's wandering eye, but was confident that he loved her too much to stray. The Reverend Richard McCree, the vicar of Thorpe Matravers, was already seated with his wife.

'Would you say grace, please, Richard?' asked Harry politely.

Banging a spoon on the table and coughing nervously, Richard asked for silence then mournfully said grace. He, naturally, took his calling seriously, and some thought him dull, for his sermons often sent older members of the congregation to sleep. Next to him, his wife, Clarissa, sat very straight in her chair, looking as if something rather nasty was under her nose. Always looking drab, tonight she had taken no account of the festivities when dressing to go out. She wore a plain chocolate brown dress; her hair pulled back severely from her forehead, rolled into a bun and enclosed in a black net. Although appearing as if she felt herself in status above most of the villagers, she was a very hard-working woman; if called upon at any time, she would leave the vicarage and give assistance. Matilda, in particular, admired Clarissa and valued her friendship; they often worked together in the village, visiting the poor and elderly. They occasionally took nourishing broths to those too ill to care for themselves.

The place filled up quickly, and was noisy with the sound of chatter and laughter; the village band was warming up for the dancing to commence after supper. Three members of the band tuned their fiddles, whilst a fourth played a small accordion, the sound of their tuning rising above the din. When ready, they played such tunes as The Pearl Polka, Speed the Plough and The Old Woman Tossed in a Basket. The dancing was instantaneous and the villagers changed hands and partners as the jogs, reels and polkas decreed; the Gay Gordons; Cumberland Square Eight; Circassia Circle; the Family Waltz. The whole place was sent into a whirl, apart from the widows and elderly, who sat watching the spectacle and remembering their youthful days. The aroma of dancers becoming warmer and perspiring freely, mixed with the scent of the flowers, pipe tobacco and hay soon filled the marquee with a pungent atmosphere.

'My dear, time we went,' announced Harry after a short while. 'Let's leave these good people to their fun.' Matilda glanced anxiously at Tom before she left the marquee; he appeared to be spending a lot of time with Daisy, Jane's daughter. Oh, well, she thought, as she made her way to the house, he knows how to behave.

Tom, meanwhile, was certainly enjoying the evening. He was fully aware of his mother's designs to find him a suitable wife, but he didn't feel ready to settle down yet. He enjoyed dancing with pretty girls, and whilst Victoria was a marvellous shot with the guns, he didn't really fancy her as his wife. He was pleased she married Digby, he was much more her type of husband, and he looked forward to hearing about their honeymoon in Italy.

Daisy Evans sat on a bale of straw surrounded by other young ladies. Her beauty and her wonderful auburn hair singled her out from the other girls. Daisy knew she was pretty and she always tried to make the best of herself in a proper, demure way. Usually, she wore her hair pinned up when at school or out, tonight she had just tied it back with an emerald green ribbon. When she let her hair down completely at bedtime or when she washed it, it cascaded down her back like a shiny, silky mane.

'If, at going to bed, a girl puts her shoes at right angles with each other in the shape of a T, and say "Hoping this night my true love to see, I place my shoes in the form of a T" they do say she be sure to see her future 'usband in a dream,' said Emma excitedly.

'Well, I be gonna try 'en' explained Mary, I be looking fer an 'usband.' The other girls all laughed and chattered prettily.

I need to see Daisy Evans without it appearing obvious, thought Tom, as he stood with his hands in his pockets watching the other dancers. Why do I want to see her? What possible motive can I have? There can be no future with her. I can't be seen with her, yet I really do want to be with her. So, taking his time, he sauntered across the marquee and approached her.

Noticing Tom walking towards her, as she stood at the edge of the dancing, Daisy flashed a broad smile.

'Any man who would leave you standing on your own at the edge of the dance floor clearly doesn't deserve you,' whispered Tom, thinking how pretty she looked in her new pale green floral printed cotton dress. 'Dance with me?'

'Yes, that I will. But why do you ask me? There are girls here far prettier than me.'

'No one's prettier than you, Miss Evans.'

Daisy felt pleased at the compliment and excited to be asked by the young master; after all, being a teaching assistant she felt herself just a little above the other girls in status. Her friends, she noticed, were eyeing the young men gathered around the beer barrels in the hope of finding partners themselves. Taking her by the hand Tom led her into the circle. Holding her around the waist, he now inhaled the smell of her, a mixture of soap, lavender and of the grasses she wore around her hair. He was intoxicated by her presence. She, in turn, felt a surge of blood through her veins that made her temples throb and tied her stomach in knots. Off they went into the dance. He was an adept dancer and led her expertly. What was it about him that induced this physical reaction in her? She wanted to curl up in his arms and be pampered by his caresses. She wanted to feel his arms around her all night – every night. After dancing a reel, then a jig, their breathless energy leaving them sated, Tom suggested they take some air outside. Stepping out of the marquee they both noticed the change in temperature; the heat from their bodies following the energetic dancing dissipated in the cool evening air. Holding her hand, as Tom walked Daisy to a seat on the lawn, she glanced around and took in her surroundings. Bats flew around in the distance, feeding greedily on the midges. Lanterns hung from decorated poles and their brightness disturbed many moths, which blindly fluttered towards the light. Tom wanted to hold her, to run his hands through her thick hair and to dress her in fine clothes. Suppressing a shiver, she wrapped her shawl around her shoulders.

'You look cold,' said Tom casually, 'let me warm you up.'

'Oh, Master Tom, you mustn't be so forward.'

'Why not, I'm only going to put my arm around your shoulders. There, see, do you feel warmer now?'

'Yes, Master Tom.'

'Call me Tom, don't be stuffy,' he laughed. He leaned closer to her and brushed his lips upon hers, so fleetingly that Daisy wondered if it had really happened.

'We should get back to the dancing, Daisy.' Aroused, Tom was suddenly on his feet and holding out his hand to her and helped her to her feet. A frightened blackbird flew off, having been perched on the top of the marquee. The sound of him calling echoed in the still evening air.

Inside a reel being in full swing, Tom took her by the waist and pulled her into the dance, moving easily on feet lighter than anyone would have thought. Her friends looked on in envy as Daisy danced every dance with Tom; in between dances he attentively brought her drinks of mead. When she said she was hungry, he filled a plate full of tasty food and attentively brought it to her, before going back for a plate of food for himself. They sat together on a bale of hay and ate heartily. Tom was so handsome, every girl at the supper wanted to dance with him, to be held in his arms, but he had eyes only for Daisy.

At midnight it was time for everyone to leave the supper and dance. Going home was a two-mile walk along a dry, chalky road. The brightly lit full moon made the going easier. The men wandered drunkenly, whilst the women walked sedately in a party together. Some of the young men and girls having paired up during the evening straggled behind the adults, whispering and giggling.

'Now, Davey, you can stop that,' exclaimed Ivy, as Davey started pinching her bottom again. 'Stop pestering me. I aint gonna walk with you alone, so go away.'

'You'll change yer mind, Ivy, I know yer will one of these days. I knows yer fancies the pants off me,' laughed Davey, full of himself.

Ivy tutted and, catching up with her friends slowly sauntered home, feeling tired.

'Yer, Daisy, you be doin' alright tonight with Master Tom. We's all envious,' Mary remarked. 'Did he kiss yer when yer went outside?'

'Mind your own, Mary. We both enjoyed the evening and that's all.'

Daisy realised that it would be difficult being careful not to let her friends know how much she liked Tom. She didn't want to be the victim of gossip around the village. That night, as Daisy lay in the bed she shared with Ivy, she couldn't sleep for thinking about Tom. She had met the man of her dreams and was excited. He was so handsome and danced with her. She remained awake for the rest of the night, reliving the whole evening, the words they spoke to each other, the dancing, and the smell of him. She never felt happier in her whole life, despite her apprehension at the thought that he was unobtainable.

CHAPTER TWO

A few evenings later, as Daisy left the school, and walked through the heath towards her home, she heard footsteps behind her, then her name spoken.

'Hello, Daisy.'

'Hello,' she replied, turning around to see who it was, and feeling slightly startled.

'Meet me at the railway crossing tonight at nine and we can go for a walk. I know where we can listen to the nightingales singing. There's no need to tell anyone else,' he said abruptly.

'I'm not sure about that, Tom. Why must we keep quiet about meeting?'

'My parents won't like it.'

'Well, neither would mine,' sniffed Daisy. She felt affronted. 'I won't meet you, it wouldn't be right.'

'Of course we should meet. I like you. Do you like me?'

'Yes, I do. But I'm only a teaching assistant, and you're from the big house. Goodnight, Tom.' She walked quickly away.

Feeling dejected and rejected, Tom decided he had no option but to walk back home. He would woo Daisy some other way; perhaps he had been too bold.

Daisy felt let down. She hadn't expected Tom to take such a tone with her. He had been quite abrupt. She understood that it wouldn't be right to tell everyone that they were keen on each other, but the way he spoke to her was most unsettling. She was disappointed. Perhaps her attitude should have been different. Now she would worry that he wouldn't want to see her again.

Two evenings later, leaving the house after she and Ivy had cleared the dinner dishes, Daisy took a walk along the lane towards the heath. She took a deep, satisfying breath. The smoke from the pottery was being blown by the wind away from the village, for once. This is the best place in the world to live, she thought. As she passed the field holding Farmer Bright's bull, she had to walk carefully around the puddles. She had been walking for about ten minutes when she saw a horse and rider coming towards her. She stood on the grassy verge to let them pass, but the rider slowed, and as he reached her, lifted his hat. 'Miss Evans, we meet again!' Tom looked down at her. 'She's very gentle.' He patted the sleek brown neck. 'Say hello to Miss Evans, Aurora.' His mount obliged by nodding her head and snorting through her nostrils, making Daisy laugh. 'Will you allow me to walk with you?' asked Tom.

'All right,' she said. 'I would like that.' Daisy's heart began to beat faster. Just the sight of Tom was enough to give her palpitations. He looked smart in his riding clothes of beige breeches and russet coloured tweed jacket. His white shirt collar was tied with a cream cravat. She noticed he was wearing soft leather gloves. Jumping down from Aurora, he held her reins in one hand and gently held Daisy's hand with the other as he steered both her and the animal around the next puddle.

They walked on in silence for a while, both appreciating the clumps of cowslips, celandines and early primroses growing along the banks of the lane. After a while, the heathland slowly receded as darkness fell. Tom still held onto Daisy's hand.

'I must go back…' stated Daisy at the same time as Tom was saying 'How are…' Realising that they both spoke at once, they laughed together.

'Go on, Daisy, what were you saying?' encouraged Tom.

'I must start to go back. My parents will wonder where I am.'

Without speaking, Tom turned Aurora around and they headed back the way they had come. He halted at Farmer Bailey's field, where he tied his horse to a wooden fence post.

'Thank you, Tom. I enjoyed your company,' breathed Daisy, quietly. She really enjoyed being with him and Aurora was so funny.

'Can I meet you here again? Tomorrow night? Please.' Tom leaned forward, before mounting his horse, and kissed Daisy on the nose.

'I'll try, but I can't promise. It depends on whether my mother leaves me chores to do.' Saying which, she strode off up the lane, dodging the puddles. The joy of this evening would stay in her mind for a long while. Tom looked at her retreating figure and smiled.

'Come on, Aurora,' he said, as he turned her round again. 'Home to your warm stable and my dinner.'

Daisy turned after a few yards and watched Tom as he cantered away on his mount. She was pleased they were friends again. He had acted a gentleman this evening. By choice she was still a virgin. She could have had her pick of youths from the village but she had spurned them all. She was setting her sights higher than village yokels. Tom was interested in her and just maybe they could become very good friends. She doubted much else would happen.

As their clandestine meetings continued in the following weeks, Daisy realised that she loved Tom, he was all she had ever dreamed of in a man; but where was this leading? Every time she heard black birds shrieking, she was reminded of the harvest supper and their first kiss. As their romance continued through autumn, they found different places and ways to meet. One Sunday afternoon Tom helped Daisy pick blackberries. Sitting on a boulder with her, he licked the blood-red juice that was dribbling between her fingers, as she looked at him with love in her eyes. She never let him go further than kissing; after all, she went to church regularly and been warned by her mother what happened to girls who allowed men to take liberties. But she would feel weak-kneed when he took her in his arms, and when he kissed her on the lips she would feel his breathing coming harder and faster and in turn she felt she would swoon with desire.

One Saturday, Tom took Daisy to Weymouth on the train. They walked hand in hand around the harbour watching the fishermen unload their boats hauling the fish they caught onto the quay. The smell of the salty sea and the pungent aroma of the dead fish stayed with them both for hours, which made a talking point on the return train journey. Arriving at Wareham Railway Station, Tom was met by his coachman for the drive home and Daisy walked. Tom felt unhappy about the situation, but it was a necessary precaution if they were to keep their meetings secret.

'It adds to the excitement and mystique of the day,' Daisy told him just before they arrived at the station.

Another day, they caught the train at Wareham and travelled in the opposite direction from Weymouth, to Corfe Castle. The small tank engine huffed and puffed its way up the inclines.

'It's travelling so slowly that I'm tempted to jump out of the train, pick wild flowers growing on the embankment, and then climb back in,' joked Tom, making Daisy laugh. Arriving at the town and after discussing the story of Lady Bankes, who had defended her castle without success against the army during the Civil War of 1643, they climbed up the steep path to the top of the Castle and looked down to the old town, all the houses being built of stone with grey walls and stone roofs. Then, having eaten lunch at the Greyhound Inn, they wandered around the narrow lanes, visited the beautiful, very old church and the old town hall, before returning to the railway station.

As autumn approached and evenings became colder, Tom and Daisy would watch the wildlife on the heath preparing for their migration; the swifts and swallows darting overhead, catching the last of the flying insects. One evening they watched a skein of geese flying in short formation, calling their croaking, anxious cry.

'They've flown in from the harbour,' said Tom as he stood with his arm around Daisy's shoulder. 'By next week they will be gone.'

'I can feel the salty breeze beginning to rise. Autumn is certainly in the air.' Daisy enjoyed the beauty of the changing seasons.

'Listen. You can hear the rustling and whispering of the grasses.' Tom was appreciating nature even more now. 'Before I began to love you, Daisy, I enjoyed being outdoors and building my follies and designing the Park. But since we have been walking out together, I have begun to appreciate nature in a deeper sense. You have taught me so much. I didn't realise just how much beauty there is in the heathland.'

'I love bringing the children out here for nature walks. Their enquiring minds are delightful. We collect grasses, cones, empty birds' egg cases, anything else we find for the nature table.'

'I love, you, Daisy Evans,' smiled Tom, as he kissed her gently before taking her back to the lane leading to her home.

In winter, on cold evenings and Sunday afternoons, they would wander through the follies, Daisy wrapped in her heavy shawl and Tom in his greatcoat and then they would move to the hermitage, where Tom had left a blanket and cushions. Here they would just sit and cuddle. The need to keep their love secret added just the right flavour of excitement to their meetings. At Christmas he had been impressed in the way she organised the nativity with the children at the school. She was firm, professional, and yet fun to be with when they were alone together. As winter turned into spring, Tom became convinced that she was the woman he could spend the rest of his life with. He sent her an embroidered card for Valentine's Day which she treasured.

CHAPTER THREE

As the late spring sun dipped behind the stonework of the largest folly in the park, Tom gave a huge sigh of satisfaction as he stood on the path looking at the view. Intricate pathways led uphill and down again, past ravines, arches and bridges, towering red sandstone cliffs and follies, the hermitage and numerous caves. These caves were built during the Iron Age, when the ancient peoples mined down into the hill in what is now inside the Park boundaries. The follies were designed by Tom and built of the red sandstone that men quarried from the cliffs at nearby Wareham at great expense and transported to the Park. Imposing follies reaching forty to fifty feet in all shapes and sizes glinted in the setting sun. A Roman villa had recently been discovered in the grounds of the house, much to the delight of Tom, who was the main instigator of the dig. He was an avid member of the Dorset Natural History and Archaeology Society, founded in 1846 to protect the natural history, geology and archaeology of Tom's beloved county. Made mostly from Purbeck stone and sitting on top of a hill, the imposing house could be seen from the river Frome in Wareham, the nearest town to the village of Thorpe Matravers. Standing under an oak tree and taking in the view Tom almost gasped, due to the lump in his throat. Tomorrow he was leaving Dorset and was heading for the unknown wilds of Alaska where it was known gold had been discovered.

William, Thomas's elder brother had gone there over a year ago, and was missing, no one having heard from him since the short letter he wrote:

...Heavy snow has slowed us down and we are waiting at the Canadian border for the weather to improve. The Indian I hired to take our goods has explained that the river Yukon is still frozen and we need to wait for the thaw before we attempt to take our ponies, goods and sledge along. It is very busy here; hundreds of people are hanging around. I have formed a friendship with another traveller, and we have taken the Chilkoot trail, which we have heard is shorter but tougher. Before we left Skagway I encountered a character called Soapy Smith who owned John Smith's Parlour and ran all the 'scams.' He was named Soapy because he once ran a racket in which he sold tablets of soap, many of which he claimed had a dollar bill tucked in the wrapper. He would organise a crowd around his stall and sell a marked tablet of soap to a stooge in the crowd, who shouted out he'd found a bill. Everyone clamoured for the soap, but there appeared to be no more dollar bills! Soapy also ran a telegraph racket in Skagway. There are no telegraph lines to Alaska, but he opened a small telegraph booth down on the shore with a cable running into the sea to make it look real. He would take several dollars from people then pretend to send their message home. People even had fake replies from their loved ones begging them to send money home. Soapy gained a lot of money from this, but he's also generous in that he feeds stray dogs and gives hand-outs to the sick and widows. It's just amazing he hasn't been jailed yet! Or shot!

Some men have sold their kit to buy a passage home, others are crying in desperation and homesickness, but I intend to stick this out, it's the adventure of a lifetime, despite the freezing cold... ...

Tom was the manager of the family pottery business, a position he enjoyed, mostly due to the respect of the men who worked for him. Now, after being asked by his father to go out to Alaska to look for Will, he temporarily handed the business over to Eddy, his brother-in-law, for the duration he was away. His brother, Will was the adventurer in the family and had always craved excitement, so his trip to the gold fields of Alaska was a dream fulfilled; something he had wanted to do ever since he had read articles in newspapers and journals of the men and women searching for gold. Similar in build to Tom, he too was tanned, brown-eyed and dark-haired. There was no doubting the family resemblance. They both took after Matilda, their mother in looks and in personality; that seeking for adventure and looking forward to seeing what opportunities were around the next corner. Tom was unsure of what he would find; Alaska was hardly 'around the corner,' it was much further than that! He knew his parents were apprehensive about his journey and what he would find, whether or not he would catch up with Will, who he would meet out there, whether he and Will would both come back safe and sound. But he had to go to Alaska; the future of Thorpe Matravers depended on this trip. Will was the heir to the family estate, and therefore he needed to return, marry and have children to carry on the Thorpe line.

As the dampness of the evening descended Tom's boots became wet in the dew-sodden grass. The distant sounds of the country seemed to intensify; he could hear the barking of a dog fox, the trilling of the blackbirds as they called to each other before settling in the trees for the night. Hearing the birds, Tom was taken back in time to last year's harvest supper and his first encounter with his darling Daisy. It had been a wonderful evening. Now, he made his way along the path towards the newly built railway track that ran through the common land bordering Thorpe estate to see Stan. He leaned on the Thorpe Halt crossing gate as the steam train hurtled out of the evening mist, whistle blowing. Stan, the railway worker in charge of the Halt and who lived in a cottage beside the track, opened the gates behind the retreating train. Ada, Stan's wife, waved from the kitchen window.

'Evening, Master Tom, you ready to go tomorrow?'

'Yes, Stan, I shall be on the 8:15, make sure you stop the train for me.'

'That I will, Master Tom, that I will, and good luck to ye, I hope ye find your brother.'

Tom turned and walked back towards the hermitage, the quiet returning, only to be interrupted by the distant sound of the church bells ringing out in Wareham as the bell ringers practised their rounds ready for the Sunday morning call to worship. Thomas thought of his own journey to come, of searching and finding his brother in that vast, bleak country. A sad aspect of his travels was the fact that he would be leaving his beloved Daisy behind in Dorset. Daughter of Bert, the pottery foreman, Daisy was still Tom's secret. If his family knew, sympathetic parents though they were, he felt they would not approve of his growing love for this beautiful girl, which was why he was walking around the estate before finally going to the hermitage where they were to meet in secret.

Finally, he heard soft footsteps approaching along the stone path leading to their secret hiding place. He watched as she eventually walked towards him, a strikingly attractive, spirited twenty-year-old young woman, with a slim figure and deep auburn hair. She wore the same green dress that she had worn at the harvest supper last year, and it blended in with the foliage surrounding her. Her generous mouth was turned down at the corners and her large green eyes were brimming over with tears. Reaching him, rising on tiptoe, she slid her arms round his neck and her lips parted with a sigh. When he wrapped his arms around her, her pulse roared. Pressing her body against his, her corset seemed to tighten around her breasts and her nipples pressed against the whalebone. Their kiss was long and passionate. With the smell of the wild honeysuckle and dog roses growing around the hermitage, Daisy felt desire flame between them as they looked into each other's eyes. She surreptitiously sniffed at him to familiarise herself with the scent of him, something she could remember when he was gone, she had a feeling it would be a long time before she saw him again.

'Dear Tom, do you have to go? When are you coming back?' I shall miss you so much.' Her emotion was such that her Dorset accent was strong. Tom's lips were soft and gentle, but he pulled away from her and stood looking down into her shining, tear-filled eyes.

'You know I have to go. Parting from you is agony, but I have to admit I'm anxious and have mixed feelings about this trip, I must find out what happened to Will, if he is still alive and his whereabouts. I feel apprehensive about travelling so far away, but I take the memory of you with me.'

'I know, Tom, I do understand.'

'Marry me, Daisy.'

'Yes, Tom, I will. I do so love you.'

'I'll remember this evening, with the aroma of your hair and skin and the taste of your lips mingled with the smell of the honeysuckles. I adore you, Daisy. I won't make love to you, my darling, difficult though it is, you are so beautiful and I love you so very much. You will wait for me, won't you? Don't go off with any of the farm labourers I see hanging around the village.'

'Tom, I'll wait for you. I promise.'

Daisy put her hand in her pocket and brought out a small embroidered handkerchief. 'I embroidered this for you, Tom, so that you can remember me.'

'O, dearest, I shall wear it always in my breast pocket so that you will be next to my heart,' Tom said lovingly. 'I hope to be back this time next year.'

He kissed her again, very gently, then moved away from her and picked up a long slim box from the bench next to him.

'I don't have a ring for you, but in the meantime, until I come back, here's a present for you, and I promise I'll bring you back a real fur coat.' Daisy took the lid off the box and gasped with surprise when she removed the tissue paper to reveal a turquoise silk gown, plain but beautifully cut. She had never seen such an item in her whole life, had never worn anything so expensive.

'Keep this dress, dearest, and wear it when we are together again.'

'Oh, Tom, it's beautiful. I'll wear it on the day you return. As soon as I know you're on the train, you'll see me at the railway level crossing waving to you.'

'I'll see you there, darling, keep well, my beloved.' As they parted with a final kiss, Daisy's eyes were brimming with tears and Tom was choked as he watched his lovely girl walk away from him carrying the dress box. The old coat she wore was in stark contrast to the promised fur coat. Tom realised how proud his girl was. In turn, Daisy was thinking how lucky she was to have Tom in her life. Her thoughts turned to his return and their marriage. Where would they live? How many children would they have? How would they overcome the class barriers? All the romance and sweet talk may come to nothing if, upon his return, he told her he had changed his mind. Her head was in a whirl as she walked home, carefully carrying the box. She would need to hide the dress under her side of the bed, she couldn't imagine how she could explain its presence if it were found by either Ivy or her mother. She would willingly have given up her virginity to Tom if he had asked her, but, being the gentleman he was, he was willing to wait. She would love being married to Tom.

Once again, the quiet of the evening descended as Tom made his way through the rose garden his mother had planted. Reaching the house by the front entrance, he climbed the steps to the terrace. Tubs of early red trailing geraniums planted in stone urns looked lovely set against the pale Purbeck stone walls of the house. This house may not be the finest in Dorset, but it was certainly in a magnificent setting. Stepping into the hall he would always remember how he felt that day.

The dining room walls were white, which reflected the taste for simple, uncluttered interiors as designed by Mr William Morris, as were the lily and pomegranate design wallpaper and the Arts and Crafts furniture. The simplicity of the room pleased Matilda, a woman who was gentle, yet determined in the way she perceived her home to look. William Morris was her hero and she loved the Pre-Raphaelite paintings scattered around the walls of her house almost as much as she loved her husband and sons, not forgetting her beautiful daughter, Amy. Mr Morris had written: 'Have nothing in your house that you do not know to be useful, or believe to be beautiful' and she had tried to follow his advice in the home she had built for herself and her family.

As the family sat round the table for dinner, the atmosphere was one of sadness. Will's seat was empty, and tomorrow Tom's would be too. Matilda had moved into this house as a bride upon her marriage to Harry, a marriage made in heaven, for she loved Harry more so now than she had on their wedding day. She knew that her husband loved her too, his passion not diminished by passing years. Harry enjoyed his position as a Justice of the

Peace in the town and he was well respected as director of several businesses. Her family and this house, the servants, the land in Dorset were her world, her lifeline, yet too, was her charity work in the village. It was through her that the village church school had been built; she remorselessly worked her charm on various businessmen in the area and wheedled out of them the funds to enable it to be built. The vicar, Reverend Richard, and his wife, Clarissa, were also at her table, having been invited to supper; Tom's last evening at home. She loved visiting the school to see how the children were faring, as she enjoyed, too, visiting the families in the village with Clarissa, the poor, the elderly, those who needed a hamper of food from her kitchen. Life was good, if only Will had not gone to Alaska and Tom did not have to embark on this long venture.

'Did you enjoy your walk, Tom?' Matilda enquired. She was holding back her tears that threatened to spill over at any moment.

'It was so very peaceful, so beautiful and I met Stan at the railway crossing. He expressed his good wishes for my journey. Ada waved from her window. I shall miss all of this, the house, the land, but most of all family.'

'When you and Will return we shall have a party to celebrate'. Harry was feeling optimistic. He had had a good day in Wareham, the four youths who needlessly vandalised the Town Hall were ordered by Harry to clear up the mess and help the glazier repair the windows. He was an excellent JP, strong but fair. He doubted those youths would be up in front of his bench again.

Amy didn't hold back her tears; they ran down her pretty cheeks. She wore her favourite gown tonight, pale pink off the shoulder silk decorated with dusky pink silk roses. She looked attractive and assured. She loved both her brothers equally. 'Dear Tom, do take care, Alaska is so far away. I hear the bears can be very fierce, don't get near them.' Eddy, her husband, gently touched her hand, for once sympathetic to her feelings.

'I won't, dear Amy, I'll take great care. I've got the maps and information I need when I'm there. I'm well prepared for any eventuality,' Tom answered her softly, holding her hand tightly before kissing it.

'My prayers go with you, Tom. I shall miss you, you have been a good friend to me since I arrived in this village; God go with you,' Revd. Richard said quietly. Clarissa sniffed. She didn't hold with 'adventures.'

Eddy was secretly pleased Tom was going to Alaska, it left the way clear for him to be the boss; nobody could interfere with his plans, and one of those plans included Daisy; he'd watched her for a while now and he was well aware of her trysts with Tom. He often crept around following them covertly, becoming excited and then frustrated every time he spied her.

'Yes, Tom, do take care out there in the wilds. Be assured the business will continue as it would if you were here.' Eddy was now in full control of the pottery and the workers. He would soon bring Bert Evans to heel, that man thought too much of himself. Tom disliked Eddy and often wondered what Amy saw in him. Despite the fact that he was from a wealthy neighbouring estate, he was rough and often rude to people he dealt with. Amy was desperate to have a child, so far without success. She wondered if the fact she was unable to give him a child was her fault. She always gave herself willingly to him in bed, but no baby had been conceived.

James Hibbs, the butler served the soup keeping his face expressionless but knowing that he too would miss Master Tom, as would the servants. Tom had been down to the kitchen earlier to say his goodbyes to the staff. Cook had been in tears. 'Master Tom, now you look after yerself.

I've baked some of my shortbread for you to take. I know it be yer favourite.'

'Goodbye, dear Cook. I'll think of your cooking when I'm eating beans in Alaska.' He gave her a big hug and as he left the kitchen he could hear Aggy, the kitchen maid sniffing in the scullery.

Early the next morning, Harry, Matilda, Tom and Amy stood on the Thorpe Halt platform aware that the train would soon be pulling away. In the chill early morning air they were well wrapped up in coats and hats. He shook hands with his father, kissed his sister, embraced his mother and said, 'I'll write when I can.' When the whistle blew, he climbed aboard into his first class carriage and stood leaning out of the open window. The train eased away with a clanking of couplings and a hiss of steam and his family watched until it rounded the curve in the track and he was lost to sight. Tom threw his Gladstone bag onto the luggage rack and settling into the seat near the window he gazed out at the scenery surrounding the Park on this still chilly but bright, sunny day. He glimpsed his follies and the pottery chimney. Thinking of last night, he suddenly felt a surge of guilt over Daisy. He felt bad deceiving his family by keeping from them the fact that he had proposed to her. But he could hardly admit he loved a girl from the Terrace, whose mother was his mama's maid and her father a worker in the Thorpe pottery. As for Daisy herself, perhaps he was selfish in asking her to wait for him. He didn't know how long he was going to be away. In the meantime, she could have a chance to meet a man of her own class and marry happily. Well, if that didn't happen for her, he would certainly marry her, and face the consequences. On their first meeting last September at the harvest supper, he knew he was in love the second he set eyes on her. He had a feeling that Eddy knew of their friendship and he was Bert's boss now. There was nothing he could do about the situation, he may as well settle back and enjoy the shortbread Cook had thoughtfully baked for him.

Four hours later, the train pulled into Waterloo station. Tom alighted carrying his bag and outside found a hackney that took him to Euston. From there it was another long train journey to Liverpool Lime Street and a night's stay at the Western Hotel before walking to the docks in the morning.

CHAPTER FOUR

At the end of the garden stood the old railway carriage that Grandma and Grandpa Evans moved into when their cottage fell into disrepair. Daisy loved going in there, it was her favourite place, and it was away from Mother who was always complaining that they needed more money. She manoeuvred around a couple of clucking chickens that had managed to come in with her. Then, as she opened the creaking cupboard door that had almost come away from the hinges, she recognised the familiar aroma of mothballs. Hanging on a peg was her grandma's very aged coat. All black, it was a mourning coat that grandma had bought early in her marriage when grandpa's mother died. Daisy was determined that she would wear this garment, not sell it as mother wanted. Taking it off the hook she pushed her arms through the sleeves. The silk lining felt cold against her warm skin and the worn cuffs hung at her wrists, grandma being taller and slimmer; the waist felt tight as she did up the buttons, balding where the fabric had worn away. The coat was cut from velvet and had cost her grandma a shilling. Pulling the collar up around her chin she breathed in the mothball smell that mingled with a very faint odour of the violet toilet water grandma often used. The bottom of the coat was slightly ragged, the hem needed some attention, but she guessed this would add to the ambience of the garment. Leaving the carriage she walked down the garden path past father's vegetable garden, past the washing line, and around the pigsty. Father's sow was lying in the small space afforded her, grunting in her sleep. She was being fattened for the butcher; the meat would be salted and keep the family in meat for the year. The Evans family lived at number four, the Terrace Cottages; one of a row of cottages built by the Thorpe Estate, to house the pottery workers and their families. These cottages were compact and comfortable, with two bedrooms, front room, kitchen, scullery with a stone sink, running water and an outside toilet. Most families owned a pig and chickens or rabbits to supplement their income, the gardens were substantial and Bert, Daisy's father took pride in growing his vegetables and flowers for the house.

Walking through the small scullery and into the kitchen, Daisy saw her sister, Ivy sat in her usual place at the table in the kitchen, avidly devouring the *Hearth and Home* magazine, her long dark hair hanging over her pretty face.

'I'm off to school now, Ivy, don't you be late for work.' Ivy was a shop assistant at the local grocers shop and, being an avid reader, took every opportunity she could to read the magazines she bought out of the meagre amount of money her mother allowed her out of her wages. The books her mother was able to borrow, with the permission of Lady Thorpe also grabbed her attention in any spare time available.

An article concerning Florence Nightingale had caught Ivy's imagination, and she was reading this for the fifth time. She read how, in 1837, at the age of sixteen, Florence felt that God was calling her to do some work but wasn't sure what that work should be. She began to develop an interest in nursing, but her parents considered it a profession inappropriate to a woman of her class and background, and would not allow her to train as a nurse. They expected her to make a good marriage and live a conventional upper-class woman's life. Eventually,

Florence's parents allowed her to take up her nursing training, and after qualifying, she finally went out to the Crimea to nurse those men injured in the war.

Ivy was certain that being a nurse was the path she herself was to follow. For some months now she had been helping Mrs McCree, the vicar's wife, in her parish work. Twice they visited old Jimmy Curtis is his tiny cottage situated on the edge of the heath, and dressed his ulcerated leg. Ivy had not blanched at the sight and stench of the poor man's suppurated limb, a fact of which, she felt proud. Not many eighteen-year-old girls would be able to help Jimmy in the way she did, thought Ivy to herself. She also went back to the cottage several evenings to help Jimmy tidy up and clean his cottage; it wasn't good for him to live in such squalor. Last week, late one evening, she had accompanied Mrs McCree to the home of Mary Ellis, where the woman was in the last stage of giving birth. Ivy appeared to be a great help by allowing Mary to grasp her hand, and to mop her brow with a damp cloth as the pain increased. As the baby emerged, Ivy had been fascinated by the experience of seeing such a tiny scrap crying out her first breath. Ivy was humbled to see the miracle of birth and be part of the activity. Like Florence Nightingale, Ivy considered herself to be called by God to do this work. She found her job in the shop tedious, but the family needed the money. She was going to ask Mrs McCree to have a word with her parents in the hope that they would allow her to start nursing training. Lady Matilda was such a kind lady and was often seeking ways in which she could help the villagers; maybe she would fund Ivy in her quest. Mrs McCree could help her too; she had a good relationship with her ladyship.

Her courtship with Davey Barnes was going nowhere; all he wanted was the thing that she was not prepared to give in to. He even hinted at marriage, but Ivy needed her freedom if she was going to fulfil her ambition. Noticing the time on the mantle clock, she rose from her seat, and making her way past the furniture in the crowded kitchen to the door, Ivy was now determined to follow in Florence Nightingale's footsteps. The vicarage was going to be her first port of call after work this evening.

Daisy was a teaching assistant at the village church school. This school was built with money donated by Lady Thorpe. The main room of the building was 'the church', there being screens to divide the room into two smaller classrooms. On Fridays all school equipment was packed away and early on Mondays, set out again. Coats and hats were hung in the tiny vestry and on wet days, the smell of drying clothes hung in the air. Across from the vestry a small classroom had been built on the side of the building for the older children. Their desks, benches and equipment were set out permanently; around the room were cupboards and at the far end a large blackboard stood proud on a stand. This room was where Daisy spent her days as a classroom assistant, helping the teacher, Miss Lucy Martin. A large wood-burning stove heated the room, which, for many village children, was a luxury. Outside, a large playground allowed the children to run free and play during their break times.

Daisy was sad. She was missing Tom dreadfully, and wondered where he was today. He couldn't write to her in case his letters were discovered. Keeping their romance secret was not easy. Her parents wondered why she mooned about the house and rarely went out nowadays, whereas not so long ago she was out some evenings and Sunday afternoons. Daisy knew they would never agree to her relationship with Tom. They believed that people should know their place in life, and that was not marrying into the aristocracy. He once told her that he occasionally took Georgina Mellor to the theatre, or to a dance. He certainly wasn't serious about Georgina, but his outings with her kept his parents happy. Daisy rarely thought of Tom as being 'aristocracy'. He was, to her, a very special friend. He was dark-haired with heavy brows and lovely brown eyes. He had a muscular build from dragging stones around when he made his follies. Whenever they had happened to meet in public, such as church or the shop, he had been courteous, but in private had been passionate, caring and loving. She always wondered what sort of man she would marry, never dreaming he would be a man with a title. Daisy often looked up Alaska and the Yukon in the school atlas; she couldn't believe how far away it seemed, and what a vast country he needed to travel across.

Oh, how I wish I could go with him, thought Daisy, as she set out the slates ready for Miss Martin to begin lessons for the day.

A concern was Mr Eddy. She was aware that he watched her; several times she encountered him riding his horse on the path when she walked home from school. Occasionally when out walking with Tom she had a feeling someone was watching them; it had probably been him. He had a peculiar look in his eyes and she didn't like him; nor did she trust him. But she needed to be polite as he was her father's boss and was aware of the hold he held over the workers.

CHAPTER FIVE

Alaska 1898

Liverpool Lime Street Railway Station was noisy, smelly and dirty. People rushed about with travelling cases and newspaper sellers called out the news headlines. To Tom, as he walked to his hotel, the buildings seemed overpowering in their size and nearness to each other. The Adelphi Hotel was in complete contrast, quiet, clean and fresh compared to the railway and the streets. Tom decided to forgo drinks in the bar and went to bed early. Next morning as he walked down to the docks he could smell the sea and feel the stiff north-easterly breeze. Moored on the dock was the White Star Line SS Majestic, the steam ship which was to take Thomas and his fellow passengers to New York. Her two funnels belched smoke as Captain Edward Smith prepared the vessel for the six-day trip to New York. Tom looked up at a crane that would hoist containers full of luggage onto the ship. After checking in at the departures desk in the terminal building amidst the cacophony of people and noise, Tom climbed the gangway and joined the crowds on board.

The sky was a sullen dark grey and the sea was choppy whilst the stiff wind forced the passengers to cling to their hats as they waved farewell to their family and friends. As he stood at the rail and looked down, Tom saw red jacketed bandsmen playing jauntily on the quay and streamers being thrown at the ship, creating a carnival atmosphere despite the dreadful weather. Eventually the crew hauled in the gangways and prepared to cast off. People on deck were crying, as were the folk on the quay. The gangways were stowed away; sailors cast off, and then coiled the ropes away and suddenly the gap between ship and shore widened. The band struck up a jolly sea shanty, the last of the paper streamers were thrown and at last they were at sea.

Tom left the deck and went below where he settled into his first class cabin pampered by soft carpets and polished wood doors with brass fittings. White-jacketed stewards carried trays of drinks to the passengers as he enjoyed lunch in the dining room, his first meal aboard ship. Exploring the amenities on board made a pleasant afternoon. That evening, after dinner, as the orchestra played in the first class saloon, Tom met up with a couple from New York who were on their way back from Hampshire, having visited their newly married daughter. Emily Harwell was drenched in diamonds and wearing a white fur stole over her beautifully cut gown. When Tom explained his mission, they were enthralled, but sympathetic.

'Your poor parents, Thomas, must be very anxious, one son missing and one on their way to the dangerous Yukon,' said Mrs Harwell.

'If you need help, you just call on us. We'll give you our New York address.' Clyde Harwell was kind and Tom knew they meant what they said. It might be helpful to have acquaintances in America.

'It's a long journey; I did hear you need a lot of endurance. But at least the weather will be all right this time of year. ' Clyde said diffidently. 'You won't catch me doing anything like that; I prefer all the luxuries when I travel.'

By the following morning they were out in the Atlantic and as the sea became rougher many people began to suffer from seasickness. Tom, however, was thoroughly enjoying his trip; he appeared to have good sea legs. Enjoying the Harwell's company helped to make for a pleasant crossing; Clyde was a mine of information and explained to Tom the processes of embarkation and customs. Meeting other passengers in First Class enabled Tom to also enjoy the company of several young single ladies, who enjoyed sharing his company and dancing with him in the evenings. During the daytime, if the Atlantic weather allowed, they played quoits and deck tennis. Then, after six most enjoyable days, land was sighted. Rain poured down, but it didn't stop the people pushing and shoving up on deck to catch their first sight of New York. Wearing an astrakhan coat and hat and looking very dapper, Tom watched from the saloon. He knew the ship was to lie at anchor in the Hudson River for immigration officials to come aboard for health and documentation checks on the passengers and monitor for diseases. There was no need to rush.

Eventually, there was New York spread out before him, looking just as he'd imagined it. He could see the spire of Trinity Church, which was the highest building and an important aid to shipping. Other buildings were tall, too, taller than any he had ever seen before. The sheer volume of ships amazed him and he lost count of the number of piers jutted out into the East River. The quay was crowded with every kind of wagon and carriage imaginable. Hundreds of men were loading and unloading cargos. The noise was deafening; barrels were being rolled over the cobbles, horses' hooves, and the rumble of wagon wheels, ships' engines and human voices. Hundreds of craft, from tugboats to old sailing ships were out on the river.

Tom was eager to continue his journey. Once they were through immigration and customs he joined the Hartwell's who insisted that he stay with them for at least one night. Tom felt unable to refuse, so sat back in their carriage and enjoyed a short journey through the city, feeling overawed by the size of the tower blocks. His friend's mansion was impressive, as were the furnishings and antiques which invaded every room. Privately, Tom thought it ostentatious and overpowering, but he couldn't fault the kindness of his hosts. That night, after a delicious dinner, Tom joined Clyde in his den for a cigar.

'I don't envy you the trek to the Yukon, Tom, I've heard all sorts of stories of scams and violence. You'll do it well, though. I've only known you a short while, but I have the measure of you, and if your brother is as tenacious as you are, you'll both do fine.'

Next morning, after bidding his friends a fond farewell, he continued on his journey, which took him from New York to Ottawa on the railway. The scenery was not unlike that of Dorset, with pine forests and lush green landscape. Crossing the St Lawrence River the train steamed on along the New York Central railway line. Although the scenery was familiar, the trains certainly were not. Tom was impressed by the size of the locomotives, far larger than any he had seen before. From Ottawa he took the Canadian Pacific to Vancouver, and whilst on the railway he wrote home to his parents… *I'm on an incredible journey travelling right across this huge country, where astounding scenery takes in snow-capped mountains, vast lakes, and prairie and pine forests. Many of the stations we stop at are small, made of timber with tin roofs. The steam hauled trains setting fires with chimney sparks is a hazard, and I'm interested in seeing these buildings, especially as this could have been the route that Will took on his journey to Alaska. The wildlife I can see through the train window is fascinating; golden eagles, ospreys nesting in trees, beaver swimming in the rivers, their flat tails acting as rudders and only yesterday I observed a stampede of caribou, kicking up dust with their incredible speed. We could only imagine the noise their pounding hooves would make.*

Travelling through the huge prairies in Saskatchewan we passed a Blackfoot Indian settlement, their tepees standing out in bright contrast to the scrubland. This morning we were held up in Eatonia Station due to a herd of buffalo on the line. What gigantic fellows they are……

Arriving in Calgary, after spending two days resting at a hotel close to the station, Tom boarded the Canadian Pacific Railway for his onward journey to Vancouver. Riding through the Canadian Rockies, Tom was humbled by what he saw; the breath-taking scenery of glacier-fed lakes, majestic mountains and ferocious rivers. They travelled through old forests, deep valleys and snow-capped peaks. Removing a letter from his bag that Will had written home, Tom read ... *The Rockies were sculpted by enormous glaciers, which advanced and retreated, shaping the faces and peaks of the mountains. The first recorded instance of a white person sighting the Rockies was in 1754, when fur trader Anthony Henday glimpsed what he called "The Shining Mountains" from Red Deer, Alberta. Over time, the fur traders established a few arduous routes through the Rockies...* Looking up from Will's writing and glancing out of the carriage window, Tom could only gasp at the scenery surrounding him. He agreed that the men who surveyed and built this railway were indeed extremely brave with an incredible vision. *'At Kicking Horse Pass I discovered that at this spot Dr James Hector was kicked by one of his pack horses and knocked unconscious for several hours. Although in severe pain, he continued with the expedition....'*

Following Will's journey through these mountains by railroad, Tom travelled the route past Castle Mountain; at just over eight thousand, nine hundred and fifty feet, the bulky turreted peak was an example of a castellated-type mountain, and onto Big Hill. '...*The very first work train to travel down Big Hill after the line was completed ran away and plunged into the Kicking Horse River, killing three workers. Another engineer won the dubious honour of riding a runaway engine all the way down the Big Hill. When his light engine lost control, he threw caution to the winds and made a joy ride of it, a reaction typical of the boisterous mountain division railroaders. Shouting to his terrified fireman, "Here goes for Field!" he signalled to the stunned switchman that he wanted to stay on the main rail line. When he finally brought the engine to a halt at Field, he briefly enjoyed his celebrity as the only engineer to ride a runaway train the length of the Big Hill. His glory, however, was short-lived; he was promptly fired by means of a telegram."* Tom smiled as he read his brother's letter. He was pleased that Will had written these descriptions, it made his journey so much more entertaining and interesting. Will also included a photograph of an early railway tourist who rode a velocipede in the Rockies in 1887. He also wrote, upon passing Eagle River '...*On Saturday 7th November 1885, at 9:22 in the morning, at Craigellachie in the Rocky Mountains, Donald Smith was preparing to drive the last spike of The Canadian Pacific Railway. His first blow was a feeble one and the plain iron spike bent. A spare one was quickly set up and Smith hit this one with careful, precise blows, driving it into place.*

There was a brief silence, followed by cheering and backslapping as the onlookers celebrated the completion of Canada's first transcontinental railway. The line was completed in just fifty-four months, almost six years ahead of schedule....'

Travelling through a desert area, where Tom spied a rattlesnake and some coyotes, the train stopped at Kamloops, or Shuswap, meaning 'meeting of the waters'.

Wandering through the town, before settling for the night, Tom bought a magazine in which he read an interesting article of the place: "One story perhaps connected with this version of the name concerns an attack by a pack of wolves, much built up in story to one huge white wolf, or a pack of wolves and other animals, travelling overland from the Nicola Country being repelled by a single shot by John Tod, then Chief Trader, with his musket – at a distance of some two hundred yards. The shot caused the admiration of native witnesses and is said to have given the Chief Trader a great degree of respect locally, preventing the fort from attack."

That night, as he lay in a roughly hewn bunk in a rooming house, sleep evaded Tom. It wasn't because his surroundings were uncomfortable; he knew that he would experience much more discomfort in the days to come. He had come so far, seen so much magnificent scenery and met many interesting people, including fellow travellers on the railroad; read Will's letters; looked at the photographs and articles he had sent home from this vast country, and Tom should have felt excited, but he felt apprehensive. He was missing home, his family, and Daisy. He could only wonder whether she was well and happy. He hoped that she was missing him as much as he missed her. He even missed Aurora, his horse. Yet, he felt an emotion, almost one of *dè já vu*, as if he had been there before. Maybe, he mused to himself, it is because he read so much and learned so much about this journey. His head was full of stories and legends.

Following in the footsteps of Alexander Mackenzie, Simon Fraser, another great explorer of the fur-trade era, commanded an historic expedition across the Rockies to the Pacific. He established trading posts which became the first permanent white settlements west of the Rocky Mountains. Fraser and David Thompson founded the Thompson and Fraser Rivers. Simon Fraser noted in his diary: "I have never seen anything like this country. It is so wild that I cannot find words to describe our situation at times. We had to pass where no human being should venture." These two mutual admirers and adventurous surveyors not only did much for the fur trade but also helped achieve an understanding of the difficult terrain on both sides of the Rocky Mountains....' reading out loud from a leaflet, the gentleman sitting opposite Tom in the railway carriage the next morning, introduced himself.

'Gerald Green, from Jasper. Pleased to make your acquaintance.'

'Tom Thorpe, from Dorset, England. Pleased to meet you, sir.'

'Hey, you're all the way from England? Tell me, what are you doing here?'

Tom gladly explained to Mr Green the purpose of his journey, following which, the two men talked companionably for the rest of the journey to Vancouver.

'I am a travelling salesman,' explained the dapper Gerald. He was dressed in grey worsted suit, white shirt, blue tie and shining black boots. His bowler hat sat in the rack above his head. Tom estimated him to be in his early fifties. 'I sell umbrellas, parasols and accessories. I'm on a buying trip to Vancouver, where they provide the most fashionable goods, some from Paris, France.'

'Which way did you travel?' enquired Tom cordially.

'I took the Canadian Pacific Railroad from Jasper, travelling through the mountains, following the Fraser and Thompson rivers.'

'I believe we still follow these two rivers down to Vancouver.'

'That we do, Tom, that we do.'

Vancouver was a fascinating city and after saying farewell to Gerald Green, Tom slowly made his way to Gas Town taking in the sights. Named after a Yorkshire seaman, steamboat captain and barkeeper, 'Gassy' Jack Deighton arrived in 1867 soon after the fire which had wrecked most of the town. He opened the area's first saloon. Deighton was known as Gassy Jack because of his talkative nature and his penchant for storytelling. The name stuck and the area around his bar became known as Gastown, after his death in 1875. The town of Vancouver soon prospered as a port and a 'rough-and-rowdy resort for off-work loggers and fishermen. The Canadian Pacific Railway terminated, and warehouses were built. He wondered whether Will had visited the famous saloon, the Globe, owned by the native wife of the late 'Gassy Jack'. Stalls had been set up in the street selling all kinds of food from baked potatoes and hot dogs to bowls of noodles. Music drifted out from a dozen different sources, mainly saloon bars and drunken sailors and prospectors lurched along in groups, singing as they went. Gas Town was certainly throbbing with activity, noise and less pious pleasures. In the Globe the noise was becoming unbearable. At the far end of the room dancing girls in bright red dresses, white petticoats, black stockings and no drawers, high kicked their slim legs in time to the music, watched by men drinking beer from tankards or small glasses of whiskey. Soon after entering and booking into The Globe, Tom enquired of the barman if anyone had met his brother. The bartender just laughed.

'What! Do you really think I can remember who's been in here? I've served thousands of people. Clear off. But before you do, have a word with those three men over there.' Gingerly, Tom approached the three men sitting at the table pointed out to him; George Jefferson, with his two brothers-in-law, Charlie Took and Sidney Brown. Sitting down Tom interrupted their conversation and cordially said

'Hi there, my name is Tom Thorpe, newly arrived from England. I'm looking for my brother, Will, a journalist. He was travelling around the Yukon and writing articles and drawing illustrations for various publications. I know he came here on his way up. Have you by any chance encountered him? By the way, I've ordered a round of drinks for us all from the bar.' Tom expected these rough looking fellows to tell him to 'clear off' as the bartender had done, but, after looking Tom up and down and deciding he was harmless, George informed him they recently prospected and found gold in Rabbit Creek, one of the six tributaries of the river Klondike in the Yukon Valley.

'If we don't spend all our gold in this town we might go home, back to Chicago. The women here look mighty tasty. On the other hand, we may go back up to Rabbit Creek to our claim there.'

'Yea, no hurry,' piped in Sidney. 'Too much enjoyment here to worry about home.'

'Aye, think we might have seen him. He was heading up to the Yukon, nice bloke, hear him talking to folks, great English accent, just like yours,' offered Charlie. 'My guess is, he caught the steamer up to Skagway, travelled on to Dyea then took the Chilkoot Pass trail which is where we bumped into him. But the Trail is mighty dangerous; winter is a dreadful time with snow falls eight feet high and even deeper drifts. But if you need to track him down, then take the same route. No snow now, but mud inches deep.'

'It's mighty busy still, up there, the prospectors keep on coming. There's gold to be found, we're the lucky ones, but there's thousands come back destitute,' informed George.

'Or dead,' was Sid's dour pronouncement. 'But good luck to 'ya, lad. We hope you find him alive and prosperous. 'Tis a very long trek.'

Tom was pleased he had found these three men, and after buying another round of drinks, he retired to his room, which was simply furnished, but clean. In no time at all he was asleep, despite the noise inside the saloon, which stayed open until six am, and the breaking glass and shouting from outside. Next morning he made his way to the steamship office, but had to queue to obtain his tickets to depart next day to Skagway, the nearest town to the goldfields.

Tom noticed a tall, blond, smartly dressed young man in front of him in the queue and started a conversation with him. 'Hi there, my name is Tom, newly arrived from England. I'm looking for my brother, last heard of at the Canadian border. Are you by any chance heading that way?'

'Howdy, yea, I'm Caleb Howard. I'm a prospector, taking this journey in the hope of finding gold and craving excitement. I did hear there is some gold left, though a lot of stampeders are coming back down. But leaving my home in Vancouver sure is hard.'

'In which part of town do you live?' enquired Tom.

'We have a house in Main Street. My father owns a warehouse down on the docks where he operates a logging business. I normally work there too, but I need to experience more than is on offer here.'

After obtaining their hundred dollar tickets, Tom enquired of Caleb where the best store to purchase his goods could be found. Caleb advised him of a store in Cordova Street, which claimed to be the best 'Klondike Outfitter'. Caleb warned, 'The shopkeepers are mighty proficient in fleecing their customers, so I'll come along with you and get my stuff there as well.' As they walked towards Cordova Street, Tom and Caleb took in the sights. Later he wrote home... *I am constantly enquiring if people have seen Will. As Englishmen I feel we stand out in a crowd and people may remember him, especially with him being a journalist. He would, hopefully, be remembered by the way he would have been interested in ordinary people making the extraordinary journey. From my enquiries, it appears he did go from Skagway to Dyea, which is where I am headed. Thousands of people have made the hazardous journey and so far only a handful have found gold in any worthwhile amount. When Will went up the Chilkoot Pass deep snow had made the journey very difficult. Here in Vancouver shopkeepers had galvanised into action, for news of the gold was like a virus infecting everyone. Although the furor has died down quite a lot now that the initial panic has passed, shopkeepers have put signs outside their shops 'Get your outfit here'. Sledges are out on display. Tents, coats and fur-lined boots, mackinaws and galoshes are piled up ready to sell. The dried goods store has a blackboard outside listing the items the owner has in stock which can be bought in bulk. As the Klondike is some seven or eight hundred miles from Skagway it's essential to take nails and an axe as well as tents. Sledge dogs are advertised at exorbitant prices. Caleb explained to me that booklets which listed everything needed for the trip were being printed and sold before the ink was dry. Bankers left their banks; farmers abandoned their crops, just to get to the gold fields. Did you know that the Canadian Mounted Police won't allow anyone across the border from Alaska to Canada without a ton of provisions? This is because they fear a famine. Caleb and I have bought: beef blocks, rice, sugar, coffee and evaporated eggs. A tent, mackinaw coats, wide-brimmed hats, high boots, gloves. We've packed our supplies first in burlap sacks then in waterproof oilcloth sacks. People think the Yukon is just a hike from Skagway, but I've done my homework, talked to men who have already been, and we need to be prepared for a long, arduous journey. This country is vast.*

It had taken Tom and Caleb hours to purchase what they needed, but eventually everything was collected together, packed up and sent ahead to the steamer. Both Caleb and Tom were fortunate in being able to buy their way to the Yukon; Tom's father ensured he would be financially secure especially as, hopefully, the two brothers would need money for their return journey. Harry had arranged for Tom to collect as many dollars from the bank as he needed. At the dock sat the steamer Albany on which Tom and Caleb had booked berths for their journey to Skagway. It looked extremely shabby, seedy and sadly in need of paint and the smoke from its three stacks drifted into the cold air. As they managed to get closer Tom could see it was rusty and battered – was he really travelling in this dangerous tub? There were hundreds of people milling around, Tom could hardly move. Then, just behind him, a fight between two men broke out. One man fell and the other started kicking him, but Tom noticed no one intervened. Caleb shrugged and moved away; Tom imagined that this was quite usual. Progress along the pier was blocked by wagons containing luggage and stores, all piled up high. The steamer sounded its shrill whistle letting people know they were sailing within the hour. Eventually Tom and his companion arrived on board, and finding a seaman asked him to show them to their cabin.

'First class?' drawled the steward. He was used to men expecting something fancy but what a shock this guy was in for.

'That's right; I've paid a lot of money for this trip.'

'Don't matter how much you paid, they're all the same. Of course, I may be able to find you a single cabin, but it'll cost you.'

Having settled into his expensive cabin, which turned out to be little more than a cupboard, Tom climbed the greasy stairs to see what had become of Caleb. Up on deck he was faced with pack dogs howling constantly, horses kicked and neighed in the temporary hastily built wooden stables, and he noticed the ship was so crowded that if you dare leave a space it would be taken up immediately. Crowding would only become worse as they travelled further. Looking around he could see that some people had brought the most ridiculous items; bicycles, enough wood to build their own cabins, a cast iron stove and even a piano; how on earth would they get these things up the mountains, wondered Tom. The conditions on the boat were terrible, even in so-called first class there was a lack of washing facilities, and the lavatories caused one to retch. Tom needed to push past rough sailors, lumberjacks, garishly dressed women with painted faces, old-timers from previous stampedes and clerics who appeared to be going in a missionary capacity. He noted there were Americans, Canadians, Swedes, Hungarians, Mexicans and even Japanese. This journey was obviously going to be interesting; he would have plenty to write home about. People were arguing. Every inch of space appeared to be used. All this, despite rumours that there was little or no gold left.

Eventually, having sought out Caleb the two men then settled down in the saloon for pricey meals and drinks. Even after waiting hours for food, eating meals on board became unpleasant experiences; many of the travellers just shovelled the food in their mouths, and drank a bottle of whisky in one go. Raw meat hung from the ceiling of the saloon, the fatty skin hanging down onto the heads of the diners. Hardened greasy gravy and scraps of food from the previous sitting littered the tables.

This is just terrible, observed Tom, we're being treated worse than the cattle on board. Realising that it would be inappropriate to say so, Tom thought longingly of the meals he had enjoyed on the liner, and those meals at home, of Mr Hibbs serving the best food that money could buy in delightful surroundings with his family.

'Guess we just have to put up with it,' said Tom thoughtfully. 'It's only for two weeks, but I think it will be a very long two weeks!'

'Yup, having done this before, I can tell ya, it ain't much fun. We just have to make the best of the journey, playing cards in the evening will help pass some time,' announced an old stampeder, his beard full of crumbs.

Travelling along the Inside Passage of Alaska, Tom beheld the breathtakingly beautiful scenery of virgin forests, snow-capped mountains and misty fiords on both sides of the narrow channel. On just the first day out, a family of brown bears were spotted on the far beach gorging themselves on a beached whale. The skeleton of the massive creature sticking up out of the blubber reminded Caleb of the frame of a partially built upturned boat. When a pod of humpback whales were spotted off to starboard, Tom realised he was in a special place and he would write to his family; he could describe to them all these amazing sights. Perhaps it would be wise not to describe the conditions on board this rusty tub, it was bound to cause worry to his mother. Sometimes they passed the prows of half sunken abandoned paddle steamers, which stuck out of the water like shark fins. Many of them had been there for less than a year and were rapidly rusting and disintegrating, the sad corpses of a once thriving industry. Hopefully, thought Tom, if Mama reads out some of my letters within Jane's hearing, Daisy might get to hear of his journey so far. Suddenly feeling homesick he began to have doubts; was he doing the right thing in coming here on this journey, or was nostalgia playing tricks with his mind? Would Daisy really wait for him? She was going to be lonely without him around; he hoped this didn't mean she would look elsewhere for some male company.

Eventually, the steamer pulled into the tiny dock in Skagway and the seamen tied up the ropes on the stakes attached to the wooden planking. The Indians called this place Skagus, which meant 'Home of the North Wind'. It appeared to live up to its name. The noise of the people on the steamer blended with the noise of the town, a cacophony of such unspeakably loud decibels, it began to hurt Tom's ears. Having travelled light, apart from their provisions, with just his carpetbag, he was able to descend the gangway onto the wharf immediately and make his way to the Lucky Diggers Saloon where he'd arranged to meet Caleb. Skagway was just a huddle of ramshackle shacks and tents on marshland. Pouring rain hampered his way, the streets were thick with black mud and faeces, both human and animal, which stuck to boots and soiled the hems of ladies dresses despite the wooden boards laid down across the streets. The stench hit Tom's nostrils, the smell here was even worse than on board that rusty hulk the captain had called a steamer. Men gobbed spit everywhere, to Tom's disgust. Horses loaded with supplies stood tied to railings. The boardwalks were slippery with trod-in mud; the whole town had a dingy, muddy hue. Wooden buildings were under construction, many looking deserted. Stakes and other building detritus piled up in places. Carefully walking along the boardwalk and looking around, Tom noticed an old chap sitting on a rickety stool smoking a dirty pipe so he stopped and asked, 'Hi, tell me, why are these buildings like this?'

'Well,' replied the old timer. 'It's like this – builders be 'ard to git, they're all off to gold fields. No one wants to work like this; they wanna make a quick buck. You new in town?'

'Yes, from England, searching for my brother, a journalist, who's disappeared. But at the moment I need to find the Lucky Diggers Saloon.'

'Ah, well, there be many a bloke gone missing up 'ere, but I wish ya all the best young man.' Removing his pipe and showing a few blackened teeth, he indicated to Tom the direction before spitting onto the ground.

'Good day to you,' gestured Tom as he walked on, noticing a carriage had its wheels stuck in mud, the owners faces red hot with the exertion of pushing and pulling. Noticing a scabby dog cocking its leg against one of the carriage wheels, Tom decided not to go and help. Surrounding the town were mountains, covered with forests, many still snow-capped; their beauty contrasting sharply with the grimness of the town.

Opposite the saloon was the Telegraph office, so Tom called in and after making his usual enquiry, sent a wire to Thorpe Matravers informing his parents of his whereabouts and telling them he had no further news of Will.

Gingerly crossing the road, Tom next entered the marshal's office where he made enquiries. No one had heard of Will. The marshal, a man of enormous girth and dirty, yellowed teeth, with a gun on the desk in front of him, sat reading a pamphlet. He appeared to be totally uninterested. 'Don't trouble me 'less ya got some kinda real trouble.' It was obvious Tom had interrupted his perusal of a somewhat dubious story, judging by the picture of the scantily clad woman on the front page. The marshal started to scratch his crotch as Tom walked out. Next to the marshal's office Tom noticed a building with *Skagway News* etched on the window. He entered the building, waiting for a few moments as his eyes adjusted to the gloom. Sat behind the counter a middle-aged man with a brown apron tied round his waist was thumbing through an issue of the local paper. He looked up as Tom entered.

'Do you want to place an article? I'm just about to set the print for this week's issue,' he said gruffly. A last minute item had to very interesting for him to be impressed at this late stage of the proceedings.

Tom took a deep breath then asked, 'Do you hear of everything that happens in Skagway?' The printer nodded as Tom continued, 'Have you come across the name Will or William Thorpe? He's a journalist and my brother. He was writing articles about the people here and the Yukon. Thought he may have come in here to speak to you or to offer you some articles? He's missing, last heard of at the Canadian border about a year ago. We're from England. I've just arrived here.'

'Nope, ain't heard of him. Quite a few Englishmen came through. I've a good memory. Have you tried the marshal? Mind you, he 'aint interested in much, other than girls.' Tom nodded and left, feeling dispirited. No one appeared to have heard of Will, or if they had, they weren't telling. Perhaps, pondered Tom, Soapy Smith had something to do with the attitudes around this town. Will having written last year telling us about his hold here in Skagway.

As he entered through the swing doors of the saloon, Tom coughed due to the smoky atmosphere. He could see the place was packed with men dressed in dirty brown chequered shirts and old trousers, most with months' growth of beards. Squatting in a corner one man played a violin, another, with a really long, straggly beard played the mouth organ. Suddenly, a fight broke out, one man accusing another of stealing the gold dust he had just that minute placed on the bar to pay for his drink. The accused had quickly covered the gold with a filthy handkerchief, scooped it up and pocketed it, thinking he hadn't been seen in the crush of men at the bar. The victim started throwing heavy punches. As customers stepped out of the way, a table and a couple of chairs splintered like balsa wood as the men threw themselves across the room. The barman, a huge bear of a man, wearing a soiled apron over a once white shirt, leapt over the counter and separated the men, one of whom dripped blood from what looked like a broken nose before physically throwing them out, one by one, into the mud outside. The other occupants of the saloon appeared to be oblivious of the scuffle; they must have been used to it all, thought Tom. A dirty unkempt woman wearing a purple off-the-shoulder dress, one hand on her hip, sashayed through the crowded room looking for possible punters to take upstairs. Who knew what diseases she could spread, Tom thought with a shudder.

Caleb was drunk on whiskey already, and he was excited; 'On board the steamer, I made the acquaintance of Jake, here,' he slurred as he placed a friendly arm around the shoulder of a young chap, in his twenties, Tom guessed. He was dressed in the 'uniform' of a trapper, thick trousers, fur jacket and hat made from a dead skunk, or some such small animal. Tom almost gagged at the smell emanating from Jake, but listened politely as he told a story of two ships that arrived simultaneously in Seattle and San Francisco in 'ninety-seven called the Portland and the Excelsior. They'd sailed a month before from St. Michael near the Yukon River. On board the ships were scores of miners who unloaded three crates full of gold. No one had ever seen anything like it before and nothing like that had been found since. That was the start of this quest for gold. Caleb asked, 'Have you been trapping or prospecting, Jake?'

'A bit of both,' he replied, 'but it's the thought that we might find gold to keep us going. I found ten ounces, cashed it in, and wasted it all on wine, women and song. That's why I'm going back again, it just gits to yer.' Jake was laughing and animated. 'There's definitely gold to be found out there. If yer can stand the freezing cold, the discomfort, violence, and, this time of year, mosquitoes, and then ya'll survive. It's the joy of finding a nugget and the heartbreak of finding nothin' what keeps ya goin.'

'Well,' announced Tom, 'I guess we'd better book a night here, then collect our packs from the quay tomorrow and set off. I don't want to waste time.'

'Shall we just get some fresh air before we turn in?' asked Jake, who, hanging around, now considered Tom and Caleb to be his friends.

'No,' said Tom. 'But I'll wait here for you.' It was a chilly, damp evening, the stars hidden by the fug of fog and smoke from the fires. Walking along the decking of the sidewalk, Caleb suddenly tripped and slipped down the three steps onto the road. Slithering in mud and sawdust, he was thrown off balance and ended up on his backside. Jake held a hefty stake of wood in his hand and in one smooth movement brought it up and slammed it into Caleb's chest. Finding it difficult to breathe, Caleb staggered, but got up and crouched, in position ready for the next onslaught, feeling as though his ribs were coming through his chest. Jake didn't move but stood looking down on Caleb, sneering nastily.

'Ya son of a bitch. You an' yer posh English pal. Think ya can come in here and lord it over us. Making it known ya got money. Well, mister, ya can just hand over your cash now.' Caleb gasped for breath again. He had three choices – to run, to give the money, or to fight. There was nowhere to run. Give up the money? No way. He'd worked hard for the money he earned in his father's warehouse. The only thing left was to fight. Fighting seemed to be the way of life here in Alaska. It wasn't the first time he'd fought. The school he went to in Vancouver had been tough. He'd learnt to literally fight his own battles. Caleb looked up, opened his mouth to shout at Jake and received a handful of mud full in his face. He flung himself forward, still blinded by the mud, and grappled with Jake's knees. One of them came up violently, crashing into his mouth, and he went over backwards. Blinking rapidly, he gained a little vision, enough to roll out of the way of the huge stick aimed at his head. He realised that he was now fighting for his life. As he tried to stand up, hoping to gain advantage of height, he was again thwarted by the slippery, disgusting mud, spit and blood. A relentless volley of punches was being hurled at him. Jake had thrown the wood down and was now depending on his fists. The onslaught slackened which gave

Caleb the advantage, so he grabbed a foot and knocked Jake off balance. His enemy was now slithering about in the mud searching for a foothold as Caleb punched him firmly in the jaw. Jake went flying backwards, having almost given up the fight. As Caleb stepped up ready to give another punch, the improvised weapon Jake had used suddenly descended upon his own head. Tom stood over both men, grinning.

'Wondered where you'd got to, Caleb. For an American you sure gave a good fight. Didn't think you had it in you.'

'Well, he took me unawares,' Caleb replied. 'We'll have to take care in future. I thought we'd done well by keeping out of trouble and avoiding incidents until now. Thanks, Thorpe, I guess you saved my life. He was determined to get to my money regardless. Pity he didn't realise it was all safely in the bank, ha ha.' With that, Jake opened his eyes and stared blearily at Tom and Caleb. Leaning menacingly over him, Caleb muttered, 'Good, he's still alive. Don't want any problems with the law.'

'Now, partner, let's get to bed,' smiled Tom.

'We'll leave this ruffian to get himself to wherever he's headed. Now that it's raining again, he'll have difficulty getting up from the mud – good!!' Caleb enunciated each syllable with great care, his jaw felt on fire and he might have a few loose teeth. He was covered from head to foot in the street mud and he could taste the blood pouring from his nose. Finding the thug's disgusting animal hat in the mud, he picked it up and painfully flung it at him. Inside the saloon, taking a good look at them both, the barman charged Tom and Caleb three times the going rate for the room and bath. It would take at least two of his men to lug the tin baths up, fill them, and then lug them down the stairs again before throwing the contents out into the street. These luxuries had to be paid for.

'And you have to be out the room by six in the morning, the sheets are needed for tablecloths for breakfast.' Tom and Caleb looked askance at each other, but obviously all the saloons were the same, they'd just have to grin and bear it.

Next morning the sky was a clear blue, the rain having cleared during the night. After a quick breakfast, the two companions with trepidation and excitement headed for the wharf, wading through the muddy streets, keeping a lookout for thugs who were out to thieve. Fortunately there was no sign of Jake. As they approached their packs, which had, remarkably, not been stolen, a man jumped out from behind a bale of straw right in front of Tom making him almost jump out of his skin. Wearing a grubby red padded jacket and baggy grey trousers, his small, brown wrinkled face lit up and his black eyes twinkled under his tiny red tasseled hat, as he stared up at the men; 'Me Ling, looked after your pack all night. I take you up Pass. Me velly good guide. Me velly good cook, cheap too.' Caleb and Tom laughed; this china man seemed quite a character. He proved his worth when he carried heavy packs without appearing to use much effort.

As Tom remarked to Caleb, 'For a small man, he sure can shift!'

CHAPTER SIX

At three o'clock, the released pupils walked sedately through the Dorset village school doorway, aware that the teachers were watching them from inside the classroom, only to erupt in a babble of sound as soon as they reached the gates, which they ran through and then dispersed to their various homes. Each child carefully carried a brown paper wrapped package. Daisy was tidying up the schoolroom before walking home. The stove was going cold and the room felt damp and clammy, despite the warmth outside, and, feeling tired, she was looking forward to being home with the family. As she worked, she thought back to the day's events. That morning Lady Thorpe and Miss Amy had visited them unexpectedly. Jane accompanied them, carrying a large basket. As the visitors had confidently walked into Daisy's schoolroom, following their visit to Miss Martin's class, the children had risen from the benches and, as one, said 'Good morning' so politely that Daisy could only stare. Realising how bad-mannered she appeared, she quickly dropped a curtsy to Lady Thorpe. 'I am so pleased to see you, children,' Lady Thorpe smiled delightedly.

'Good morning, Miss Evans.'

'Ma'am,' was all that Daisy could reply. This was Tom's mama and here she was, behaving like a dumbstruck child herself.

'We are so delighted at your politeness, children, we have brought along buns and fruit for you. You may take them home with you for yourselves and your families. Now, you must show us what you have been learning.' Daisy felt proud of the children. Albert had been the first to show the visitors the sums he worked on, on his slate. Susan pointed out pictures pinned to the wall of birds the children drew. When asked what the birds were, the children confidently answered. Miss Amy was interested in the sewing the girls were going to be involved in that afternoon, whilst the boys would be outside learning the game of football with the older boys. The children stood politely as the visitors left. Their families could enjoy the little parcels of food later in the day.

Emerging from her reminiscence and having collected up the slates the children had used, she stacked them on top of the cupboard ready for the lessons on Monday morning. Suddenly, Daisy jumped as the door burst open with a loud bang. Standing there was Mr Eddy, looking very angry, his cheeks ruddy, his breathing laboured. His eyes were glazed and evil looking. His threatening bulk dressed in his riding breeches, stock and jacket filled the door. He moved inside, grabbed the door and slamming it shut, he turned the key in the lock. 'Who have we here? Well, if it isn't Daisy, Tom's precious whore.' He was sounding very ugly indeed.

Daisy was filled with fear as she moved towards him, hoping to get near the door, but he backed away, tossing the key teasingly in the palm of his hand. 'Not so fast, Daisy dear, we'll enjoy ourselves before you leave here. You must be missing Tom and I am a good replacement. I know all about the secret meetings, watching you both made me feel frustrated and I need to relieve the agony of seeing you being kissed by him, when it should be me. I want you, Daisy and I think it's about time you stopped mooning over him and started enjoying yourself.'

'Let me go home, my family's waiting for me, I'll be late.' She was beginning to panic. Eddy was looking at her in a way that made her skin crawl. 'We are alone together now and I've waited so long for this, Daisy. I'm sure you're not a virgin, you know what to expect. You know what I want. I intend to get it.' He pocketed the key and held his arms splayed wide from his sides; his palms open in an apparent gesture of welcome. He moved towards her.

'Please, Mr Eddy, let me go.' Misery broke out in her voice. She backed away around the room towards the cupboard. No one would hear her if she screamed. She had stayed behind to tidy up. 'Stay there, stay away from me.' Her voice was soft and plaintive. She tried to think if there was anything she could use in self-defence. But he was a big man and surprisingly agile. Her hand suddenly felt the pile of slates, so she seized the top one. A flimsy article but it may help her. As he moved suddenly to grab her, she swung the slate and hit him across the face with it. As it broke over his cheek drawing blood, shards went flying all over the place. She realised then it was the wrong thing to do, Eddy became even more inflamed. He hit her on the side of her head with the flat of his hand and sent her hurtling across the floor. She was in pain but suddenly alert; everything was very clear but somehow moving slowly as she had time to think. She didn't want to be raped. She wanted to be home with her family, not here with evil Eddy. As she attempted to get up off the floor, at the same time watching Eddy, who was sneering, her thoughts went straight to Tom. She needed him here to protect her.

'I want you, young lady, and I'm going to have you. Fighting will only make it worse and no one can hear you, I'm going to have you.' With that he pushed her back down and attempted to kiss her roughly on the lips. The smell of him, of his drink sodden breath made her feel sick. Now he was on top of her and pulling her skirts and petticoats up past her waist. Her head was reeling and she felt dizzy. She bit his lip hard and in retaliation, he grabbed her round the throat with one hand whilst undoing the buttons on his trousers with the other. As he thrust into her, the pain was excruciating. She'd never felt anything like this is her life. She felt as if she was being torn apart. She beat on his back with her fists but the strength of her resistance was ebbing away; she drifted in and out of consciousness. As he finished with a loud groan, she lay still, numb and dazed. It was too late to fight him anymore; he had done something to her too despicable and disgusting.

'Well, what a surprise, a virgin! So Tom didn't deflower you before he left, but I have and I must say it was most enjoyable. I will have you again. Tell anyone about this and your family will pay the price. Your father will no longer work at the pottery. I can find a new foreman. Your mother will lose her position in the house. Your sister isn't as pretty as you, but I daresay she will fight like you did, I shall enjoy her. So watch what you say, you belong to me now; Tom won't be back for ages if at all. I for one, hope he never returns.'

As he uttered the words, he tucked his shirt in his trousers, did up the buttons and replaced his hat on his head. He found the key, unlocked the door, and, as he left, threw the key at Daisy, slamming the door behind him. As Eddy walked back to the house, he pondered on the situation; how was he to explain to Amy the bruise on his cheek from the slate she threw and the bite on his lip from that trollop. Daisy had asked for it, the way she repelled his advances. He smiled wryly to himself, it has been a most enjoyable experience despite my injuries. Next time she won't injure me, I'll make sure of that.

Daisy lay on the floor, still and lifeless. How long she lay there she didn't know, but eventually she painfully got up off the floor and rearranged her clothes. Looking in the small mirror on the wall by the door she put her hair back into a semblance of tidiness and pinned on her hat. She looked the same but she knew she was different; she was spoiled after such a vicious attack, even if Tom came back he wouldn't want her now. The future looked very grim indeed, Mr Eddy was sure to see to that. He had a hold over her – a hold that involved not just her, but her family. They didn't deserve the lives of poverty that Eddy would be sure to inflict. Still distressed and stunned, she carefully put on her coat and made her way home, walking slowly but upright so as not to invite questions should she meet anyone she knew. Despite the warmth of the late spring afternoon, she turned up the collar of grandma's coat. She was shivering and felt cold due to shock.

Reaching home she quickly lifted the kettle of warm water from the kitchen and took it upstairs to the room she shared with Ivy, who, mercifully, was out. Daisy stripped off her clothes and pouring the water into a bowl, scrubbed her body clean with an old washcloth. The pain between her legs made her gasp, but she had to carry on. Dressing in her spare blouse and skirt, she took her soiled clothes down to the scullery and washed them in a fresh bowl of hot water, then hung them on the line outside to dry. When they were dry she would have to secretly mend the tears in the blouse and skirt that evil Eddy had ripped. No one in the family need know what had happened to her – the shame was so great; whatever would she say, how would she be able to explain. Wiping tears from her eyes, she managed to pull herself together and start preparing the supper. She must act normally. She must get on with her life.

CHAPTER SEVEN

Once through Dyea without incident, Tom, Caleb and Ling
endured three days of painfully slow progress as they and a
few hundred other stampeders hauled their carts and
sledges up a pot-holed track. The sheer volume of people,
carts, dogs and pack animals made the path rutted and
treacherous. The hastily improvised bridges were so
ramshackle that on one occasion they all ended up on their
knees in icy water. Drying their clothes proved to be
difficult on the trail, and as a consequence they wore damp
clothes for days on end. They crossed the river several
times. Ling explained that the stampede had quietened
down. Six months ago there would have been thousands of
people taking this trek. Along the trail they came across
primitive shacks, many abandoned, which were handy for
shelter, were it needed. Abandoned heavy items such as
stoves, chairs and trunks lay around. Torn tents and
mountains of piled up goods were awaiting removal. Sheep
Camp, which was the last 'town' of any substance that they
would see until they reached Lake Bennett, lay in a hollow
at the end of the timber line, encircled by mountains and
consisting of a large campground accommodating about
eighty people. Here, they set up camp for one night. Ling
was left to start cooking supper and make their
surroundings as comfortable as possible under the
circumstances.

Noticing a grog tent, Tom entered through the low entry to be greeted by the smell of stew wafting around his nostrils; what kind of stew was anyone's guess. He needed to ask around but the place was empty except for one woman. The owner of this establishment eyed Tom, he reminded her of someone; someone she'd seen quite recently.

'They call me Slack Gertie, What d'ya want my 'and some?' asked the woman as she approached Tom. She was wearing a filthy brown thin cotton dress and she had a gleam in her eye which slightly scared Tom. Her pendulous breasts hung down below her waist. Lying with Slack Gertie would mean he really was down on his uppers – you'd need to be well down-wind of her even on a breezy day. She spat tobacco into the spittoon.

'I'm looking for my brother, Will. He came to the Yukon but hasn't been heard of for over a year. Apparently he looks like me. Have you met him?' asked Tom.

'Maybe I 'ave seen 'im, maybe I 'aven't. There's a nice mattress out back, you come on wi' me and I'll give ya such a good time ya'll fergit everything else.'

'No, thank you, ma-am, my priority is to find Will.'

'An Englishman, nicely spoken, came in 'ere, O, what, coupl'a weeks ago. Real 'ansome he were, just like you.'

Tom was cheered by this news. 'Do you know where he was headed?'

'He said Dawson City; he was on his way up. Lotta people are now on the way back. All the gold's gone, so I heered,' said Slack Gertie gloomily, her hands on her hips. 'Men are committing suicide, all sorts a things goin' on. You wanna take care. Come and see me again.'

'I will, and thanks for the information about Will, I just hope I catch up with him, I'm really looking forward to seeing him again.'

Tom left the tent, confidently striding away to his companions. He was elated that at last someone remembered seeing Will. He just hoped that his brother would still be in Dawson when he arrived there. Ling explained to them that if they fed scraps to the Whiskey bird that was pecking around their feet, then it will bring luck and the bird will clear up camp for them. Laughing at this and squatting around their camp fire, after supper, several other stampeders joined them, encouraged to do so hearing Caleb playing the mouth organ. His bright and jolly tunes echoed through the still evening air and bounced back from the mountains. When the sun shone, it now stayed light twenty hours a day. There were cookhouses here, but as Ling provided all they needed, they decided to save their dollars; everything was charged at exorbitant prices. For instance a dozen eggs cost sixty-two cents. Tom was surprised to see women on these trails; he had assumed, wrongly, that this was just a male-dominated event.

Chalkey was a man with a craggy face, broken nose and broad hands with short stubby fingers, with which, nevertheless, he played the banjo. In between stories, he admiringly told them; 'I heerd of a woman who made a lot of money by trading hats and dresses with native women in exchange for furs. These she sold to steam ship passengers as they disembarked at Skagway. She then bought hot water bottles and fabric which she took over the Chilkoot trail and sold in Dawson City. She had enough money to build what is now the best hotel in the whole city. Ya gotta admire her,' he chuckled.

The next morning, ascending Long Hill, the two and a half mile section between Sheep Camp and Scales was hard going for the three of them; it ascended sixteen hundred feet over the distance. They climbed with all their equipment strapped to their backs, and thankfully, the snow had melted, but the going was still tough. Jagged rocks and large boulders constantly hampered their progress. Ling was proving to be a good hire, he was a good cook, making the most of the provisions, although they lived mostly on bacon and beans. He added various spices, which he kept in little pockets sewn on the inside of his padded, quilted jacket the two men had never tasted before and were impressed.

On the fourth day, they woke to blue skies; it was going to be a fine, bright day, albeit a chilly and windy one. The sunrise gave off a faint hint of rose which washed the sky and fluffy clouds scudded by. They decided to have a day's rest and continue their journey the next day. They had only travelled about fifteen miles, but with the rocky, uneven, mountainous terrain it seemed double that distance. Ling was attending the fire to make the first brew of the day. It was Caleb's turn today to go and chop some trees for wood. Tom offered to do it instead, but Caleb insisted, despite the fact his ribs were still painful from the fight back in Skagway. Whilst waiting for breakfast Tom wrote home...

At last, someone has seen Will. A woman who owns one of the cookhouses here remembers him going in there for his meals but that he left about two weeks ago. She said he was a nicely spoken English man and the description I gave her fitted Will. He was making his way to Dawson, which is where we're headed. I'll go straight to the North West Mounted Police station to see if has registered a claim on some land, or if they know him or his whereabouts and I'll write again as soon as I have news. As I sit here on a fallen tree trunk admiring the view, in the distance I can see a female elk and her calf. A little further on are moose, they really are magnificent creatures. We are making slow progress; there is a great deal of mud where the snow has melted, which hampers us. The permafrost, which is soil at or below the freezing point of water for two or more years, has killed smaller trees. It makes one's feet cold to walk on it. Bluebells and rock roses remind me of home as do the swallows and plovers.

Ling is an inventive fellow; he makes torches by wrapping stout stakes in burlap sacking – after we've used up the beans the sacks contain, and, also, makes less for us to carry – and dipping them in kerosene. They shine brightly at night. He makes the most delicious tea from Labrador leaves; tastes like green tea we have at home. It's a good source of vitamin C, so as you can see, we are keeping well and fit. Later I shall go and collect pine cones for the fire. We seldom have the luxury of a full night's sleep and we take turns getting up to tend the fire which needs to be kept burning to deter predators, mainly bears. Last night we heard a couple of wolves eerily howling. I haven't seen a wolf yet, they sound fearsome. We have heard lots of tales, mainly about the women up here. The ones we have encountered work just as hard and share the same primitive living and working conditions as men. They have adapted and can cope with the same hardships. Dressed in high-heeled boots, corsets, bloomers, ankle-length skirts and blouses and jackets with leg-o-mutton sleeves and hats, they appear incongruous against the background of the primitive surroundings. Sometimes they have children with them and are still expected to perform all the domestic tasks expected of a woman. Occasionally the women will discard their impractical female clothes and dress in men's garments. Acting like men makes them feel safer.

One of the women round the fire was called Alice Birch. She had left her family in Washington in order to accompany her husband Jeff on the same journey that we are taking. It is an arduous journey for her, helping to drive a herd of five hundred sheep and fifty cattle. She's been married less than a year, she told us cheerfully. Last night we were attacked by a ravenous flock of mosquitoes. They were hungry and blood-thirsty and the noise of their humming nearly drove us mad. It's so important to sit near a smoky fire to keep them at bay, unless you have a veil to cover your head. ... ...

The next stage of their journey took them up the Golden Stairs; fifteen hundred steps cut out of the ice in the winter. Now, in early summer, with most of the ice having melted, the stampeders climbed up rugged steps hewed out of the rocks. With no shelter, they were buffeted by wind and the hot sun burned their skin. Exhausted, they stumbled on up. The Pass was almost vertical, rising to over two thousand, six hundred feet. Despite the breath-taking scenery, Tom found this journey taxing, his body ached, muscles he never knew he had, hurt. His shoulders felt as if leaden weights had been tied to them. Caleb felt that the sheer strain of dragging himself and the heavy packs up the mountainside was taking its toll on the injuries he received in the fight with Jake. It was so exhausting that all he wanted was to stop, sink to his knees and rest. Stopping, however, was not an option anywhere until they got to the top.

Eventually they reached the summit where everyone was able to stop. Tom took the canteen from around his shoulders and, removing his felt hat, after taking a deep swig of water, looked around him. The views were breath-taking, mountains surrounding them, covered in pine trees and huge boulders, in between which early purple and white spring flowers budded. Glaciers of bottle green overhung rocks in the distance and Tom could hear the cracking sound of the ice melting causing avalanches. Looking up, he spied a bald eagle circling above, his feathers shining in the bright sunshine, his "kwee, and kwee", call echoing around the mountains.

CHAPTER EIGHT

One late afternoon in May, Daisy walked home from school. Although late spring, it was one of those miserable days when the smoke from the flues of Thorpe had barely strength enough to emerge into the drizzling rain and hung down the sides of the chimney pots. She was thankful she wore a coat and hat, as she decided to walk along the heath road to check out the ponds and large pools. If the tadpoles were plentiful, she could bring the children here for their nature lesson next day. She smiled as she walked, thinking how the children enjoyed any outings they were able to go on. She still missed Tom and the outings they had enjoyed together. She felt sure when he realised what Eddy had done to her, it would be the end of their romance. She felt deep shame every time she recalled the day evil Eddy attacked her. She still kept the secret to herself, and so far no one knew.

The first pond she arrived at was Bottomless Pool, so named because it was, apparently, bottomless. Legend had it that a coach and horses had ploughed into the pond one frosty, winter night. No one had survived; the carriage and contents had sunk to the abyss. Daisy shivered, as if a ghost was nearby; local folk said it was haunted in these parts. The crunching of carriage wheels and the neighing of horses could be heard on still nights. Moving along the heath, and bending down as she was looking in the smallest pool, a large raindrop plopped in the water, to be followed by more drops. Seeing that there were, indeed, tadpoles, as well as a few froglets, she decided she had better get going. As the rain started to come down heavily, Daisy saw in the distance the little square brick building she had seen many times before. Today, however, nearly invisible smoke came from the puny chimney of the hut. Deciding to seek shelter until the rain shower eased, Daisy rapidly approached along the path. Stepping over the threshold and moving towards the fire, she heard someone behind her. As she turned and saw Eddy she jumped slightly. He was dressed in shooting clothes; sage green tweed Norfolk jacket tied with a matching belt, green wool plus fours, wool stockings and sturdy brown boots. On his head he wore a deerstalker. There was a simmering anger and fear in Daisy, as she knew what would happen next.

'Keep away from me, you horrible man, you've already damaged me, just leave me alone.'

Removing his hat and throwing it onto the ground, Eddy quickly grabbed her, put a hand round her mouth and dragged her backwards by her hair. He threw her to the dirty ground as she kicked and screamed. Eddy hissed into her ear, 'Stop screaming, no one can hear you, bitch.'

It was warm in the hut; he'd lit the fire especially for their rendezvous. The log he'd put on the fire was still green and it spat and crackled and then cast out a spume of dense smoke. The floor was composed of hard packed dirt. As she lacked resistance, being too scared to fight back, this time the attack was rapid. He pulled her coat and blouse open and, releasing one breast, he bit her, leaving painful marks. Enraged that she was still unresisting, he slapped her face.

'I don't know why you won't respond, Daisy. I am a wonderful lover; if only you would respond in the way I'd like you to. We could be friends. You know I can take you whenever I wish.' As he spoke, spittle from his mouth sprayed Daisy. She tried to turn away but he was still pinning her down.

When he had finished raping her, completing the act with a disgusting groan, he got up, dressed, picked up his hat and his gun from the corner of the hut where he had propped it and left without a word. Daisy felt, again, totally degraded and in pain. Blocking this attack from her mind, she couldn't help but wonder what Tom's lovemaking would be like. In her imagination, he would be gentle and loving, not brutal and causing her pain. She felt, until Tom came back, she was living in a dangerous world; a world that included hateful Eddy. Tidying her clothes and stumbling out of the hut she walked back home through the rain, which by now was pouring down but Daisy barely noticed. There was no one she could tell of her ordeal, and who would believe her anyway?

The next day, the rain having ceased, Daisy stood outside the open door of the schoolroom, naked pain in her eyes as she called out, 'Children, line up, boys in one row, girls in the other, and keep quiet. Jim Slater, stop kicking Isaac and line up.' She was taking them on their nature walk to the ponds; those ponds now held bitter memories, but the world still revolved. Children deserved their time looking at the newts, tadpoles and any other wildlife they found. She must put Eddy out of her mind and allow the beauty of the countryside surround her.

Three weeks later, after visiting the outside privy situated in the yard of the house, Daisy was concerned that she hadn't yet received the 'curse' that came regular as clockwork to her every month. A few mornings later, as she rose from the bed she shared with Ivy, nausea rose in her throat. Rushing to the, mercifully empty, privy, she tried to vomit, but despite retching, produced only bile. Her concern that she was pregnant by the repulsive Eddy caused her to retch again. 'I can't be,' she mumbled aloud. But as days passed and the retching continued, and still no smear of blood showed in her drawers, the dreadful realisation hit her: she must be pregnant. Hiding this fact from her family was not going to be easy. Her mother would know if she wasn't using her rags, and eventually, one member of the family would hear her retching in the privy.

At the end of the second month she knew it wasn't her imagination playing tricks, but that it was something far more serious. Each morning she heaved at the smell and sight of the porridge her mother placed in front of her. Daisy accepted the fact that she was, indeed, going to have a baby. She wondered how she was going to break the news to her mother, who so far, had said nothing on the matter; but had commented several times that Daisy was looking unusually pale and unwell. Daisy had replied that school was busy and keeping twenty children under control was tiring. She was unsure if her mother believed her, but although she ached to confide in her mother about her condition her courage always failed her. She was well aware of how horrified she would be because of the shame and disgrace it would bring on the whole family.

At night she slept badly, feeling rather fat and uncomfortable. Repeatedly she ran her hands over her stomach, conscious that her shape was changing and fearing the time when she no longer had an hour-glass figure. Each time she drifted off to sleep, she awoke suddenly, finding herself trying to decide which dreams were real and which reality. There were times when she imagined she had already faced her parents. Then she fantasised that they welcomed the news and told her that they were delighted. She didn't know how long she would be able to continue working at the school, or how Lady Matilda would take the news when she found out. Eventually, she decided time would tell, but for now, she would try and carry on as normal and take each day as it came.

Thoughts of Tom were never far from Daisy's mind; the memory of being in his arms and the love they had for each other. He was a special person. She wondered where he was, what he was doing. Had he found Will and were the two men coming home together? What would he say when he found out she was having a child by Eddy? Would he believe her when she explained what happened? Was anyone going to believe her when she eventually told the truth? What would her parents' reaction be? They had a lot to lose if she was believed. Eddy would almost certainly make her father's life a misery, and her mother could lose her job at the house. It was all so difficult, but, eventually, Daisy decided that she would tell her mother at the first opportunity. Her figure had expanded, her breasts were sore and she was no longer able to hide the terrible facts. Her friends were also concerned that she no longer went out for walks with them, or joined them at the sewing circle. She was spending too much time on her own in her bedroom. Although Daisy was on the verge of telling the girls about her predicament the last time they met, she held back, believing they would say she was making it all up. Now, she was lonely and scared and longing for Tom.

CHAPTER NINE

Harry, sitting at his desk, stared out of the study window. The estate gardeners wearing cotton hats to keep the bright autumn sun out of their eyes were trimming the yew hedge bordering the lawn. Although he was looking at the sunny, early morning view, Harry wasn't actually seeing it; his mind was completely occupied by the papers he held in his hand. The files of paperwork dealing with the house and estate, the pottery and school were piled up in front of him. Moments earlier he glanced at the file of household accounts that sat to the right of his blotter; neatly notated by him in columns, which all added up. One thing he noticed was the amount of money being spent on wine and spirits. His and Matilda's consumption was moderate and Amy drank very little, preferring soft drinks. That left Eddy. Harry decided he would have to speak to him about his drinking. Several evenings he had drunk so much that he was put to bed by the servants. It would have to stop. But all that were discarded as he once again read the contents of the envelope from Alaska that Mr Hibbs had brought to him on a small silver salver:

The Brown Dog Saloon
First Avenue
Skagway
Alaska

10 August 1898

Dear Lord Henry Thorpe

It is with regret and the deepest sympathy that I write to inform you of the death of your son, William Albert Henry Thorpe. As you will see, your son died during an act of selfless bravery.

Mr Thorpe was staying here at the time of his accident and amongst his belongings I found his notebook, which contained family details. Your son is buried in the cemetery in Skagway.

He died an honourable death and I also enclose a cutting from our local newspaper describing the incident in detail, and a copy of the inquest report. I have also enclosed a bill from the undertakers, which I have paid. I feel sure you will pay me back. Please let me know what to do with his personal belongings.

Yours sincerely,
Michele Parsons (Mrs)

Proprietor

Heroic Death of English Aristocrat

On July 8th, only days since the first White Pass and Yukon Railroad Company train left Skagway for Lake Bennett, an act of bravery took place. Mrs Wilmott, a visitor to the town, was holding the hand of her daughter, Marie, aged four years. They were standing near the waiting room. Mrs Wilmott was suddenly jostled due to a robber attempting to steal her bag, which she was holding loosely in her other hand. Marie, having freed herself from her mama, ran to the edge of the platform just as the train was approaching. Seeing the danger she was in, the Honourable William Henry Thorpe, an English aristocrat, rushed to the child, pulling her clear of the train. The child was unharmed, but unfortunately, Mr Thorpe's silk scarf became entangled in the driving rods and he was dragged under the wheels of the train to his death. Thorpe was the eldest son of Lord Henry and Lady Matilda Thorpe, of the county of Dorset, England. He was working as an independent journalist and sent several articles describing the Gold Rush to various English newspapers and periodicals, travelling to Dawson alongside stampeders and gold prospectors. He returned via the new White Pass and Yukon Route. He was boarding with Ma Parsons at her infamous brothel.

An inquest has been held and it has been found that the White Pass and Yukon Railroad Company are in no way to blame for this tragic incident. Mr Thorpe has been buried in Skagway Cemetery by the Baptist minister and Lord Thorpe informed of his demise. Mrs Wilmott is still shocked by the incident, but acknowledges her gratitude to Mr Thorpe and is humbled by his bravery. Following the incident, a man was arrested and is being held in the jail for attempting to rob Mrs Wilmott.

As Harry unfolded the newspaper cutting, tears blurred the corners of his eyes; he was unable to focus on the piece. He wondered how he was going to be able to break this news to Matilda.

'Harry, dear, I've just seen the post boy. Is there any news from Will or Tom?' asked Matilda croakily, as she entered Harry's study. Despite the warm August morning, feeling chilly, she was wrapped up in a shawl.

'Sit down, my dear. Yes, I have a letter here, but it is very bad news.' Harry explained kindly. After blowing his nose in a copious handkerchief, he led Matilda to a chair in front of the empty fireplace. Matilda looked up at her husband, realising immediately his distress.

'Tell me, Harry, please tell me, is it Will or Tom?'

'It's Will. He's dead,' Harry said abruptly. Realising how his words must sound to her, he then gently told Matilda all he knew. He read the newspaper cutting out loud to her but omitting the fact that Will had been boarding in a brothel. Matilda was a sensitive woman, and as a mother, would not want to hear about her son's sex life. Harry held her in his arms as she crumpled.

'Our dear Will, our first-born child, dead. He may have died a heroic death, but that is little comfort,' she sobbed. As she removed a small, lace trimmed handkerchief from her sleeve, Harry gently took it from her and wiped her eyes in an act of such love that it caused her to cry anew. She cried and cried, copious tears streaming down her face. Leaning on his shoulder she mumbled, 'He died in Alaska, Harry. So far away. Where is Tom? Do you think he knows?' She was beside herself and unaware of her surroundings for a moment, being in deep anguish.

'I can't answer those questions, my dear,' Harry muttered. 'However, I will write to the various people involved, thanking them for informing us and pay Mrs Parsons straightaway.'

They sat quietly for a while, comforting each other in the silence. Nothing like this had ever happened to them before this; it was particularly trying for Matilda. Dealing with death and distressing situations was part of Harry's work as a magistrate, but this was different; this was his own beloved first born son, his dear Will. He thought back to the times when they had attended shooting parties, joined the local hunt, enjoyed a quiet brandy together at the table after dinner when the ladies retired to the drawing room. He couldn't believe it would never happen again. Suddenly jumping up quickly, Matilda tugged the embroidered bell pull from beside the fireplace. She needed to summon Hibbs; he would find Amy and Eddy for her. She and Harry would break the news to them together she thought, as she bravely straightened her shoulders and set her stiff British upper lip in place. They also needed Richard, the vicar to come over. A memorial service would be appropriate; they could hold it in the church; maybe it would help Matilda grieve, thought Harry. He was going to be busy informing people who knew Will of their dear son's demise. Even though he was a hero, it was little compensation for the loss they are now enduring.

On Wednesday 21st September, 1898, a memorial service for Honourable William Albert Henry Thorpe was held in the Parish Church of Lady St. Mary's. The Reverend Richard McCree officiated and the address was given by Mr Harold Jones, a friend and fellow student of Mr Thorpe's at Rowborough School. He and Mr Jones had become firm friends over the years since leaving the school. Harold praised William for his tenacity in travelling all the way to the Yukon to bring news of the Gold Rush to the small corners of the British Isles. He commended Will for his courage in saving little Marie's life in an act of unselfishness. Matilda, dressed entirely in black taffeta with a veil and picture hat hiding her features, sat stiffly throughout the service. Occasionally she delicately wiped her eyes with a black edged lace handkerchief. Amy, however, was to be heard sniffing loudly; finding it difficult to hold back on her grief. Sitting with the women in the hard-backed pew, Harry and Eddy stared straight ahead. At the back of the church, the staff from Thorpe House sat with the workers from the pottery and those villagers who were able to take time off to attend. Daisy sat with the schoolchildren, who were finding it difficult to sit still through the long service. Two hymns were sung, *The Lord's My Shepherd* and *Guide Me O Though Great Jehovah*. Following the Memorial Service, Lord and Lady Thorpe hosted a tea back at the house, to which all were invited. However, the villagers and workers soon dispersed back to their homes, enabling the family to spend the rest of the day quietly together.

'It went well, I thought, my dear,' said Harry, as he kissed his wife. It was the end of the saddest day of their lives, and they were relaxing together in Matilda's bedroom, where she was sitting up in bed. She was exhausted.

'It was a lovely service, Harry. I just wish Tom was home. Where is he?'

As she closed her eyes and drifted off to sleep, Harry crept out of the room and joined Eddy in a whiskey before retiring himself. He wished he could answer Matilda's question – where was Tom?

CHAPTER TEN

The scenery around Lake Bennett showed that the worst of the weather was behind the stampeders. Trees and flowers grew in abundance and geese, sparrows and robins twittered around. A beaver dam blocked part of the lake nearby. Men were fishing, hoping to catch a pike, trout or grayling for their supper. On the shores of the lake a small town had been set up. Every possible amenity was here, including bath tents, barber shop tents, a church, casino and post office, along with shops selling everything from bread to gumboots. Some businesses were held in hastily erected cabins made from roughly hewn wood; yet because of the Mounted Police's vigilance there were none of the crimes seen in Skagway. Soapy Smith's henchmen had been sent back with dire warnings not to return. Tom, Caleb and Ling had been visited by the Superintendent of the Mounties and details logged of their next of kin, along with the name of the boat they were travelling on up the lake to Dawson.

They made camp near large boulders, which sheltered them from the wind, pitched the tent and unpacked the cooking gear. Each man knew his task by now, no need for anyone to give orders. Tom visited the post office and sent off his letters to Dorset, knowing that his parents would be anxious to hear from him, particularly as he found news of Will. He was now most eager to be in Dawson and to seek out his brother. Thoughts of Daisy entered Tom's mind, as he walked back to their own small camp area where Ling was starting the fire by scraping bark shavings from a silver birch log prior to cooking supper. He wondered what she was doing at that very moment, was she well, was she missing him?

'Beans and bacon again, Ling?' he called out as he saw his friend bending over the tripod set over the fire.

'No, sir, we got beef tonight, me buy from shop. Velly nice beef. I cook it with potatoes me bought, too.'

'Well, while there's still daylight, I'm going to take a short walk and collect some wood and see if we can catch some game whilst you cook, Ling. Are you coming with me, Caleb?'

The two men wandered through patches of bluebells and lupins, appreciating the greenery and trees and colours after the stark terrain of the Pass. An elk and her calf were spotted in the distance, and, though he carried his rifle, Caleb was reluctant to shoot a mother who was not a threat to them. It would leave the calf to starve to death. Noticing a flock of geese flying overhead, Caleb took aim with his rifle and, to his delight, brought one down.

'Supper tomorrow, what a difference this will make to our meagre rations.'

'I'll go and get it, Caleb,' said Tom cordially, as he ran off into the brush. Suddenly, without realising what was happening, Tom had wandered into the path of a female brown bear and her cub. The bear came lumbering up to Tom, who, shocked, just stopped in his tracks, unaware that looking a bear in the eye was a sign of aggression to the animal. They stood looking at each other, eye to eye for a second, then the bear attacked, charging and snorting. Tom tried to dodge the bear, but it rammed him up against a pine tree, smacking his head. The beast then mauled Tom's head and the arm he put up to protect himself, tearing the blue denim cloth of his shirt. Screeching with fright, Tom felt helpless against this onslaught; the bear then shook him as if he were a rag doll. Hearing Tom's screams, Caleb ran to the scene and, quickly cocking his rifle, fired at the bear. Unsure whether he had hit the fearsome animal, Caleb fired again, but was too late; the bear was carrying Tom off. Then, dropping his prey, the bear made a beeline for Caleb, who, dropping his gun in fright ran like the wind, as if the devil himself was behind him, which, indeed he was. Caleb reached camp as the bear veered off and loped back into the trees, back to her cub, or to finish Tom off, Caleb was too scared to know which.

Making his way, feeling shaken, in the dusk of the evening, to the North West Mounted Police hut, Caleb realised that tears were streaming down his face. His dear friend, Tom, had been horrifically attacked.

'Come quick, please, a man has been attacked by a bear,' screamed Caleb. 'She was enormous, I fired my rifle, but don't think I even winged her. Come and help me find him.'

'Stay here, sir,' soothed Sergeant Wilson and he and a scout took details of the location, then, with rifles at the ready, they disappeared into the woods. Ling collected Caleb from the hut and led him to their tent where he sat him in front of the fire. Shaking with shock and pale-faced, he gratefully accepted the mug of whiskey offered him by he knew not who. A crowd of stampeders gathered around Caleb as he recounted what had happened:

'The female bear was huge. Had a massive jaw and teeth, which she sank into him. Tore at Tom's face and arm, then carried him off. He must be dead. She came after me, and then veered off, don't know where. Don't know if she got Tom again.'

'There have been attacks like this many times,' offered a man in soiled dungarees worn over a ragged chequered shirt. 'Ya' have ta' be real careful.'

That night Caleb got little sleep, as he said to Ling next day, 'I can still see it every time I close my eyes. 'Tis an awful thing to happen.'

The Mountie and his deputy returned to Caleb and Ling's tent after an hour. 'No sign of a body, but blood everywhere, can only assume the bear got him. Found some fragments of his shirt. Probably dragged him off to its lair. I'll telegraph his family and tell them. Not the first time I had to do this,' he stated pragmatically. 'People just don't realise the dangers here.' He took out his tobacco pouch, packed his pipe, lit it, and, puffing away, walked back the way he had come, leaving behind a pungent trail of smoke.

CHAPTER ELEVEN

Matilda sat in her favourite armchair watching through the window, as her daughter played with Florence, her dog. Amy laughed as she threw the ball time and time again for her pet to retrieve. It was difficult to imagine the trauma they were experiencing, but it was a treat to see Amy happy for a while. Picking up the heavy silver coffee pot, and pouring herself another cup, she sipped her coffee and thought back to the conversation held last night between herself and Jane, her maid. Matilda had sat up in bed, her pink bed jacket tied at her neck with a matching ribbon, mesmerised as her maid's story unfolded.

'I need to talk to you, please, ma'am,' announced Jane the day after she and Daisy had endured a difficult conversation. 'I have to tell you something very personal and unpleasant.'

'Go ahead, Jane, I am listening. Bring the dressing table stool here and sit down next to my bed.'

'I am so worried, ma'am. It's our Daisy. She told us yesterday she's in the family way. She said she had been attacked and raped twice.' Jane swallowed, trying to shift the lump in her throat. Telling the truth to her mistress was not easy. Jane paused as she wondered how her mistress was going to react. Worse still, how was his Lordship going to take the news?

'Go on, Jane,' murmured Matilda as she shifted uneasily, dislodging a pillow slightly.

'Daisy…' Jane paused, swallowed, then, with trepidation, started again; 'Well, it was Mr Eddy who attacked her. The first time in the school room, it was after school the day I came with you and Miss Amy to visit the children. The second time in a hut at the factory. Daisy was out walking and looking at the ponds on the heath. Bert and I don't know what to do. Bert is fearful he'll lose his foreman's job at the pottery. Mr Eddy may not want Bert there anymore. Oh, ma'am, what shall we do?' Jane swallowed again; she mustn't break down in front of her mistress. Lady Matilda was very good to her and the family. It was she who had obtained the teaching assistant's job for Daisy at the little school.

'Do you believe her, Jane?' asked Matilda.

'I do, ma'am, my Daisy is a good girl, and she wouldn't tell lies. She has found all this very frightening and painful. Now, her reputation is about to be destroyed and her father and I are at our wits end. It's so unfair,' Jane said, her voice raising an octave.

Matilda felt anger begin to fill her, but she remained straight-faced; she had heard various stories recently about Eddy's proclivities. 'When do you estimate the baby will be born, Jane?'

'It was in May, the second attack happened. By my reckoning it should be February, ma'am.'

'Leave this with me, Jane; I'll speak to you again soon. Help me to dress, then you must go and tell the Master I wish to see him here in my room.'

When Harry arrived, he pulled a comfortable chair up to the bed and held Matilda's hand. Jane having left the room, Matilda tearfully related the sorry story. Harry left his seat and sitting on the bed, took his beloved wife in his comforting arms. Sobbing against his chest and inhaling the smell of the sandalwood soap he always used, she spluttered, 'How will Amy feel about this? She is desperate to conceive a baby and now it appears Eddy has one easily through his fornication.' Sniffing, she continued, 'Poor Amy. I do love her so. We do not need a scandal, Harry, we must contain this embarrassing disaster to within the house. But, if the story is true, as Jane is adamant it is, what can we do for Daisy?'

Harry, naturally, took it badly, and, like Matilda, felt angry. 'I've seen him flirt with village girls quite often, but I wouldn't have thought that of him. I've also heard how unpopular he is at the pottery; apparently he treats some of the workers badly, and pesters women. I'll have to have it out with him and I'd better invite Bert Evans up here. We'll get it sorted out, my dear, don't cry, please.'

As Jane walked down the stairs towards the kitchen, where Cook would share a pot of tea, she thought back to when Daisy had broken the news of her unfortunate pregnancy to her. It was one evening following Daisy's walk home from school. Jane was enjoying some rare time off from her work at the big house and was just laying the table for supper. Bert was in the back yard smoking his pipe and talking to his pig as was usual. Ivy was visiting friends.

'I notice you haven't been using rags for your monthlies, Daisy, and you've been sick a few mornings. You haven't eaten much at breakfast. I hope this doesn't mean you are in a certain condition? ' Jane had blurted out as Daisy hung up her coat on the hook on the door of the kitchen. Daisy had stared at her mother, her face turned pale and she fought back the tears, which were threatening to flow over her cheeks. Jane had realised that she was, indeed, with child. Daisy hoped to tell her mother before she mentioned it, but now the time had come for the truth to be spilled out. Jane sat down heavily on a ladder-back chair and faced her daughter.

'I should have told you sooner, Mother, but I was scared.'

'Tell me now, Daisy, tell me all about it.' Jane's voice had an angry edge to it. 'Does this have anything to do with that box stored under your bed? You've never told me who gave you that dress.'

'No, Mother, the dress has nothing to do with this. I'll tell you what happened. Do you remember the evening in May you were late home from the big house? Lady Matilda needed you to help her with something?'

'Yes, yes, I remember, I had to tidy the wardrobes and the room. She'd had some new dresses made. So, what happened?'

'Well, that day Lady Thorpe, Miss Amy and you visited the school. The children all went home with buns and fruit. I was tidying the schoolroom when Mr Eddy came in. He locked the door and cornered me. I couldn't get past him and then he raped me. It was so terrible. I felt so ashamed. I just couldn't speak of it.' Jane saw that Daisy's cheeks were burning pink with embarrassment and that tears weren't far away.

'Am I supposed to believe you, girl? You must have led him on; he wouldn't just thrust himself upon you.' Jane was angry and Daisy was mortified at her mother's words.

'I hit him on the cheek with a slate in self-defence when he first grabbed me. It made him angry. I just couldn't fight back. He was too strong.'

Jane just stared at her daughter, pink spots appearing on her cheeks. 'Oh dear, I find this difficult to take in.'

Daisy, now feeling embarrassed, looked at her mother. 'That was the first time. Then it happened again. The second attack and rape happened three weeks later. I was walking back from school and went around to the ponds to see the tadpoles. That day it had poured with rain; I was getting soaked to the skin. As I walked past the hut the men use when it's raining, I noticed smoke curling up from the little chimney, so went to investigate. I thought Dad might have been in there. He wasn't. It was Mr Eddy. He pulled me inside. He'd been shooting; I saw his gun propped up in the corner. I was helpless and couldn't do anything. He threatened me, told me Dad would lose his job, you'd be thrown out of the big house and he'd get Ivy next. What could I do?' Daisy's voice raised and then Jane turned to see Bert standing in the doorway.

'I'll kill the bugger that I will,' he shouted.

'Now, Bert, you know that won't help, we have to think this through.' Jane was still stunned. Daisy was crying as if her heart would break; the shame and humiliation of it all. It broke Jane's heart to see the effect all this was having on Daisy and longed to be able to do something to help her.

Jane was gratified that Lady Matilda had allowed Daisy to still work in the school, which had been a blessing; it meant her work helped her take her mind off the coming baby and also allowed her a small salary to help the family finances.

Harry told Eddy he wanted to see him in his study early the next morning. Eddy was eager to get to the pottery; he had a feeling he knew what was about to happen. He was right. Standing in front of the fireplace Harry confronted Eddy who stood next to a chair covered in tartan cloth. On the walls hung Harry's stuffed animal head hunting trophies.

Looking Eddy straight in the eye, he said, 'Jane Evans has told us they believe what their daughter has told them – that you abused Daisy. I want the truth now, Eddy, did you attack Daisy, not just once but twice, as she says?' Harry stood tall and straight, his stance so aggressive Eddy looked uncomfortable and shifted from one foot to the other. He was right, his father-in-law did know about his violence towards Daisy Evans. He wondered if Matilda and Amy knew. Mother and daughter were very close; he would be very surprised if Amy didn't know.

'I deny these allegations. Who has been telling you these lies?' Eddy stated sneeringly.

'Her mother, Jane, told Matilda yesterday. We both believe Jane, and we believe Daisy has told her the truth.'

'She's a fine-looking girl, I couldn't help myself.' Finally, under Harry's dark scrutiny, he admitted, 'Yes, the child in all likelihood would be mine.'

'She claims you raped her the first time in the school room and the second time in a hut near the pottery.' Harry was so angry he was virtually spitting.

'She asked for it. A girl like her, with her good looks should be married by now. I didn't know she was a virgin. I had been drinking, both times.'

Eddy was beginning to run out of excuses. He could see the anger in Harry's face, his right eye was twitching. Also, Harry's hands were clenched by his sides as if he were about to hit out at Eddy. Pausing for a few moments, Harry finally said, 'We will tell Bert Evans to come here and to see what is to be done. I am very disappointed in you, Eddy.'

'What's done is done,' replied Eddy. 'Now, if you will excuse me, I'll be on my way to the pottery. The stable lad has my horse waiting outside.'

'With regards to the pottery,' claimed Harry, 'I understand that business is dropping off. We haven't secured any new contacts recently, and it's important we do so. When Tom returns he will want a flourishing business, not one going down the drain, literally.'

'I will do what I can. I don't seem to have the same personality as Tom when it comes to meeting clients. They all ask for Tom, rather than do business with me!'

'If you stopped drinking so much and you were more business-like, I am sure business would improve. Now, get out of my sight before I do something to you I may regret.'

Eddy stormed out of Harry's study, strode down the hall and slammed out of the front door. The stable lad, Jack, was ill prepared for the kick and thump Eddy gave him as he climbed onto the horse and galloped away. 'Wonder why he did that?' sniffed Jack as he ambled back to the stables. 'I've done nothing wrong.'

Bert had been summoned up to the Big House after dinner that evening. He felt out of his depth. The scale of this family's status and wealth made him feel small, everything surrounding him in this study was large and expensive, including these two men. He also felt ill at ease in his Sunday best suit in contrast to the expensive rug he was standing on and looking at the way his supposedly "betters" were attired. Both Harry and Eddy were dressed in black velvet dinner jackets and pristine white shirts. Eddy's top shirt button was undone and his black tie hung loosely around his neck. Shiny patches showed on the knees of Bert's trousers from his kneeling in church, despite Jane's careful ministrations with the iron and brown paper. Although feeling at a disadvantage, Bert stared at Eddy with hatred in his eyes, how could you do such a thing to my daughter? She's an innocent girl. What has she ever done to you? Her life is ruined. Our family is ruined. Eddy arrogantly stared back at Bert but kept silent, showing no indication of shame. Harry, looking straight at Bert, said kindly; 'We must avoid scandal at all costs. Matilda and I have discussed this problem at length and believe we have a solution. Of course, Bert, we need your agreement.'

'Go on, sir,' said Bert.

'Nanny Smith has now retired and lives in a cottage a distance from Thorpe. We've written to her explaining the situation and she has agreed to have Daisy stay with her until the child is born. After that, we shall find a good home for the child. Nanny will be quite capable of handling this situation; we have every faith in her. Before her retirement she looked after me, and all the family since, having been a part of Thorpe House since she was thirteen years old.'

'Well,' muttered Bert after some consideration, 'it does seem a good solution. What about after, when the child is born, what then?' he went on flatly. 'We have to think about Daisy.'

'Of course,' said Harry in a matter-of-fact way. 'We have, actually, found a good home for the child. You needn't concern yourself. It's all been thought out.'

'Oh, yes, and just what does that mean?' Bert felt deflated and tired standing in front of these two intimidating men. He had to be careful what he said, but he must do right by Daisy and the family.

'My wife and I are going to take the baby. We can't have children, through no fault of mine, obviously,' sneered Eddy. 'I will break the news to my wife at an appropriate moment. There'll be no gossip from the servants and villagers,' he announced defiantly. 'We'll just say the baby has been adopted by us. All you have to do is sign the papers our lawyer will draw up and the matter will be settled. Daisy will need to sign a legal paper as well. All done and dusted, no harm done.' Eddy, after relating this to Bert, gave a satisfied cough and walking towards the door, showed Bert out of the room before he could object in any way. Sneering as he closed the door, he turned around, walked to the Tantalus and helped himself to another whisky before walking out of the study himself.

'Arrogant fellow,' muttered Harry as he watched Eddy help himself to the best whisky money could buy.

As he left the house to walk back home, Bert, once again feeling intimidated, reflected back to the meeting. He couldn't believe what he'd heard from Mr Eddy – no harm done. Who does the man think he is? He's ruined my daughter's life and 'all done and dusted?' He couldn't imagine what Jane would say. But he was aware that their hands were tied. Would it be a case of 'No agreement? No jobs?' It was obvious they had set up plans before meeting with him; and Daisy was his daughter, not a piece of their property to be disposed of. But he couldn't fault the plan; Daisy would just have to fall in with it all. Passing the local public house, he called in for a quick pint of bitter. He couldn't tell his mates where he had been, but he could share his hatred of Eddy with them.

The day following the meeting Eddy had cornered Bert in the factory and took him out of the hearing of other workers; 'You do as I say, Bert. I can make sure you lose your job here and your wife will no longer work at the house. Be sure of it. I have the power over your whole family. Who knows what could happen to that other daughter of yours, Ivy, she's a beautiful young girl, ripe for the picking.'

Pushing Bert out of the way, he stormed out of the factory, glaring at anyone who dared to look his way.

Bert walked come home the previous evening furious and the worse for wear after too many pints and thumped the table where Daisy sat sewing. Looking at him she felt more than a little apprehensive, never having seen her father in such a temper before. He'd taken his pipe from his pocket, and then stumped off, still in his suit, to talk to his pig; the sow always had a calming effect on him. You knew where you were with pigs, not like some people. Today's threat against him and Jane was bad enough, but what he'd said about Ivy was painful, they certainly didn't want the same ordeal placed upon their young daughter. They would have to be very careful.

CHAPTER TWELVE

Amy's black silk gown hugged her slim body as she sat ramrod straight on the sofa in the drawing room. Her eyes were still wet as she sipped her coffee, the hand holding the Crown Derby saucer was shaking and the tiny teaspoon rattled. The death of her brother, Will, had hit her hard. They had been good friends, despite the fact that he always enjoyed teasing her, never letting her forget she was a girl and girls shouldn't canter around the way she used to do, sitting astride her horses instead of side saddle. She remembered the games the three of them played together; hide and seek, sardines and charades. Their perfect childhood with father encouraging them to be individuals and to explore their surroundings, as well as urging them to take up whatever activities they enjoyed. Now look what Papa's encouragement led to; one brother dead and another missing. Quietly sobbing, she placed her cup and saucer on the little side table and searched for her handkerchief. She dearly loved her Papa and it was unfair to blame him, but, oh, she did miss Will and Tom; there was a big gap in her life. Taking Florence on her lap, she buried her face in her warm, soft fur. Her pet looked up at her with large soulful brown eyes; it was almost as though she could feel her sadness. Eddy was absent again, he hadn't appeared at dinner. She wondered where he was. Harry stood in front of the fireplace. Matilda sat on the couch at right angles to the fireplace, her black taffeta dress in contrast to the paleness of her alabaster skin. She was feeling very tired, grieving was exhausting. As her parents quietly discussed the recent events, Amy thought back to the previous night, when Eddy told her further shattering news.

Sitting up in bed reading her favourite novel, *Pride and Prejudice* by Jane Austen her husband lurched into the room in another of his drunken bouts. Stretching out his hand and throwing her book on the floor, he slumped on to the edge of the bed, his eyes glazed and blurred from the amount of whisky he had drunk. Facing his wife, Eddy was slurring his words as he said: 'Amy, a young girl from the village has fallen on difficult times. She's going to have a baby, through no fault of her own. Her parents are unable to care for a new baby and the scandal through the village will be too much for them to bear. Not that I care about their reputation,' he spat. So, I decided we shall adopt this baby.' He stopped speaking for a moment and grinned at Amy. 'We can give it a secure loving home.' Eddy gazed into his wife's pretty face. Amazed at his audacity she looked at him, and then moved her head side to side in disbelief at what he was telling her.

'A young girl from some village is having a baby? You want us to adopt it? Are you completely mad?'

'I am not mad. I need a child, an heir to carry on at the pottery. You are a barren, frigid woman. We are going to adopt this baby.' Eddy thrust his face nearer Amy, and as she recoiled, he became angry. 'You will do as I say. I've already told your parents, so you can't go crying to them.' His threatening manner was scaring Amy.

'What did Mama and Papa say? Surely they didn't agree!'

'Oh, yes they did. And what's more they know who the slut of a girl is.'

'Who is the father?' queried Amy, becoming more and more suspicious of Eddy. She wouldn't be surprised if it was him, he was hardly ever around in the evenings these days. When she did see him, he was drunk and angry. It was almost as if he couldn't cope with anything. She had overheard Papa telling Mama the other evening that business was going down at the pottery. They were all putting two and two together and realising that Eddy was finding it difficult to cope.

'Well, if you must know, woman, yes, it is my child. And another thing, the girl is Daisy,' he shouted.

'Daisy? Daisy Evans?'

'Yes, perfect Daisy. Her from the school. Bert Evans' slut of a daughter. Her who was friendly with Tom.'

'Friendly with Tom?'

'Amy, you keep asking me these questions. You will take this child in when it is born and you will give it a decent home. I tell you, Daisy Evans is having my child. I attacked and raped her twice. She was a virgin. Huh, what a surprise that was. Can't tell you how much I enjoyed those encounters. Thought Tom had got there first,' laughed Eddy, as he got up from the bed and drunkenly wove his way around the furniture to the door to his dressing room.

Going into the room, he slumped down on the single bed and began snoring loudly. Amy sat up in bed stunned. She could hardly believe what he was telling her. He had attacked and raped Daisy, that dear, sweet girl from the school. Jane's' daughter. She wondered how Jane and Bert were coping. How Daisy was coping. Her head reeling, and feeling nauseous, Amy settled down under her blankets and rested her head on the pillows, attempting sleep. But sleep evaded her. She tossed and turned all night long, pondering the words she and Eddy said to each other. She couldn't believe that he was expecting her to take in his bastard child, even if the mother was poor Daisy.

The next morning at breakfast, still feeling sick, and helping herself a cup of strong coffee, then pouring in milk, she faced her parents across the crisp, white-clothed table.

'Last night Eddy told me he has made Daisy Evans pregnant by attacking and raping her.' Amy swallowed a small amount of coffee before continuing: 'Do you know about this? He says you do.' Both of her parents nodded. Amy noticed the dark shadows under her Mama's eyes. She appeared to have slept little, too. The same as me, thought Amy.

'Yes,' answered her Papa: 'It's a dreadful thing Eddy has done, and we do not condone it, but we must make the best of a bad situation.'

'Dearest Amy, it does seem a good idea,' said Matilda softly. 'After all, your arms have been aching to hold a child ever since you and Eddy wed. It could be an answer to our prayers.'

'It would mean there will be a grandchild to carry on the business and a child in the house would be very pleasant indeed,' said Harry quietly. Both he and Matilda were of one mind; if there had to be a baby as the result of Eddy's fornication, then Daisy being the mother was acceptable. She was a nice girl, and at one point they wondered if Tom was keen on her.

'It will, however, be difficult for Jane. Working here she could encounter the child, which, after all, will be her grandchild as well.' Matilda paused, as she bit into a piece of toast. 'She may only be a servant, but she has been a good friend to me. She is well respected and she does her job very well. Finding another maid would be too distressing. I must ask her how she feels.'

'Has no one considered my feelings?' pointed out Amy. 'You both appear to be more concerned about a servant, than me,' she pouted.

'Of course we have, darling. You are our first consideration, we realise this must be most distressing for you. But we have to consider the options. Sadly, you aren't with child, much as you and Eddy have tried to produce one.' Matilda coloured slightly as she said this. 'Think it over, and you will see what we propose will be all for the best.'

Harry looked lovingly at his only daughter, his eyes showing the pain he was bearing for her. She must be falling apart inside, despite her outward appearance. To hear the things she has had to hear would be tearing her apart. 'Try and think of the baby as an orphan. Put the evil way it came about, out of your mind, dear Amy. Mama and I do feel for you.'

'There will be a baby that will need to be loved, Amy, and you will make a good mother. Nanny will come out of retirement to help us all.' Matilda looked lovingly at Amy. She felt the pain her only daughter must be experiencing. 'Daisy is going to live with her till the birth. The baby will then come straight here. I believe Eddy has arranged a nurse already,' Matilda said kindly as she stood up, preparing to leave the table. Harry stood as well, and held her chair as she stepped back. Kissing her daughter on her forehead as she passed, she quietly said as she left, 'I need to see Cook about the menu.' Matilda was cautiously aware that Amy was feeling angry and disillusioned, but life had to continue in the house. Servants had to be given tasks, the families' emotions needed to be hidden; no scandal must reach the servant's hall.

Harry, too, left the room, after patting Amy on the hand, leaving her to, once again, ruminate on all the family tragedies. Amy stayed at the breakfast table, eating nothing and wondering how much more she could take.

Sitting on the stool a few evenings later, wearing a white lawn nightgown, patiently watching her maid, Elsie, brush her thick chestnut hair, Amy reflected on her life and her husband's announcement about the baby. The mirror on her dressing table reflected her large four-poster bed, dressed in pretty muslin sprigged with violets; the drapes matching the bed quilt and cushions. Looking at it, she wondered the point of having such a pretty item of furniture when to sleep in it brought so much anguish.

'Elsie, I'm sure you have realised how desperately unhappy I am.'

'Well, Miss Amy,' replied Elsie. 'I've looked after you since you grew out of the nursery. I know when you are unhappy and when you are content.'

'My marriage to Eddy is not quite what I expected. Falling in love with him at the age of seventeen, I was thrilled when he announced he loved me and when he proposed I accepted not just with my own joy, but with my parents' joy, too.'

'I remember that, miss.'

'They are acquainted with Eddy's family and the match, which joined the two families, I know, delighted both sets of parents.' Amy paused, allowing Elsie to finish brushing her hair. Still listening to her mistress, Elsie tidied the dressing table.

'Eddy, then, appeared very dashing, though not exactly handsome, but with a charisma about him that attracted the ladies. His brown hair was cut regularly and his moustache neatly trimmed. His brown eyes were fringed with lashes that were, really, too long on a man; many a woman would be envious of such lashes.' Amy closed her eyes for a moment, remembering how it had been.

'But, you know, Elsie, I realise he has changed. He's put on weight. He drinks too much. Have you noticed?'

'Well, yes, I have, miss.'

'I don't know where he goes, or who he goes with in the evenings when he's not here with me. It doesn't help that every month, when the blood flow starts I feel desolate. I just do not seem able to conceive a child.'

Amy was not sure she should be telling her maid this, but she needed to confide in someone; Elsie, she was sure, would be discreet. Elsie, herself, was feeling distinctly uncomfortable listening to her mistress, but she had enough respect for Miss Amy not to say so.

'I knew that your wedding night turned out to be a disappointment with Mr Eddy being unexpectedly rough with you. I noticed the bruises when I helped you dress,' said Elsie, gently. 'I couldn't understand why he treated his new wife so badly. I felt very sad for you.'

The morning following their wedding, before they departed for their honeymoon in Italy, Eddy cruelly confessed to Amy he married her just because she was beautiful and he enjoyed owning beautiful objects. Upon their return, he bought her the little King Charles Cavalier spaniel puppy, in part, as recompense for his behaviour. She named the puppy after the city she loved visiting: Florence. Maybe a baby would heal some of the pain of her marriage, thought Amy.

'Is that all, ma'am?' said Elsie making her mistress jump slightly.

'No, Elsie. Please stay with me for a while.' said Amy pensively, as she felt tears beginning to well up. Shivering, she wrapped a shawl around her shoulders. It had been a long day; spending her morning in a meeting with some ladies of the parish planning the Sunday school outing. Keeping her composure was most trying. As the family were in mourning for Will, she and Matilda were unable to hold their 'At Home' afternoon, so Amy endured sitting with her mama, who cried constantly. Amy loved her dearly and she was concerned about Matilda's health, she looked so very pale and was not eating properly. All day Amy was impatient to be outside in the warm sunshine. All the bad news was taking its toll on the whole family; the village was quiet too, the villagers had loved Will. He always found a friendly word to say to villagers he passed as he rode his horse down the narrow lanes. Old Miss Dean their old governess looked forward to his visits; she always had a pot of tea and shortbread biscuits ready for him whenever he called round to her cottage. The family looked after their retired staff, ensuring they were housed if they had no family to care for them. Miss Dean became inconsolable following the tragic news.

'Mr Will was a fine young man,' she wailed to her neighbour, Mrs Broom. 'His manners were impeccable and he never forgot my birthday. Oh, I shall miss him sorely.'

Finally, after supper Amy managed to take Florence, her spaniel for a long walk around the estate. Whilst walking past the follies and the hermitage she was able to reflect on the whereabouts of Tom. Florence was now curled up on the carpet, near Amy's stool, snuffling in her sleep.

'Elsie, Mr Eddy and I are going to adopt a baby. A girl from the village, apparently, is having an illegitimate child. She's due in February. We are trying to keep this quiet, but if you should hear any gossip, do let me know.'

'I will, miss. It will be lovely for you to have a child, someone you can love.'

'Yes, you're right, Elsie, I just hope I can love some other woman's child, I can't imagine it will be easy.'

'I'll be here to help you, miss. Shall Nanny be returning and coming out of retirement?'

'Yes, she has been asked, but I will write to her, Elsie. Nanny will be a tower of strength, she'll help us, I know. Dear Nanny, she is a very special person.'

Having finished helping Amy, Elsie tidied the room, and discreetly disappeared as Eddy came in through the door ready to share Amy's bed. As Eddy came in, Florence slunk out; she'd been kicked too often by that man, and made her escape. Amy shuddered, feeling a chill as she had to face her husband once again.

Amy rose and sank rhythmically with the body of her horse as it cantered through the shallows of the outgoing tide. As they approached the large pile of rocks, the usual limit of their outward ride, Artemis slowed down of his own accord, but Amy urged him on over the rocks. Surprised, he almost unseated her. She recovered, however, and brought her mount to a stop for a few minutes, facing the sea. She was comfortably dressed in beige breeches and a soft pale blue cotton blouse, denouncing the custom of wearing black for her mourning, and defiantly sitting astride her horse. A veil attached to her small hat gave her presence a small amount of anonymity. Had he been alive, Will would have teased her, but he wasn't here, and life needed to carry on.

There were several people on the beach already, sitting in the sand dunes taking in the fresh air; some women were sitting under large sunshades, watching their children. The sea was absolutely still with a soft blue haze on it, drawn up by the sun. Old Harry Rocks in the distance appeared to be floating on the water. Those paddling at the shallow waters edge appeared distant, enchanted, their voices and laughter overheard as if from another world. As she sat comfortably in the saddle of her stallion, Artemis, Amy looked longingly at the children playing in the sand. She felt certain, now, she would never have a child of her own. At least, not whilst Eddy, her despicable husband, lived. After the drunken announcement of his actions, she finally banned him from her bed. She hated him with a vengeance. Feeling forced to accept the situation of adopting his baby, along with his feeble painful fumbling in her bed she had had enough. He would no longer share her bed or be invited into her private rooms. She arranged for the servants to remove all his belongings and place them in a suite of rooms as far away from hers as possible. She would be polite to him at dinner and at social functions, but that was as far as she was prepared to accept his presence. He must stay in his own rooms in future and if the staff wondered why, well, they could just mind their own business. Most of them probably knew anyway. She could exert control over him now she really knew what he was capable of. She was no longer the sweet, biddable wife he married, she was finding an inner strength she had been unaware of, and this was empowering her to face up to him.

Turning Artemis around, Amy led her up the sand dunes, over the wide path leading to the beach, and followed the gravel road into Studland village. Coming upon the ancient church, she dismounted, tied the horse to a railing and walked into the cool, dark interior. Built by St Aldhelm in Saxon times much of the present building now was Norman. She noticed a slightly decaying smell mixed with candle wax as she waited for her eyes to adjust in the dark, and as she walked past the font and up the narrow aisle, the clicking sound of her riding boots interrupted the silence. Sitting on one of the wooden pews she closed her eyes and allowed the peace of this ancient place to surround her. Half an hour later and beginning to feel chilly, Amy emerged from the church into the warm late morning sunshine, mounted Artemis and set off at a trot. Her way home took her up and over Nine Barrow Down with its magnificent views of Poole Harbour and past Corfe Castle. They took the heath road, and, with the wind blowing in her hair and enjoying the exhilaration, she allowed Artemis to take the lead as they galloped onwards, crossing heathery open land and jumping across small streams, to the Thorpe estate. Suddenly, the thought of afternoon tea spurred her on. Amy felt that the long ride had been extremely cathartic and she was feeling stronger and able to cope with whatever else came her way.

CHAPTER THIRTEEN

Winnie Longhair scraped the remaining flesh from the beaver skin she was working on. She needed to produce a good amount of furs and garments to sell in Dawson City. Apart from the shrill voices of the women, it was quiet in the camp this morning; most of the men had left early to hunt. The food supply needed replenishing after their move from Lake Bennett to their new reserve. Moving from place to place was an essential part of Athabascan life. Staying together enabled them to hunt for food efficiently. The men were also fishing for salmon, whitefish and grayling. What was not immediately eaten would be dried and packed away by the women for future consumption. As custom dictated the women had been left behind to complete their allotted tasks and to take care of the children. The squaws worked with babies strapped to their backs, wrapped in blankets or in brightly coloured embroidered and tasselled shawls. The camp was situated in a scrub valley clearing; the short grasses allowed the tepees to be erected in a circle with space between for fires to be built. A large fire was kept burning in the central camp clearing. Behind the tepee's, racks of salmon skins hung on wooden racks in the sun. Once dried they would be packed away and used as food for the dogs. Winnie's son, Joseph was busy collecting firewood from the woods along the edge of the camp with other children; the oldest looking after the young ones. Wearing skin leggings, they were able to move around in the scrub and amongst the trees without scratching their legs. The collected wood was placed in large hessian sacks. They knew they had to be careful and be aware of dangerous wildlife. Bears had been spotted foraging for autumn berries with their cubs by their side, but the noise of the children's chatter possibly deterred the bears from coming near.

Winnie smiled as she scraped and prepared the skin. She thought how fortunate she was to be married to Grey Eagle, the Elder of their group. They married when she was fifteen and he was thirty, his first wife having died of a fever the year before. She was also proud to be the mother of Joseph; although only six years old, he was already showing signs of being strong and fit. This summer, their camp had been enlarged by visiting groups and this area was the ideal one for the gathering. A traditional ceremony called a potlatch was to be held, but first, there was to be much hunting and fishing. After her preparations, Winnie decided she would cut the skins up into the required shapes for the mittens and then she would embroider them with beads. The days were getting shorter now, but she had enough light to sit late in the evening sewing and chattering with the other women. They looked forward to being able to meet with the stampeders and those who lived near Dawson as they enjoyed the challenge of bartering and knowing that their handiwork was appreciated.

The man lying on the cot in the buffalo skin tepee opened his eyes very slowly. Luminous sunshine came streaming through a gap between the entrance flaps and threw a beam across his face. As he surfaced he felt confused as he tried to look around at his surroundings. Turning his head brought a pain so sharp that he relapsed back into unconsciousness for a few moments. Where was he? Why could he only see out of one eye? Why was he in so much pain? In fact, who was he? He felt such confusion. He also realised that his body was swaddled in lightweight skins; his left arm was extremely painful. His hips felt dislocated; he couldn't move. His face hurt.

'You are awake. That is good.' Winnie approached the cot and looked at the heavily bandaged guest who was being cared for in her and Grey Eagle's tepee. 'Will you tell me your name?' He looked at this beautiful smiling woman leaning over him. A thick plait of black hair hung over one shoulder. He could see she was wearing a simple suede dress embroidered with beads. Her dark eyes were shining with unshed tears; she felt immediate compassion for this man in her care.

'I don't know. I don't know who I am,' rasped the stranger in a quiet voice. It hurt to talk. He closed his eyes and groaned. Winnie held a goatskin flask to Tom's lips whilst gently putting a hand behind his head to lift him slightly.

'Try and drink this, it will be good for you,' she urged soothingly. He sipped the liquid, which had a slightly bittersweet taste, then thankfully she placed him gently back onto the cot and released her hand from the back of his head.

'Sleep, friend, and when you wake up again I will bring you some broth.' He gratefully closed his eyes, but sleep evaded him. Again and again, he thought, who am I? As he lay still he felt overtaken by a feeling of panic; he must figure this out. He had enough sense to be able to think. He appreciated the beauty of the woman who brought him a drink, so he wasn't an imbecile, he just didn't know where he was or whom he was, or what caused him to be in this tent. Did he always live here? Why was he in so much pain? There were a few sounds around; he could hear children's laughter in the distance and a dog barking not far away. Finally, he lapsed into a deep sleep; the herbal drink Winnie fed him was working its magic. The Medicine Man said prayers and worked some magic on the man, thought Winnie pensively. When he wakes up and is ready to understand, we can tell him what happened to him. The Elders had named him 'Bear Man', or Bear for short.

Flames from the highly piled bonfire reached up into the dusky sky, sending sparks spitting upwards and outwards. There was an edge of excitement around the fire, as many Indians from the band gathered around. The pipe was being passed around, and the women and little ones wrapped themselves in blankets for there was an evening chill in the air. The men were dressed in various styles, trousers, shirts and waistcoats, their plaited hair under large hats, the brims being wide enough to deter mosquitoes from biting their faces. The biggest of the men, Grey Eagle, stood out by the way he wore feathers in his hat. There was no mistaking the one in charge of the camp. Grey Eagle inherited this position from his father, who was now in the great camp in the sky. The women and children sat as close to the fire as they dared, to keep away from the flying nuisances. Grey Eagle's young sister, Grace sat next to Winnie; Bear had noticed how pretty she was. The evening meal had been consumed; the dogs could be heard growling as they fought over the bones thrown to them from the carcase of the elk that everyone had enjoyed eating, alongside the vegetables of cabbage and squash. It was story-telling time and everyone was eager to hear new tales and riddles. Propped up on a seat especially made out of willow for him by two of the young braves, half cot and half chair and padded with sweet, herbal-smelling cushions, Bear contemplated all that was happening around him. It was now a week since he had first regained consciousness in Grey Eagle's tepee. Winnie's care for him was humbling; she performed duties that could have been very embarrassing for them both, but she seemed to take it in her stride. He still didn't know who he was. In a funny way it made these tasks she carried out easier for him to cope with. He hadn't been told about the bear attack, fearing it would cause him to relapse, but she had explained to him that he had been unconscious for three weeks; since Eagle had rescued him they had feared he would never make it, but here he was, on the mend and outside for the first time. Grey Eagle passed the pipe he had smoked to Beaver-man sitting next to him and Beaver-man told a story: 'One fall, a group of hunters set off up the mountains to hunt. With them were a man and his very pretty wife. In the evening they were camped and a wolverine was watching them. He saw the pretty wife and fell in love. As the wolverine was very strong, stronger even than a moose he was able to kidnap the woman. As he took her away it started to rain. It was dark and rained and rained so much the wolverine didn't know what to do. He took the woman to a mountain and laid her under an overhanging rock, then covered her with his tail to keep her dry from the dripping water. She was about to freeze to death. The big wolverine saved her life. As the clouds lifted and the ground steamed, the big wolverine took her away. No one knows where they went. So that is why we sing song about big wolverine when we go hunting. When we catch a wolverine, we must kill him, so that his strength goes into us to make us strong hunters.'

The men continued puffing on the pipe as it was passed around, until Grey Eagle spoke: 'One evening two men walked through the woods near a big lake where they camped. One had dark hair and brown eyes, the other, the younger of the two, blond with blue eyes. I guess they were prospectors on the way up the lake. The blond had a rifle and had just shot a goose. The older man walked through the scrub to retrieve it; it was going to make them a good supper. Young man made way back to camp. An elder from this band was hiding in the woods, watching. There was no malice in the Indian, he was stalking the area to see what animals there were for hunting.' Grey Eagle paused in his talking and glanced at Bear. His eyebrows twitched in surprise as he saw that the white man was completely oblivious of the fact that the story was all about him. Grey Eagle continued, suddenly expansive, 'A mother bear and her cub appear. Older man is in her way and she feels threatened. What would she do to man?' As Eagle spoke, he paused for effect and glanced at the youngsters, their eyes were shining waiting for the next part of the tale. 'Well, the she bear decides that man is enemy. She runs to him, she is huge, a very big black bear. Man puts his arm up to shield his face, but bear, she claws man's arm and pushes him up against a pine tree. She claws man's face and he falls down. She bear takes man in mouth and drags him away.' Again, he paused long enough to let his words take effect. Everyone turned and looked at Bear, to see what his reaction was, but he just sat passively listening to the story. He was still oblivious to the fact the tale was true and about him. So, waving away a crowd of mosquitoes, Eagle carries on. 'But, big Indian, he ready to help. Big Indian fires arrow at she bear. She not down, so he fires another arrow. She bear lets go of man and runs off to find her cub. Big Indian gently approaches white man, and realises he not dead, picks him up and carries him, running, back to camp. Indian man's wife looks after man. She makes poultice from resin of white spruce and applies it to man, then wraps him up in skins. She sets his hip back in place. She give him healing herbs in drinks and cares for him. Man sleeps long time, possibly two moons. But he now here and getting well. Indian goes back to camp by Lake Bennett but no people know of bear-eaten man. Friend had moved on.' The final part of the story is then related. 'Indian camp soon move on. Summer is time to move to river for fishing. Man put on stretcher padded with skins and fur and pulled behind horse to new home where we go.' His tale over, Grey Eagle sat back and the pipe was passed to him. Silence. No one moved or spoke. Bear looked around at all the smiling faces; at all the Indians staring at him. He asked of Winnie, 'Why are they all looking at me?'

'Don't you know why?'

'No. No idea. Do you think the story has anything to do with me?'

'Time you went to bed, Mr Bear, we'll talk again another time.'

A shout from inside their tepee suddenly woke Eagle and Winnie, who had been soundly sleeping, wrapped together like a pair of spoons in their large sleeping bag. Joseph was still asleep; the shout hadn't come from him. Quietly, in the dusky light, Winnie approached Bear's cot. Again, he shouted and then screamed. He screamed again and again, this time waking Joseph. Eagle crawled out of his sleeping bag and gently shook Bear awake. Coming to, Bear looked at him. All became clear: He was having a very bad dream; the bear attack story was all about him. He relived it in the nightmare.

'It was horrific, it was just like I was there, and it was happening all over again,' he cried. 'I remember now, the whole scene. But the last thing I know is being pinned against the tree. I am so grateful to you, Grey Eagle, for rescuing me. And, Winnie, you've cared for me so well.'

'Do you remember who you are?' she wondered.

'No, that still eludes me. I wish I knew. The only identity I have is the name Mr Bear that is what you good people call me. I must have people who I write to. You told me I had ink on my fingers when found.' All three adults settled down in their bags. Joseph smiled sleepily, then climbed into his bag and was sleeping soundly again in seconds.

Preparations for the potlatch celebrations were well under way on the day Bear was finally able to stand up and gingerly walk around the tepee. His head still throbbed dully and he felt slightly queasy now he was standing up, but he was determined to enjoy this time. Although he hankered to know who he was, he admitted to himself he was thoroughly enjoying his time here in this settlement. One person seemed to like him very much; Grace had helped Winnie bring him back to life. Her knowledge of healing plants and herbs had grown under Winnie's teaching. As she was Grey Eagle's sister, Bear had not told anyone of his growing fondness for her, he respected the clan Elder, and there was time enough for feelings to develop in that direction. Standing in the open doorway of the tepee with the flaps tied back, he appreciated the cool breeze blowing through the tent. Inside, Winnie had made the home very comfortable. He noted the floor was covered in soft, fragrant pine needles. Skins of various animals were spread around; on the floor as rugs, on the cots as bedding and piled up to make comfortable seating. The central fireplace, made of large stones placed in a circle, was unlit. The soft late summer sunshine was warm enough. Giving an unexpected shiver, as if someone was walking over his grave, Bear took stock of his injuries; His right eye was fine, the left was scarred, his sight was slightly blurred. He was deaf in his left ear; the lobe was missing. His face, he knew, held deep scars which progressed down his neck. No mirror was available, but he could feel the deep ridges with his fingertips. If he thought himself handsome before, he certainly wasn't now! His left arm was practically useless, it just hung from his scarred shoulder, a large chunk of skin and bone had been taken from his elbow where the bear had bitten. He walked with a limp. But the most worrying of his injuries was that of his mind. He remembered the bear attack, but very little from before that time. It was obvious he was a gold prospector by the clothes he wore. Winnie often mentioned his English accent. Grey Eagle told him about the camp on the lake and the fact that no one remembered him. After all, it was estimated three hundred people were camped there. Grey also visited the North West Mounted Police hut to enquire, but they were unable to help. Bear Man was now determined to regain his full health and strength so that he could pay back in some way the great kindness shown to him by these proud people. Maybe he could help with some hunting and trapping; there must be some way he could help with the use of only one arm.

The men returned to camp with a captured and then killed moose. Athabascan people hunted moose, by tracking them. They could tell by the tracks when a moose was ready to stop, and when they would be catching up with it. At that point, they would walk in a semi-circle and if they came across the tracks again, they knew the moose was still walking ahead of them. They would repeat the semi-circular tracking until they crossed where the moose tracks should have been, and if there were no tracks, they knew they had gone ahead of the moose. When the moose walked in their direction, they could take it by surprise, and shoot it at close range with their bows and arrows. After dying, it will be picked up from the grassland, tied to poles and carried back to camp. The head would be cooked by the women and made into a soup. The rest of the animal would be dealt with by the men; skinned, cut up and cooked over the open fire on spits. If the weather was very bad and there was difficulty lighting a fire, then the meat was eaten raw, although this did not happen very often. The hunting tradition went back centuries. It celebrated the lives of those Athabascan Indians who died since the last big gathering. The women made exquisite embroidered waistcoats and slippers out of felt and leather for the men to wear, and beaded necklaces for themselves. The beads show a symbol of wealth, the women designing the patterns themselves. A party atmosphere filled the air as Bear walked over to the place where the men worked. As he cut the meat Grey Eagle spoke to him; 'Would you like to know more about us? About our lives and traditions?'

'I most certainly would, I've been interested so far.'

'Our name, "Athabascan" comes from the large lake in Canada called "Lake Athabasca". The lake was given its name by the Cree Indians, who lived east of it. In Cree, Athabasca means, "grass here and there", there are many local dialects, and we live in a regional band that is made up of lots of families. Our regional bands speak Ingalik, and they are gathered here for the potlatch. We move around at the different seasons of the year. In spring, summer and fall we move near the rivers and lakes where the fish are plentiful. So too, are the water mammals, the beaver, otter and others, that we set traps for. We fish a lot. In the fall we hunt the caribou as well. We respect the animals and their spirits. If we upset their spirits, they will hide from us and we will starve, unable to hunt them for food. Many Indian tribes have accepted white man's firewater and guns. They become just like bad white men, drunk and they shoot the animals. I do not want that to happen to us. We believe in tradition and living the way of our ancestors. It can be hot here in the summer, and then the mosquitoes and other insects trouble us. Before the snow falls we move to our winter grounds and stay there many moons. So, we will be moving on soon. We trap animals and when good weather comes again, we move on and so begin another journey.'

'So, when you move again, will I be able to travel with you? I feel I shall be well enough.'

'Yes, we like you to come with us; you are like a brother to me now. In the spring we move to place near Dawson so that women can sell the items they have made. We also barter the furs and buy other things we need. You come with us. Mounties are in Dawson; they may have news of who you are. But we winter first. Snow will be too deep to travel anywhere. Also, by spring you will be recovered more. We decide in Dawson what you do then.'

'I am grateful to you, Grey Eagle. And to Winnie and Joseph and all the others who have helped my recovery. I am, however, frustrated by the fact that I don't know who I am. All I know is that I am English and was attacked by a bear. I suppose I came here for the gold rush that you have told me about, I just don't know. Maybe I have relatives or friends in the Yukon Territories, who knows? I just hope my memory comes back soon.'

'Medicine Man came when you were first ill. He chanted prayers and we held ceremony for you. That is why you recovered. But he does not know who you are. His medicine spirit not reach that far.'

'Well,' said Bear amazingly as he shook Grey Eagle's hand. 'I am humbled.'

CHAPTER FOURTEEN

As she stood looking in the large gilt mirror above the fireplace, Matilda decided black silk was not flattering for her complexion; it caused her skin to look sallow. Her dressmaker did an excellent job speedily making dresses and coats and sourcing hats and accessories for herself and Amy. As she fingered the black jet mourning necklace hanging around her neck, she contemplated what the future held for her family. Will was dead in Alaska, so far from home. They received no word from Tom for weeks. And now, an illegitimate baby was to be part of their lives; that Daisy's pregnancy was still so far a secret within the house was a miracle, admittedly. She wondered if anyone in the village was aware of events. Clarissa, the vicar's wife proved to be helpful and Matilda was sure Clarissa would pass on any gossip she heard. Tearfully, Amy explained she had arranged to have all Eddy's possessions moved out of her rooms and into the other wing of the house. Matilda pulled the warm woollen shawl tighter around her shoulders. Due to the stress of recent events, she was susceptible to colds and germs, and having just recovered from a head cold she was feeling shivery. Just then, Mr Hibbs entered and said respectfully, 'Shall I put more coal on the fire, madam?'

'Yes, Mr Hibbs. It's really chilly for late October. I expect it's even colder in Alaska. I do hope Tom is well and safe.'

'We all do, madam. Cook was only saying so earlier. All of the staff miss the young masters.'

'Ah, there's the doorbell, Mr Hibbs. Please bring me the post, Lord Harry is in Wareham today.'

'Certainly, madam.' Hibbs placed the coalscuttle back on the hearth and made his way slowly to the front hall. Upon opening the door, he found the young post boy standing on the doorstep.

'Letter for Lord and Lady Thorpe, Mr Hibbs. Another one from Canada, can I have the stamp? I'll wait here.' Knowing the boy would wait patiently for the stamp, Mr Hibbs allowed him to sit on the windowsill in the vestibule. This was a common occurrence, the boy waited for all the foreign stamps. Placing the letter on a silver salver, Hibbs slowly made his back to the drawing room; his arthritis was painful today, must be the damp weather, he mused.

'A letter from Canada, madam. The boy is waiting for the stamp,' intoned the butler, offering the salver to Matilda. Taking the envelope in one hand and slitting it open with the paper knife in the other, she pulled out a single sheet of paper and read it. Seconds later, her face turning even whiter than usual, she fell to the floor in a dead faint. Her faithful Hibbs pulled the bell pull before painfully kneeling on the floor beside her and gently lifting her head.

'Find the smelling salts, Elsie,' he shouted as the maid entered the room. 'Quickly. The mistress has fainted.' As Elsie found her mistress's bag and passed the salts under her nose, Hibbs ran to the door, opened it and shouted to the post boy to go to the stables and fetch the groom. Rounding the corner of the house, having heard the butler shouting, the groom strode into the room. Taking in the situation, he panted; 'I'll ride to Wareham to the magistrates' court and fetch Lord Thorpe.' The post boy scuffed the stones as he sauntered back to the post office.

'Huh, no stamps today. Hope Mr Hibbs saves 'em fer me,' he said to himself.

Just as soon as Matilda recovered from her faint and was resting on the sofa, she indicated to her butler; 'Read the letter. I'm sure I read it correctly. Elsie, find Amy, quickly, there's such bad news.' Matilda then, having exhausted herself again, fell back against the cushions on the sofa.

Mr Hibbs' countenance was one of deep sympathy as he read the letter:

North West Mounted Police

Dear Lord and Lady Thorpe

I write to regretfully inform you of the death of your son, Thomas Thorpe. The information I am about to impart is distressing. Whilst camped at Lake Bennett, in July, in the company of a friend, Caleb Howard, and Ling, a Chinese porter, Thomas was attacked by an enormous bear and dragged away. Mr Howard fired his rifle, but the bear escaped. Having searched the area where the tragedy took place, we could find only broken shrubs and traces of blood. Other than the aforementioned, no other people were around as witnesses, so therefore, I have come to the conclusion that your son has died.

Mr Howard told me that your son was a fine, upstanding, brave man. I understand that Thomas was searching for his brother, William, which is the reason for his being in the area. I believe that William was in Dawson City for a short while, but then travelled back to Skagway. I trust that you have had favourable news regarding him.

We are very much isolated here, in the Yukon. Being dependent on the river travellers to bring and take post and messages, news takes a long while to reach us, hence the delay in informing you of the tragedy involving your son.

I send you my condolences,

Yours truly,

David McCulloch
Inspector

'Madam, I don't know what to say. This is dreadful. Elsie, stay with the mistress whilst I arrange refreshments for her. A cup of tea with a dash of brandy will do the trick,' murmured Mr Hibbs as he hurried out of the drawing room and down to the kitchens. This was a difficult situation, if only his Lordship were here.

Cook was busy baking cakes and pastries for afternoon tea and every so often she sniffed and blew her nose into her handkerchief. The house was so sad since hearing Mr William had died. There were also undercurrents of something happening upstairs; some event no one was talking about. Both Jane and Elsie knew what was going on, but they remained tightlipped. It was all so frustrating. Mr Hibbs came into the kitchen so quietly that he made Cook jump.

'Cook, sit down. It's a terrible situation. Bad news, again. Madam has just received a letter from Canada. I can't believe what I've just heard. Master Tom is dead! Oh, my, dreadful news.'

'No, James, I don't believe it. What 'appened?' Cook removed her already soaked handkerchief from her apron pocket again.

'Well, it's hard to believe, but he was killed by a bear, apparently. Out in the wilds, by some lake. He had read, apparently in Mr Will's letters, about the dangers of the bears.'

'Are you sure?'

'Of course I am. I read the letter myself. Make some tea, Cook, and I'll take it up. Madam fainted upon receiving the letter. Elsie is with her ladyship. I'll take her a cup as well. As if this family hasn't had enough tragedy.' As he left the room, Mr Hibbs gave a sigh, 'Oh dear, whatever next.'

Lord Thorpe urged Falcon, his horse, on at a gallop as he rode from Wareham to Thorpe Matravers. The groom had insisted he return home immediately, there was some kind of tragedy. Dismounting outside the front door and leaving the horse for the groom to sort out, he strode into the drawing room. Looking around and seeing no one at first, he then became aware of his wife lying on the chaise, a large fringed shawl draped over her knees. Elsie was kneeling in front of her mistress, holding her hand and murmuring soothingly. Upon seeing her husband, Matilda burst into a fresh round of weeping, holding a black edged handkerchief to her eyes with one hand, whilst with the other she held out the letter to her husband, patiently waiting whilst he read it. His face betrayed his feelings for once, tears springing to his eyes and his cheeks turning pink.

'Both boys have gone, Harry. What shall we do without them?'

'Oh, my dear. I don't know what to say to you. Elsie, get Jane in here, then get Mr Hibbs to contact the vicar, Richard needs to be here. I think he should contact the doctor too, ask him to call.'

'Yes, sir,' murmured a tearful Elsie.

'Tilda, where is Amy? Eddy should be at the pottery, I'll send for him.' Although his heart was breaking, Harry was in control. This was a terrible tragedy. He wished he had been at home when the letter had arrived; he could have protected her by keeping the worst parts of the letter from her. But now she knew. She would probably never get over it, the demise of Tom following on the death of Will. There was also the Daisy episode to get over, too. He was aware of Amy's anger towards Eddy and how the atmosphere changed when they were both in the same room. In a few months there would be a baby in the house. Well, the baby could be a blessing in disguise; help Matilda take her mind off these tragedies. Taking his handkerchief from his trouser pocket, he dabbed his moist eyes. It was important he still acted as master of this household. The house, the pottery, the school and the village all depended on them. The future would be worked out in time. Meanwhile, another memorial service must be prepared. He would talk it over with his dear Matilda tomorrow morning. Jane was putting her mistress to bed now to await the doctor's arrival; he would, hopefully, give her a sedative to enable her to rest.

CHAPTER FIFTEEN

The huskies whined as they strained at the chains tethering them together; the chains being attached to a metal pole that was dug deep into the ground. The winter had passed slowly, dreamlike in its unreality. Before leaving for winter camp, Grey Eagle arranged a small, simple but important ceremony, welcoming Bear into the clan. Since then, it had been a time, for Bear Man, of sitting around fires listening to fables and legends; of smoking pipes and drifting off into dreamlike trances; also a time of recovery, a time when he was able to gain strength in the wasted parts of his body mauled by the bear. Whilst Grey and the other men went hunting for beaver and elk in the deep snow and ice, Bear was forced to rest. Now, the snow had ceased to fall, although it was still piled up around the wooden huts huddled under the shelter of the mountain. This winter camp was made up of several households, each house varying in size, but made of the same basic structure. Bear was amazed when he saw where he was to live for the next six months. The homes were semi-subterranean structures made from whale ribs and driftwood frames covered by birch spruce bark, which itself was then covered with moss and topped with dirt. All that was visible of Bear and Grace's house from ground level were mounds of snow with smoke curling out of the centre. The many layers of insulation ensured the homes were warm and cosy. Bear often felt cold, especially when he ventured outside of necessity. He was becoming used to the nomadic lifestyle of these Indians. The only constant belongings of the people were the winter huts and their totem poles. A totem pole served as a reminder of a family, or clan, its unity, and as a link to their spirit-ancestor. They were carved in various designs, telling the history of the clan. Several of these poles were erected in the middle of the winter camp, adding colour to the otherwise drabness of the mid-winter snow-covered surroundings. Each pole was topped by an eagle, or Dakhl'awèdi the family symbol of this clan. Inside his own home, he stood in front of the stove warming his hands on the tin mug of strong coffee. The shelves around him held just a few items now; winter was almost over and the Athabascan Indians, of which Bear was now a member, were preparing to move on to their spring camp. The meagre amount of provisions left were stacked in the smaller hut next to this one; dried salmon skins for the dogs; squashes and onions; coffee beans in hessian sacks and a few bunches of dried herbs. Because they had to move around a lot, the Athabascan people didn't accumulate a lot of material goods. They carried around with them their clothing, made of skins, and their shelters, which were also made of skins and a few tools and utensils. The women had decorated the skins with fine beadwork and porcupine quills coloured with natural dyes, wild flowers being a basic motif. Their moccasins, tunics, baby-carriers, gloves and hats were all decorated with beadwork. They wove blankets from buffalo hair. Bear was dressed in Indian clothing, the same as other men, skin trousers and jackets. As he often felt cold, not being acclimatised to the harsh winter weather, he wrapped a blanket around his body, rather like a shawl. The clothes he was wearing when found were destroyed, having been mailed to shreds by the bear. They preferred to use caribou hide for clothing because of its warmth and pliability. They removed the hair from the hide for summer clothing. For cold weather clothing they left the hair on the hide and turned it inward.

Winter clothing for men and women included trousers with attached moccasins, a long coat with belted waist, a separate hat and mittens. Their underclothes were made from skins of the snowshoe hare. Wide straps held babies to mothers' backs to free their hands. That winter, they had caught fish through holes in the ice, with spears, lures, hooks and dip nets. Grey Eagle tapped on the cabin door before entering and saying: 'I come to collect you, Bear, we move these provisions to the dog sleds ready for move to summer camp. Later, after the buffalo hunt, we go upriver to Dawson City and sell much furs. We unable to go now, it still cold, the river is still thawing and we will be able to follow the current up to Dawson in summer. It will be rough, we have many items to sell, we should get good prices.'

'I feel nervous, Grey. I don't know why, perhaps I shall find out who I am in Dawson, perhaps it's the anticipation of the future. I don't know.' Swallowing hard, Bear's eyes filled with emotion. He was in a quandary; he needed to find out who he was on the one hand, but on the other hand, if he knew who he really was, his life may have to change dramatically. Before leaving their last camp of the summer, Grey gave his sister, a young squaw, called Grace to Bear. Grey recognised Bear still needed care and it made sense for Bear to have a wife of his own. Their winter wedding being a noisy celebration; everyone feasted, played games, danced, sang and told stories. The traditional games were related to hunting, strength, exercise, agility and courage. His wedding night was a revelation to Bear; Grace gave herself freely, without any inhibitions at all, she enjoyed coupling with her new husband. Bear was also wearing a bracelet around his right wrist, made by Grace by plaiting beads with strands of her own hair into a circle. This was a symbol of their partnership. He thought how her name suited her; she was small, lithe and graceful. Now, putting down his mug of coffee, and going outside with Grey to check on his dogs, Bear saw her. Wearing her snow shoes made of birch and rawhide, and sliding over the packed snow, approaching Bear, she held his eyes with her own. Despite this marriage of convenience, she loved this man. His scarred body made no difference to the way she felt when she held him during their lovemaking; he was a handsome man in her eyes. Grey Eagle had given her, his sister, especially out of all the other squaws to be his companion. Bear recognised the honour that Grey bestowed on him.

All through the long, dark winter, they were companions, Grace teaching bear more of the ways of the group. Bear was surprised when, two weeks after their wedding, Grace insisted on sleeping with other squaws in a separate house. She explained that, above all, she needed to avoid contact with him and other men because her menstrual flow contained spiritual power that could alienate animals and bring on scarcity. Grace could well remember winters where food was scarce; hunting being fruitless and several members dying through starvation. So, she explained, she must obey the spirits, they could not risk another famine.

The move to spring camp was not easy. The snow melted considerably, which meant the dogs found it difficult pulling the sleds through slush. It was easy going on snow or on dry ground, but slush stuck to the sled frames. Eventually, however, the clan made it and set up camp in a valley sheltered by the spruce covered mountains. The men set out to hunt. To catch caribou, they built corrals out of spruce logs and herded the animals into them to be shot with bow and arrow, knifed or speared. Bows were made from birch, black spruce, or willow branches four to six feet long. Bear felt strong enough to help a little with some of the hunting. Knives and spear points were made of stone. The group also drove caribou into lakes or streams where they were more easily killed. This early in spring, they trapped smaller fur-bearing animals, including rabbits, muskrats, beaver and squirrel.

The Athabascans used all parts of the animal. They ate the meat and the fat, then crafted bones into tools and weapons. When dried, the tendons provided sinew which the women thread into bone needles for sewing. The hides were used for clothing and tent covers. They also used all parts of the fish, drying skins to feed the dogs. Bear had learnt a lot during his year with Grey's people; he realised just how resourceful their life ran through the seasons.

'We will be going up the Big River soon, Bear.'

'It will be an adventure, Grace. I know you have been busy making items for sale; I do so admire you and the way you work so hard. The winter, I must admit, has been difficult for me. I would have liked to help with the hunting, but haven't been well enough.'

'You needed the rest, Bear. I was happy to care for you. You are my man.'

'I have to go with the men up to Dawson. Will you be coming as well?'

'Yes, there are many women to stay and help move camp whilst we are gone. But you must be aware; many white men do not speak with Indians. They think we are on their land, but it has always been our land. They use guns to frighten us off, but we are strong and still go to Yukon.'

Bear helped with the making of the canoes and rafts, using birch bark for the frames which were then covered in moose skins and the seams stitched with spruce roots, then waterproofed with hot spruce pitch.

When summer finally arrived, the Indian men and women selected to leave camp packed their belongings and set off for the big river. As the Indians paddled their canoes up the Yukon, the sound of water from the melted snow and ice surrounded them, the sound echoing around the mountains. It was going to be a very warm summer; the sun was now shining twenty-two hours a day. Bear thought the waterfalls fascinating, the colour of the icy-blue water tumbling over the greenery and flowers. Although his canoe was very light and made of birch bark and he could carry it in one hand, paddling was a different matter. It was hard work paddling his canoe as he followed Grey Eagle and the other Indians; his shoulder and arm were painful. He was using muscles unused to exercise. Grace helped by using her own paddle. The physical scars had healed, but he was still weak. Most of the women, children and squaws were left behind, in summer camp. When this group returned from Dawson they would all move again to take advantage of the late summer fishing and hunting.

At evening time, they hauled the canoes into a suitable camping spot and prepared for the night ahead. As there were few hours of complete darkness it was easy enough to light the fires, cook supper and erect rough shelters. Then, in the morning, after a breakfast of coffee and freshly caught halibut they dragged the canoes back to the Yukon and set off again. As they paddled, the Indians sang songs and laughed, making the work seem less arduous. Bear was pleased to hear Grace sing, and she taught him some of the songs as well. Along the banks, they saw fishermen with fish wheels, consisting of two large baskets strung across the opening and each attached to opposite sides of an axle. Between each axle, was a paddle, the same width as the baskets. The fish wheel sits on a pedestal between wooden pontoons and placed in a river so that the water hits the paddles and the basket, and causes the wheel to turn. As the basket revolves around the axle, it catches fish swimming up river. The basket has a slanted chute on the edge nearest the axle, and as the fish drops into the chute as the wheel turns, it slides down the chute, out of the basket, and into a large box resting on pontoons. Bear was fascinated; it seemed such a simple yet effective process.

Cabins had been hastily erected all along the river banks, and along with tents of all shapes and sizes, small communities were forming. None of the people panning in the water spoke to the Indians as they paddled past, as far as they were concerned the Indians were invisible. The only time they communicated with them was when they bartered for the Indian goods. Grey Eagle didn't seem bothered. All along the river, other river traffic, canoes, rafts and steamboats joined them.

Eventually, after four long days, Dawson City rose up through a gap in the mountains as they paddled around a bend in the river. A smell of sawdust assailed Bear's nostrils, and the noise of building works drowned all other sounds. He became aware that the city had not so long ago been damaged by fire and was now being rebuilt. Blackened masses of burned wood and detritus floated in the river. Grey Eagle signalled to the canoeists to pull up their crafts onto a bank nearby. They were going to Moose hide Camp, then return to set up their stalls here, no need to go any further. If, as they suspected, the fire had damaged shops and stalls, townsfolk would be eager to come and buy what the Athabascans had to offer whilst the town rose from the mire. It was an opportunity not to be missed.

CHAPTER SIXTEEN

Bear Man and his squaw wandered around the stalls set up by their tribe, on a patch of scrubby ground close enough to the Yukon river for convenience, but not so close that the stalls would be flooded if the river rose and broke its banks. Tents made of animal skins and similar to the tepees had been erected and the items to be sold or bartered were laid out on skins and blankets. It looked colourful and, hopefully, would attract townsfolk to the area. A mangy black dog sniffed around, as it was about to lift its leg ready to urinate on a beaded waistcoat laid out for sale; Benny kicked it brutally out of the way. Whining, the dog left the scene in search of better pickings. Grey had previously advised Bear not to go away from their stalls. Indians were barely tolerated in Dawson, and although Bear looked and spoke as a European, his clothes marked him out as a native Indian. He could be beaten up and thrown out of town. Word having spread that the Athabascans were selling and bartering goods, people, women in particular, soon arrived to pick out a bargain. Grace could drive a hard bargain with the women who were purchasing her goods; she had no intention of giving her produce away, but she needed to sell at a reasonable price.

As townsfolk started to arrive and inspect the goods, standing just inside a tent that Grey had erected in case of rain, and looking out at the activity, Bear felt someone's eyes on him; someone who was intently staring at him. He shivered, not from cold, but from a feeling he could not understand. The man looking at him seemed familiar; had Bear met him before? How could he have, not having been anywhere other than the Indian camp. A memory crept itself into his mind. The face of this man was one he had encountered in his many nightmares. 'Hopefully, this chap knows who I am,' muttered Bear out loud.

Grace had come quietly up to him and, standing by his side, she put an arm around his waist. 'You say something, Bear? she asked quizzically, looking up at him with a puzzled expression on her little face.

'Grace, I just think someone is watching me. You see the man with the yellow hair? I feel I know him.'

'Go ask him. He may know who you are.'

As Grace watched the man approach Bear, a sense of apprehension filled her. What if this man knew Bear and he unlocked Bear's memory? What would happen then? Would she lose him – would he go back to his home? She could not imagine losing him, he was her whole life, he was her man, her partner, her everything. As the winter snow had covered the land and the huts, they had shared close companionship, but more importantly, friendship. She had told them much more about their customs and heritage. He had been eager to learn the Ingalik language and was now so fluent he could converse with any member of the clan. He was an exceptional man. The way he coped with his injuries from the bear attack was inspiring. She remembered him being brought to the camp by her brother and Winnie caring for him. Grace herself often helped to mix the creams and lotions that were applied to his skin. When the wood splints made by Benny were applied to his broken arm, Grace held him down and eased his screaming by wiping his brow with cool water. Medicine Man obviously placed input to Bear's recovery, but it was also the women's skill and his own tenacity that made him well and be the man he now was. She also had to consider what to do if he did leave the clan. She was almost certain that she was with child. She hadn't told anyone yet, but if Bear did decide to return to his former life, at least she would have her family around her and his child to love.

'Tom! Tom Thorpe! Is it you?' shouted Caleb Howard as he strode towards Bear, arms outstretched in greeting. Bear shrank back into the tent momentarily, he needed time to think. Grace moved slightly to just behind Bear so that she gave him space to talk to this man who was calling Bear 'Tom', but she was still around to hear what he said. From past experience, most of the Indians were wary of white men, but this white man appeared to be friendly and harmless. Caleb followed them, a smile widening his face.

'Don't you remember me?' Looking at Bear intently and noticing his badly scarred face and ear, he said, 'My name is Caleb Howard and I travelled from Vancouver to Lake Bennett with you. We shared real good times, though it was hard going with such rough terrain at times. It is you, Tom? I thought you were dead. I was sure that great bear killed you. Boy, this is a shock.' Caleb looked around for something to sit on; his legs suddenly felt wobbly. Noticing this, Grace picked up a small stool made of birch wood; the seat woven with reeds and placing it near Caleb, indicated to him to sit.

Bear faced the man who claimed to be a friend. 'Forgive me, Mr whoever you are. Yes, apparently I was mauled by a bear and almost died. These Indians nursed me and accepted me into their family, as my memory has been damaged, I don't know who I am. I suffered a head injury. By all accounts you know me. You called me Tom.'

'Know you! My dear friend, back from the dead. I knew you very well. As I said, we came here, to the Yukon together. How amazing.'

As Caleb spoke, Grey Eagle entered the tent, investigating. He could hear a man's raised voice and was concerned for Bear and Grace. Caleb, standing up suddenly and tipping over the stool, explained all to Grey; how he thought Tom had been killed and carried off, and now, the shock of seeing him alive.

'We sit and spoke the pipe. You stay, Mr Caleb, and help Bear with memory. I call others. We pleased Bear has a friend.' With that, Grey Eagle organised a fire to be quickly built and lit; after all, there was plenty of driftwood lying around amongst the detritus of the ruined city. Food was prepared by the women and the sale of goods abandoned. The tribe men sat around, eager to hear what Caleb had to say, after all, they loved tales and legends around the fire. The pipe of peace was set up and as smoke ascended from both it and the fire, a pleasant atmosphere descended on the group. All evening Caleb related the story of his meeting with Tom in Vancouver, their travels all the way to Lake Bennett and the help they received from Ling. He told them what he knew of Tom's background in Dorset, and finally, the encounter with the bear. As he spoke, Bear became aware of returning memories. Some clear, others faded around the edges; gradually he was beginning to understand who he was. The herbal substance he was smoking may have helped his memory, on the other hand, maybe he was hallucinating and his memory returning was just an illusion. He had heard this Caleb Howard talking about him and where he came from, perhaps the pipe was playing games with him. Bear began to wonder what was real and what was not. Finally the stories ran out, everyone was tired.

The glow from the fire contrasted with the twilight of the night. Wolves howled hungrily in the distance and a fish plopped, unseen, in the river. It was turning decidedly chilly as the Indians in the camp settled down in their fur lined sleeping bags, Bear and Caleb having retreated to a small tepee, alone. Grace recognised that the two men had much to discuss, she would sleep with the single squaws for that night.

'Caleb, can I ask you something?'

'Of course, dear friend, anything.'

'I know you mean well, and you are excited at finding me, but I would prefer to have some time to myself,' said Bear cordially, hoping that Caleb wouldn't be offended. 'I need to gather my thoughts and see what I can actually remember. The years since Grey Eagle saved me are very clear in my mind, but before that there is a black hole of amnesia. So, if you can keep quiet and curb your excitement for tonight, I'd be really grateful.' As he said the words, Bear turned to Caleb. All he could hear was a gentle snuffling; Caleb was sound asleep. That night, or what passed for night in the summer so far north, in a spectacular display of sound and light, the skies opened, noisily emptying their contents on to the mountains, valleys and the camp tents. Pebble-sized hailstones bounced down, as flashes of light bathed the landscape in luminosity, sending the dogs howling and keeping everyone, except Caleb, awake.

The next morning Tom sat with Grey Eagle, drinking coffee and eating freshly caught salmon, aware that some of his memory had returned. Grace still kept away, even though she was eager to know what happened. In his mind's eye he pictured his home in Thorpe, his parents and sister there. He thought of Will, somewhere here in the Yukon. If Caleb's letter reached them, then they would all believe him dead.

'A gift from the spirits,' announced Grey. 'Knew memory would come back. This very difficult news, Bear. I understand if you want to go back to kinsfolk in England, but I feel you are part of this family. We don't know what Grace will think, what she will do. We should have another pow-wow with Elders to smoke again and discuss. Grace loves you and I know you love her. We must decide best way.'

Grey sat up straight, looking proud and in charge. As leader of the band he had responsibilities, both to family and the whole group. After all, Grace was his sister, as well as wife of honorary family member. Bear having been with them a year now, he grew very fond of him. Yet, as a member of the family, he had to do what was best for Bear; he felt he was still vulnerable. To move away now may cause him to regress. If only Medicine Man was here, he would do his magic and know the way ahead.

'Best way is for you to go away for a few days with friend Caleb. Talk to him. Go to Dawson City away from here and us. Your mind will be clear which way you choose to go. Whatever you decide, we will help.'

'Do you know where Caleb is? He must have left early.'

'He say he go to Dawson, do business. He come back soon. You want to go home to your Dorset?' Grey asked. 'You go with my blessing. Spirits go with you. Keep you safe.'

'I am unsure of what to do, Grey Eagle. I have Grace to consider. What will she do if I go? Do you think she will come with me?'

'You must ask her when you come back if that what you want to do. I won't hold you back.'

'I feel I should go, Grey. I want to find my brother. Also, I must write to my family and explain I am not dead after all. It will be a shock to them. I will ask Caleb to come with me, if he can sort out his business here. He was a good friend.'

'He will still be good friend, I know this.'

Caleb returned an hour later with a bundle of men's clothing. 'Will your Indian father be upset if you change into these, Tom? I want to show you Dawson City, take you to where my business had once been before the fire. You'll be accepted in western clothes, the Indians here are a despised people, as I'm sure you know.'

'I'll wear them. I must find Grace and explain to her that I am going away for a short time. Then I must let Grey know I am accepting his suggestion that I go to Dawson to seek information regarding Will.'

Tom found Grace collecting firewood in amongst the piles of wood washed up on the shore. She looked up as he approached, and she knew then her Bear was going away.

'Bear, are you going with Mr Caleb?'

'Yes, Grace, but not for long. I will be back before you move to summer camp. I'm only going to Dawson to try and find information regarding my brother, Will.'

'I will miss you, Bear. Keep safe and come back soon.'

Tom embraced Grace and kissed her quickly, before turning back, leaving her to continue collecting wood.

Saying goodbye to the people he considered family turned out to be harder than Tom imagined and very humbling. Each handshake and hug proved painful, especially when it came to Grey Eagle. 'I will never forget you, Grey Eagle. You saved my life. I'll never forget Winnie either, I'm sorry not to say goodbye to her, please tell her how much I love her as a sister. I will miss you all.' He strode over to Caleb and the two men caught the paddle steamer into Dawson.

Stepping carefully onto what passed for the dock, but was in fact just a few planks precariously nailed together to make a platform, Tom and Caleb made their into the city.

'Before the fire, this place wasn't much different to Skagway: a sprawl of tents, log cabins, false-fronted buildings and piles of lumber. The same mangy dogs. Same fights. Do you remember the fight in Skagway between that

Jake character and myself? You saved my life, Tom; I'll never forget that.' Tom stared at Caleb; he had no memory of the incident Caleb was talking about.

'Well, I'll tell you about it one day.'

'One hundred and seventeen buildings were destroyed in one night last April.' Caleb explained as they waded through the same black oozing mass of mud and sodden sawdust stretching from the shoreline to the boardwalks.

'We're just passing Paradise Alley, where the whores plied their trade out of small huts called cribs. Most of them were dance hall girls exploited by ruthless pimps. The Mounties try to curb their business, but it happens very covertly. Looks like they're rebuilding the Alley already. The prostitutes poured out of the cribs naked and screaming into the arms of the fire fighters. What a sight that must have been. The fire started in the bedroom of a dancer in one of the saloons, and with the city being made of wood, flames quickly spread to other premises. It was a freezing cold night, but that didn't stop it. In the end, they blew up a row of saloons and hotels to make a wind break.' Caleb halted outside a hotel that appeared to be little damaged beyond a sooty exterior. Inside was opulent; good flock wallpaper, heavy furniture and gilt framed pictures hung around the walls. A crystal chandelier hung from the ceiling. In one corner, an old man was playing an even older piano. The only thing to spoil the ambiance was the sawdust covering the floor, necessary due to the amount of mud and horse dung brought in from outside. Relaxing in chairs in the bar and having ordered two whiskeys, Caleb continued his tale:

'When I left Lake Bennett, believing you to be dead, I decided to join other stampeders. We ended up in Bonanza Creek, being just in time to stake and pay for a claim. My mate, Percy and I were lucky. We struck gold almost straight away. We made our way to Dawson, cashed in the nuggets and gold dust and bought a bar that we named The Boon Saloon. Funny name, but we liked it. Percy died in the fire.' Caleb paused at this point, and downed his whiskey in one go, calling the bartender for two more tots. Tom had a job keeping up with Caleb on the whiskey. Not having had a drink for over a year, he was enjoying these drinks. He hoped the alcohol would dull the headache he endured since his accident.

'So,' continued Caleb, thoughtfully. 'Perce and I made a great deal of money from the Boon Saloon. He had no family, so I copped the lot. It's all in the bank safely, a mail boat took it down the river and onto the Bank of Vancouver, and accompanied by a North West Mounted Policeman I trusted who was going that way anyway. I've had the receipt from the bank, so know it arrived safely. Tom, I'm rich and free, and, my friend, if you decide to return to England, then, if you want me to, I will come with you.'

'Are you sure, Caleb? But, the thing is, I'm not at all sure I shall go back. I need some time to consider.'

'Course you do. Whatever you decide I will stand by you. If you don't go back, what will you tell Daisy?'

'Daisy? Who is Daisy?'

'Only the love of your life, man.' Caleb looked at Tom, aghast that he had forgotten the beautiful girl he left behind in Dorset. During their travels, Tom had talked non-stop about Daisy; he couldn't believe Tom had forgotten. That bear attack must have been really dreadful to have affected Tom's memory so badly. He just hoped that Tom would realise who Daisy was before he started the journey back to England; if that is what he had decided. Daisy would be delighted to know Tom wasn't dead after all, but it would be a shock for her and for everyone back there. On the other hand, she may have met someone else and be married by now, only time would tell.

'Tell be about Daisy some time, please, Caleb. Knowing about her may jog my memory. There is so much I don't know, it's frustrating.'

'She gave you an embroidered handkerchief when you left England. I know, because you showed me several times. In fact I was getting fed up hearing about it. Did it survive the bear attack?'

'So that is what Grace gave me. It was a bit tattered, but she said she found it in my shirt pocket, so she washed it, guessing it was important to me. Daisy must have made it.'

'Well, now I can tell you, you saved my life when I had a fight with a character called Jake, back in Skagway. I am definitely coming to England with you. I can see you're not completely fit, you need someone to look after you and I will do that. I owe you. We'll go down the Yukon on a steamboat, that'll be restful for you. Then, we make our way to Carcross and travel on this new railroad everyone is talking about. It'll be a real adventure.'

Tom thought he'd had enough excitement in his life so far, but kept quiet. 'What would you suggest I do about letting my people know I'm alive? Should I telegraph? Or would it be better to surprise them?'

'Look at it this way. If it was you, say, and you got a telegram saying you were alive, would you believe it? Or would you think it was a practical joke?'

'I see your point.'

'The other thing is, it takes so long for mail to get anywhere, and you could be home before a letter. I wrote to your people, but didn't get a reply as I had moved on. It's not easy finding anyone. Like looking for a needle in a haystack, but you got to get through the haystack first.

Another thing, there is so much corruption; mail gets stolen along the routes.'

Tom rose and went in search of the washroom. Looking in the mirror for the first time in a year, he was shocked at his appearance. It was a miracle Caleb recognised him; the left half of his face, neck and shoulder were reddened and the skin puckered. His left eye was badly damaged. He had only half an ear. It was still difficult to use his arm and shoulder, but he managed. His limp was noticeable, but he was able to walk perfectly well. Walking around Dawson he appeared no different to many other people burned in the fire, but back in Skagway and other places, he thought he would probably get pitying glances. 'I'm alive,' he mumbled to himself as he joined Caleb in the bar.

'I want to go to see the Mounties; they may have some information about Will.'

'Sure, let's go now.'

Constructed of wood and tin, with the Union flag flying from the roof, Fort Cudahy could be seen quite clearly as the two friends made their way up the street towards it. Although sympathetic, Sergeant Peter McNeil was unable to help. Despite the fact the Gold Rush was practically over and even though Dawson was a law-abiding city, where guns were prohibited, the Mounties were far too busy to keep track of people passing through, particularly since the fire.

CHAPTER SEVENTEEN

'Nanny Smith, you are so kind,' sniffed Daisy as she sat at the window, looking at the view through the lace curtains, remembering the past before Tom left for Alaska. Over the past months, she felt the baby stirring inside her womb. Sometimes he was quiet, other times he kicked constantly as if he were swimming around in the fluid surrounding him.

'You are looking after me so well. Just as soon as this ordeal is over I'll be able to go back to Thorpe Matravers and the lovely school again. You are a treasure and your cottage is a delight, but living here and not being able to go out much is getting on my nerves. I feel I am running out of patience, now I just want to have the baby and be away.'

'I know, my dear. The past five months have been difficult for you.' Nanny was sitting in her wing chair enjoying the heat emanating from her fireplace. She was beginning to feel her age, and although she had grown to love Daisy, she too, wanted the baby to be born. The thought of coming out of retirement to go back to Thorpe to be in charge of the nursery again, was not something she was looking forward to. But the family were extremely good to her during her employment, and now they paid her a small pension and gave her this cottage rent free to live in, so she felt obliged to help. She would make sure that at least two nursery maids would be employed to help her with the new baby. It was the least she could ask for under the circumstances. She would be able, then, to sit by the nursery fire, as she did now in her own cottage, and tell the maids what to do. Also, her meals would be found, and Cook, she knew from old, would provide nourishing meals. Nanny reflected on the times she spent with Cook, in the privacy of her room, sharing a bottle of sherry, and gossiping about the doings of the house. Maybe she would enjoy those times again.

'Perhaps it will not be so bad after all,' ruminated Nanny out loud.

'What did you say, Nanny?' enquired Daisy.

'Nothing, my precious, nothing.'

Beatrice Smith, known as Nanny, went to work as a nursery maid in Thorpe Park at thirteen years old. She was born in Poole of middle class parents and since very young loved being around babies. When her parents were killed in a boating accident, she was sent to live with an elderly maiden aunt. When she, too, died of heart failure, Beatrice was offered the position by Lord Harry's mother and risen from being the nursery maid to assistant Nanny, then to being Nanny herself at the age of twenty-five. She looked after every baby born in the Park, and loved every single child. Once or twice she thought she might enjoy being a wife and mother herself, but as no man ever came close to asking her to marry him, she grew content with her life as it was.

'Nanny, my pains are coming every five minutes or so. I really don't want to go through with this, having to give birth to the bastard child of Mr Eddy,' spat Daisy with such venom that Nanny was shocked.

'Daisy, that is no way to speak. We know the circumstances are difficult, but you must pull yourself together. It will make the birth more painful if you won't relax.'

As she remained seated at the window, staring at nothing, Daisy thought back to the events of five or six months ago. She knew discussions on what should be done about 'the problem' went on intermittently and at first, neither her parents nor the Thorpe family, it seemed, were prepared to listen to a word she said. She convinced her mother, yet again, she was telling the truth. She'd cried for weeks. She was a good Christian woman, why did she have to endure all this? Oh, she missed Tom. She'd heard he was dead too, now, which she found difficult to believe.

'Nanny, do you believe that Mr Thomas is dead? I don't think he would have been so silly as to let something as dangerous as a bear to get near him, he was strong and sensible.'

The thought of him no longer being part of her life caused Daisy agony and heartbreak. Thankfully, if he was dead, he would never find out about the attacks and this baby, what would the truth have done to their relationship? Sitting quietly and knitting with Nanny in the evenings caused her to reflect long and hard about 'the problem' and to mull over all the scenes happening up to this point, it was all going around and around in her head.

'Nanny, how do you think I will feel when the baby is born and taken away from me? You know I have become used to feeling it kick inside. One part of me feels the baby is part of me, the other part of me hates this child because of that evil Eddy.'

'So many questions, child, I can't answer. Now, just be patient, it will soon be over. Come and sit by the fire, there is nothing to see out of the window. Nurse will be here soon and she will help you.' Nanny picked up her knitting and calmly started to count her stitches.

As far as the actual birth itself was concerned, Daisy didn't feel too scared having been present at a few births in the village. Occasionally, women called upon her mother for help and Daisy went along to calm the mother or to look after the other children in the family. Fathers were hopeless when it came to childbirth; the pub was the best place for them.

Getting up and going to sit beside Nanny, Daisy gasped as another contraction caused her to double up. Thinking back to her last moments with Tom was helping her take her mind off the pain ripping through her body. As he bent and kissed her for the last time, gently and almost reverently, the blood had rushed through her veins as his mouth touched hers. She gave him the embroidered handkerchief and in return he gave her a beautiful turquoise dress. Oh, a thought suddenly struck her; where was her dress? Was it still safely in the box under her bed at home in Thorpe Matravers? Despite her mother's curiosity, Daisy managed to field any further questioning; there were too many other things on her mind concerning the baby, to worry about a dress. The thought of the dress made her realise how she missed Tom. The thought of never being able to see him again, to see her wearing that dress, was heartbreaking. What was her future without him? Her misery was increasing every minute; she was tired of thinking; her head hurt with it all.

Daisy looked down at her huge body encased in a capacious white cotton nightgown. Her slender ankles had puffed up and her once small breasts swelled beyond the capacity of every dress she possessed. The skin of her belly was so stretched beyond its limits; the outer layer seemed to split apart, leaving dozens of pale streaks. She wondered if she would ever become slim again.

'Nanny, will I ever regain my figure?' she questioned.

'You will, my pet, you will, given time.'

'What does it matter, anyway, no man will ever want me.'

'Who knows what can happen after all this trouble, Daisy. You may meet a young man and marry. No one need know you've had a baby.'

'No, Nanny, I'll never meet anyone. I shall never marry.' Tears sprang to her eyes as she thought about Tom. Even if he were alive and came back, she would be too ugly. She felt certain she was ruined for life.

Her back ached and the pains in her abdomen had intensified, so much so, she almost passed out.

The next contraction was so strong and painful that Daisy was encouraged by Nanny to get into the bed in her small room. The bed was warm, Nurse Mabel having placed a stone hot water bottle under the covers earlier, before popping out for a walk.

'You tell me everything that slut Daisy says, and everything she does,' uttered Eddy to Mabel, as he buttoned his shirt. 'If you do as I ask, you will be well rewarded, with money as well as my prowess in the bedroom.' He laughed at his own cockiness. Oh, yes, he was always good in bed with a slut.

'I will, Eddy, I will. I'll come here to our own little cottage tomorrow,' replied Mabel. 'I expect the baby will have been born by then and you can have it. I'll bring the child here and wait for you. On the way, I'll collect the wet nurse you told me about.'

'Good. Now, remember, not a word to anyone about this, my beauty.'

Mabel had fallen under Eddy's spell the moment she set eyes on him. Walking through Wareham, after calling at the post office for her employer and dressed in her nurse's uniform, she accidently tripped over a small dog being led on a piece of rope, by a child. Eddy caught her and was immediately taken with her soft brown eyes and curvy figure.

'Glad to be of service, miss,' he said as he helped her up. 'May I buy you a cup of tea to help you steady your nerves?' he said, holding her firmly by the arm. So, over tea in a tea room in South Street, she fell under his spell. When sober, Eddy appeared to be the perfect gentleman, and as such, treated Mabel with respect.

'I notice you are a nurse,' he said, as Mabel poured the tea from the big brown tea pot. 'Are you currently in employment?'

'Yes, I am a qualified nurse. The family I work for are going abroad tomorrow, and will no longer need my services. I shall have to find another position.'

'Well, as luck would have it, I am looking for a nurse.' Eddy leaned closer to Mabel and flashed her one of his winning smiles. She noticed how well dressed he was, and felt she could take advantage of this stroke of luck. It only took two days for Eddy to persuade her to bed him in The Laurels, a small cottage he secretly purchased just half a mile from Nanny's place. It hadn't been too difficult; she was ripe for the picking.

Now that the birth was imminent, he needed to know what Daisy was doing to bring his plan to fruition. He didn't want to see her walking about the village or working in the school after the birth. Not only had she refused his advances last spring, which forced him to rape her, but she was pregnant. Every time he saw her, he would remember what she had done to him. Stupid girl, she should have got rid of the baby and not told anyone. By telling her parents, who then told his in-laws, he lost the love of Amy. Now, all she talked about was the baby. She was telling all their friends, telling them she was looking forward to holding the child in her arms. Good job she wasn't telling them he was the father, which would be too much. She wouldn't let him into her bed, she spurned all his advances. Also, he was

145

forced to live and sleep in the other wing of the house, away from her. She was his wife, damn it. So, he needed to get rid of the trollop. If he could show that Daisy was mentally unstable and therefore incapable of coming back to Thorpe Matravers, then he would arrange for her to be put away. By befriending the matron at Melbury Hall all he needed to do was pay her a substantial amount of money and she would ensure Daisy Evans never walked the streets of Dorset, or anywhere else, for that matter. She would be kept in the home for imbeciles the rest of her life.

'Damn it, this fiasco with that slut, Daisy, is costing me a fortune, what with buying this cottage, paying you and the mental home she's going to end up in,' Eddy explained to Mabel. 'Let alone the two doctors who will sign the forms. They have asked for a fortune. Now, get out of here, and act normally,' he told Mabel as he slapped her bottom in an aggressive manner, to which, being in love with him, she was oblivious.

Eddy having borrowed heavily from friends and acquaintances, realised most of them were pressing him for repayment. 'Well, they will just have to wait.'

As she dressed, Mabel laughed to herself; she was being paid a generous amount of money by Eddy to look after Daisy. Unbeknown to him, she was also being paid by Lord Harry, who didn't know Eddy was also paying her. Easy money, and who knows, she could be Eddy's wife one day. He mentioned his wife was useless, time would tell what would happen in that direction. She understood that Eddy needed her to spy on Daisy and to report back anything she thought unusual; anything she said he could use against her. She agreed as she would do anything for Eddy, she thought he was wonderful.

Now Mabel was back in Nanny's cottage, and as she came into the room, the three women prepared for the birth, Daisy having been in labour for a good twelve hours by now. Mabel was under strict instructions to ensure the mother was, under no circumstances, to see, let alone hold, the baby. Daisy had never experienced pain like this, and as the contractions strengthened, she put her hands behind her head, grabbing the iron bedstead. She felt she was being ripped in half and being drawn into a dark tunnel of pain that would take her away from the world.

'Take this, Daisy,' said Nanny, as she folded up a small flannel and placed it in Daisy's mouth for her to bite on, whilst mopping her brow with a damp cloth.

The bed was now wet with sweat and with the liquid that burst from her body like a flood. Daisy felt herself drifting almost out of consciousness. The only thing seeming real to her was the pain. Every part of her being felt the urge to push, but it seemed as though she was pushing her body inside out.

Half an hour later, the baby girl slipped easily into the world and exercised her lungs at full pelt. Daisy's pains ceased so she knew the wail did not come from her. This was a new sound. Within seconds nurse Mabel took her away; Daisy held out her arms to hold her. She was ignored.

'She's not your child any more now, Daisy. It's best you don't see her. She belongs to Mr Eddy and Miss Amy.' Nanny kindly told her. 'You will have to accept this and get used to the fact.' As Mabel had wrapped the baby in a shawl and whisked it out of the room, Daisy just glimpsed a tuft of red hair, the same colour as Mr Eddy's. She could hear the baby's cries as she was carried away.

'I can't bear this,' Daisy cried weakly. She was so tired, still in pain and feeling miserable. 'Nanny, how will I cope, seeing my baby in Miss Amy's arms?'

'Now, you just stop this!' cried Nanny. 'You must forget all of this!'

'Forget, how can I possibly forget? I can't forget the way she came about any more than I can forget what I've just been through.'

'Now, my girl, pull yourself together, you are doing no one any good by getting worked up. You're going to have a few weeks' rest, and then you can go home as if nothing untoward happened. Your mother will visit you in a few days.'

'But, Nanny…'

'No buts. You just sign the papers when they ask you to, and that's that, all done and dusted. A fine, healthy baby is just what they want, and that's what you have given them.'

'I can't even give her a name?'

'Her new parents will do that. Don't forget, she's with her real father.'

Daisy burst into tears. 'I feel so tired, so miserable. It's so unfair.'

'You just rest now, my girl, and don't forget, when you leave here, not a single word to anyone, do you hear? We all have too much to lose if this all gets out.' Nanny shook her finger at Daisy to emphasise the point, then after tidying the room, left to allow Daisy to sleep. Her imprisonment would soon be ended. What then? At last, exhausted, she fell into a fitful sleep, the tears still glistening on her lashes and her head resting on the pretty lace pillow.

CHAPTER EIGHTEEN

Amy stood in the drawing room and looked down at the beautiful child held in Nanny's arms. The baby girl was sleeping, her long eye lashes curled on her cheeks. Amy gently brushed her finger against the baby's skin; it felt so soft, just like the skin of the peaches the gardeners grew in the hot house.

'Nanny, I love her already, and I will call her Rose, as she looks just like a little flower. Thank you, Nanny; you can settle Rose in the nursery now. But bring her down to see me every evening at six.'

Daisy was still safely in Nanny's cottage and being cared for by Mabel, and would be there for two weeks. Then, having recovered from the birth, Daisy was to return to her home in the Terrace. People in the house and village, when they enquired of Daisy, were told she had gone away to care for an elderly aunt. Having returned, after Easter, Daisy would go back to her teaching post in the school. That was the plan laid out by Harry and Matilda.

Eddy, however, found other plans for Daisy. They didn't include her parents, the village, or the school. She was going to be pronounced as being mad, and put away. Mabel would do her part in making sure Daisy never returned home.

'Open your mouth, and swallow this medicine, Daisy, it will make you feel a whole lot better.' Mabel was experiencing trouble with this patient; she just wouldn't do as she was told. 'If you don't do this voluntarily, then I will tie you down and force it down your throat.'

The calomel elixir that Eddy gave Mabel to give Daisy caused her to sleep more than she wanted. Worse, it also gave her hallucinations. She suffered dreadful nightmares and when she did wake up, her throat felt on fire.

'I can't understand why you are doing this to me,' slurred Daisy, as she tried to sit up in her bed. She was still in Nanny's cottage, in the room where she gave birth. 'Where is my baby? I want Tom.'

'Stop talking rubbish and swallow this, or else.' Mabel was becoming cross now. It was three days since the birthing and the baby given over to Nanny. Eddy was due soon, she needed to get this nuisance of a woman asleep so that she could go to the other cottage and be with him; he was her obsession. She enjoyed going to bed with him, but just lately, he'd slapped her around. Although this heightened her sexual tension, she was worried he would go too far and her bruises would show. He promised her he would leave Amy and set up home with her, but so far, this promise had not materialised.

'Good girl,' muttered Mabel as Daisy reluctantly swallowed the contents of the spoon. 'I can hear his horse; he's on his way to the cottage. Be quiet and sleep.'

Just to make sure Daisy couldn't get out of bed, Mabel wrapped strips of muslin tightly around Daisy's wrists and tied them to the bedstead.

'That will keep her here!'

Jane was worried. She needed to see Daisy; it had been two weeks since the baby's birth. The only time she had seen her was the day after Rose had been born. For some reason the family were keeping her away; they made sure she was too busy to leave the big house. Occasionally she could hear the baby crying; they allowed her and Bert to see Rose, but only the once. Mr Eddy said Daisy wasn't at the cottage any more, and Nanny didn't know where she was. Rumour in the kitchen was that Daisy was not in her right mind. Cook had heard two kitchen maids giggling together in the scullery.

'She be right daft, so John the new footman told me,' said Ruby. 'He 'eard it when Mr Eddy was talking to the master.'

'Go on, she never is. Are you sure?' giggled Lucy.

'Yup, 'tis true, Daisy Evans be gone away, no one do know where she be.'

'Talking about the new footman, that John, he be 'a 'some, baint 'e?'

'No good you looking there, Lucy, he already got eyes fer Elsie.'

'Trust 'err, she allus goes fer the best 'uns.'

Jane, having been told by Cook what she heard regarding Daisy, was by now really worried. It was true she didn't know where Daisy was. She would ask her Ladyship when the moment was right.

'Nurse Mabel informs me that Daisy Evans is causing trouble in Nanny's cottage,' Eddy informed Harry after dinner one evening as they sat at the dining table drinking port and smoking. Matilda and Amy were relaxing in the drawing room and enjoying their coffee. The baby, Rose, was the main topic of conversation between the two women.

'What sort of trouble, Eddy?'

'She's becoming hysterical and threatening to go around the village telling everyone that I raped her and that I am the father of her baby. Then, she says Tom is in love with her. Nurse Mabel has to sedate her with calomel to keep her calm. Last night, she became violent and needed to be restrained,' lied Eddy as he drew on his cigarette.

'We can't have Daisy doing that, there are enough rumours circulating as it is. I've heard a lot of gossip in Wareham. I was eating lunch in the Red Lion and overheard two local women talking about an illegitimate baby being born to a girl in the Terrace.'

'We need to do something, Harry.'

'What do you suggest, Eddy?'

'We get her into Melbury Hall for a while until she feels better. I would be willing to pay for Daisy's treatment; after all, I am to blame for her problems.'

'Arrange it, then, Eddy. You are probably unaware, since it happened before you married Amy, but I founded Melbury Hall before you joined the family. It was originally a large family house; it still has the original Elizabethan wood panelling. Following the owners' death it was put up for sale and I bought it, refurbished it, re-modelled the gardens and turned it into an exclusive home for unfortunates. It is the perfect place for Daisy Evans to stay until she is well again and stops all this nonsense'. Harry sucked on his cigar and blew out smoke as he spoke. 'The place has high stone walls and heavy wooden gates so she should be safe. Some of the inmates have become trustees, they have done so well. I am quite proud of the place.'

'So, she'll be safe in there, Harry?'

'She will that. I'll write to the matron, as I am the main benefactor, it'll cost you nothing, though why I don't make you pay the fees, I don't know! Then I'll hand the arrangements over to you. I have enough to cope with, Matilda is taking too much on her shoulders, and she will be making herself very ill if we're not careful.'

'Consider it done, Pa-in-law. No need to tell anyone. We'll just say Daisy decided to go up north to be a governess. Jane and Bert will understand, once I have a word with Bert. Now, shall we join the ladies?'

As he followed Harry along the hallway and into the drawing room, Eddy grinned slyly to himself. It was all going smoothly, just as he wanted. Harry believed all the lies he'd told him. The bitch Daisy would soon be out of his way. Once in the Institution, Daisy is likely to become mentally ill anyway; a few visits from me and she'll be sure to be mad. Bert Evans would do what I tell him. He has too much to lose not be obey me.

Eddy was at The Laurels when Mabel arrived. She had sedated Daisy to the extent that the girl wouldn't wake up for at least ten hours; plenty of time for her and Eddy to complete their plans. In just one hour a horse-drawn van would arrive at Nanny's cottage. The two strong men driving it, would enter the cottage, pick up Daisy and put her in the van. If she woke and caused a fuss, they would restrain her. She would then be taken to Melbury Hall where she would spend the rest of her life. Whilst this was happening, Mabel would be busy keeping Eddy happy. No more Daisy, no more problems.

'May I speak with you, please, madam?' Jane felt this morning was a good moment to ask about Daisy. She had just put away Matilda's nightclothes after helping her dress. All the clothes in the wardrobe were made of black fabric, bombazine and crepe; very depressing, thought Jane. There seemed to be no end of grief in this house.

'Yes, Jane, what is it?' Matilda was in no hurry to go downstairs today; Harry left early for the magistrate's court, Amy and a friend who was staying for a few days were out riding. Having breakfasted in bed, she was, for once, feeling calm.

'I don't want to speak out of turn, madam, but I am worried about Daisy.'

'In what way are you worried, Jane?'

'I would like to know where she is. The rumour downstairs is that she is mentally unwell and has been whisked away. Is this true?'

Matilda swallowed, and then informed Jane Daisy was a governess in the north of England. The family felt it was the best course of action under the circumstances. Matilda felt sure that Daisy would be happy there; Mr Eddy made the arrangements, the family being friends of his parents. Matilda said she was sure Daisy would write soon and tell her parents about her new position.

Later that evening, Jane was most perturbed. After a supper of cold meat and pickles, and still seated at the table, she related to Bert what madam told her. She said, 'I just don't trust that Mr Eddy. There's a nasty streak to him. I have my suspicions. I just hope we hear from Daisy soon.'

Jane stood up and started collecting up the dishes. Bert, too, stood up and put his arms around Jane, resting her head on his shoulder.

'I need to be very careful, Jane. Mr Eddy is a difficult boss at the pottery. He's very unpopular and can be really nasty at times. To lose my job would be a disaster, we'd be certain to lose this house, and it could be Christmas Close, the poorhouse in Wareham, for us.'

CHAPTER NINETEEN

Daisy slowly woke up, feeling as if she were in a different world. Looking around her she realised she was in a large room, the walls of which were bare and distempered. She rested in a canvas hammock which appeared to be arranged on a metal frame in a bath filled with warm water. Her whole body was covered with a canvas sheet, with a hole for her head, which was resting on a rubber pillow. Daisy had no idea how long she had been there. The last thing she remembered was being in Nanny's cottage and being forced by Nurse Mabel to swallow a noxious liquid.

Daisy carefully turned her head to look around, but all she could distinguish were more contraptions the same as the one she was in. Turning her head back, suddenly, making Daisy jump, a face appeared right in front of her. It was the face of a man, a hairy man. He had black fuzzy hair, spiky eyebrows and staring green eyes.

'Where am I?' whispered Daisy. 'Who are you?'

'I am Doctor Jones.' His voice was deep and gruff. 'You are in Melbury Hall, a mental institution. We are going to look after you for a while.'

'But, why? I am not ill. I was really well until Nurse Mabel started forcing me to take that horrible stuff. I need to get out of here.'

Struggling to move, Daisy realised she was trapped in the contraption and couldn't understand why she was incarcerated inside it.

'Please let me out of here. I want to go home to my mother. She will worry about me and wonder where I am.'

'Now, Daisy, you need to understand you are not going anywhere. In a moment we will let you out and show you the room you are going to stay in. This contraption is to help calm you. The warm water has a soothing effect, wouldn't you say so?'

'I don't understand why I am here. Who put me here? Why?'

Daisy began crying, large teardrops running down her cheeks, which she was unable to wipe away. Doctor Jones walked out of the room, through large glass doors, and Daisy was left alone again. The room a nurse took her to looked pleasant. In fact, thought Daisy, it is larger than the room she shared with Ivy at home, and this room was all hers. She had been taken out of the water bath, the canvas dress taken off of her, and been allowed to towel herself dry. Now, she was dressed in plain cotton underwear under a shift made from blue flowered cambric. She was given a pair of woollen slippers to wear, before the nurse, without a word, left the room, locking the door behind her. Daisy walked to the large picture window and looked out on a view of pretty gardens. The house stood on a hill, with lawns stretching as far as she could see. Trees dotted the landscape and uniform flower beds surrounded the lawn. A river in the valley glistened in the sun. Here and there, wooden seats were occupied by women dressed as she was. They were sitting still, just as if they were statues. 'Perhaps they are statues,' she muttered out loud. Daisy tried to open the window, unsuccessfully, until she noticed the locks attached to the latches. Sitting in an armchair she looked around, taking in the features of the room in which she appeared to be incarcerated. The floor was polished wood covered with a patterned carpet in shades of brown and beige. The walls were oak panelled; beige brocade curtains hung neatly at the window. The bed was plain wood, with a beige quilt and looked reasonably comfortable. A small bedside table held a Bible. Next to a wash basin stood a large light wood wardrobe, upon noticing which, Daisy rose and opened the doors. Inside, hangings on a rail were another dress similar to the one she was wearing, a blue wool coat and a blue tweed jacket. On the floor of the wardrobe sat a pair of canvas shoes. Hearing a key turning in the lock, she quickly closed the wardrobe door and sat in the chair.

'Hello, Daisy. My name is Nurse Fox and I will be looking after you,' announced the woman, coming into the room and closing the door behind her. She was dressed in a uniform consisting of a grey striped dress, large white cotton wrap-around apron and sturdy brown boots. Her grey hair, which was arranged into a bun, was topped by a starched cap. In her hand she held a metal kidney-shaped tray on which lay a small bottle of liquid, a medicine glass and a teaspoon.

'You will be free to wander the house and grounds during your time here. The public rooms are pleasant, there is a piano for you to play, if you so wish. You may talk to any of the women patients, provided you do not make a nuisance of yourself. Meals will be taken regularly. You will be given a job of work to do.'

Nurse Fox paused for breath, giving Daisy the opportunity to ask, 'What sort of work?'

'You will be informed in due course. The one thing we insist upon is that you take your medicine when I come to administer it. If you refuse you will be given a bath similar to the one today, followed by time being spent in a padded room. Do you understand?'

'Yes, Nurse Fox, I do. But, I still cannot understand why I am here. I have done nothing wrong.'

'You can protest your sanity when you see Doctor Jones later. Now, drink this.'

Nurse Fox placed the tray on the bedside table, opened the small bottle and poured a teaspoonful of the liquid into a small glass, before handing it to Daisy. Reluctantly, she swallowed the noxious medicine and handed the glass back.

'Now, come with me and I will show you around the house.'

Glancing through the open doors of rooms as they passed, Daisy noticed they all looked the same inside. On the outside of the doors, slates hung, on which were written in chalk, the name of the patient and nurse. At the end of the corridor Nurse Fox opened double doors and ushered Daisy inside. What she saw made her gasp. She could almost have been in the drawing room of an aristocratic lady. There were flowers and pictures everywhere, with comfortable sofas, armchairs and small tables. The windows were large and dressed with gold brocade curtains. Along one wall books were placed on floor to ceiling shelves. Three woman, dressed the same as Daisy and therefore obviously patients, sat around the room. The only giveaway to the institution's purpose was locks on all the windows.

'You can come in here at any time and read or chat. Bad behaviour will be punished. You can order tea; you can read any of the novels or magazines.'

'May I stay here for a while?' enquired Daisy.

'You may. You will be collected by me when Doctor Jones is ready to see you.'

Perching on the arm of a sofa, Daisy glanced at her fellow patients. One was a beautiful girl who looked just like one of the Pre Raphaelite paintings she once glimpsed in Lady Matilda's drawing room who sat serenely flicking through a magazine. The second woman was elderly, with greying curls and eyes that appeared to be made of green glass. Her mouth was deformed, with two long yellow teeth protruding over her lower lip. She stood at the end of the room near the bookshelves and stared most disconcertingly, at Daisy. Sitting on the floor under the window sill, a young girl sat rocking backwards and forwards and dribbling; the saliva running unheeded down the front of her dress. Suddenly, through the haze of her mind, due to the amount of elixir she had been forced to take over the past days, she realised these women were mad. She was imprisoned in a place full of mad people. She wasn't mad herself, so why was she here?

Later, she was summoned to Dr Jones's office. He sat behind his desk and Daisy sat on the other side facing him. He looked less frightening sitting there than he did the first time she had seen him. His tweed suit, white shirt and tweed tie gave him the appearance of a kindly, middle-aged, gentleman.

'Why do you think you are here?' he asked, opening the conversation.

'I have no idea.'

'You are here because you have been promiscuous and have given birth to an illegitimate child. You have also been violent to the nurse caring for you, and have caused trouble for the Thorpe family who were so very kind to you during your pregnancy.'

'That's not true. I was attacked and raped and forced to give up my baby. I don't know how I got here, who brought me, or who wants me to stay here.'

'Do you feel you are being kept at Melbury Hall against your will, Miss Evans?'

Bursting into tears, Daisy was unable to reply for some minutes. Doctor Jones waited patiently.

'What's the good,' she sobbed. 'If I say yes, you'll think I'm mad. If I say no, you'll think I don't want to go home.'

Showing no reaction to her words, Doctor Jones placed his hands on the desk, and clasped them together, making an arch with his fingers, before announcing, 'You will stay here until such time as Mr Harris-Fletcher considers you are well behaved enough to return to your family. Go to your room now.'

Stunned, Daisy slowly ambled back to her room. So, it's Mr Eddy who has me locked up here, she thought. He needs me to be out of the way; I must be a liability to him. I hate him even more than I did before. I must find some way out of here.

As the days passed, the bromide elixir that Daisy was given twice a day, sent her into a lethargy she found difficult to overcome. She had been given the task of helping in the garden, which, had she not felt so tired, she would have enjoyed. Deadheading flowers and weeding flower beds were pleasant tasks. She enjoyed being out in the fresh spring air.

'Why don't I have any visitors?' she asked Nurse Fox one morning. Daisy found the nurse to be amenable and kind, once she came to know her. Occasionally, when time and duties allowed, they would sit together in the drawing room and chat. 'Foxy', as Daisy fondly called her, enjoyed talking about her aunt with whom she lived, and who was an eccentric character.

Some of the tales Foxy told, caused Daisy to laugh, much to the consternation of any other patient who happened to be within earshot.

'Mr Harris-Fletcher has said that visitors will trouble you and impede your progress. As he is paying for your stay here, we have to do as we're told.'

'How I hate that man, he's just pure evil. He's imprisoned me in a place full of mad people. When I eventually get out of here, I shall move as far away from him as possible.'

The realisation that she was not, in actual fact mad, just incarcerated by Eddy, caused her to experience an intense loneliness. Apart from Foxy, she was utterly without friends. The other patients being mostly mad she needed to restrain herself from copying their behaviour. One patient believed she was hiding from potential assassins, whilst another said she was a duchess and was so convincing, Daisy began to curtsey to her. Even the trustees were strange and exhibited weird behaviour. Back in her room following lunch a few days later, chilled by a sudden unease, Daisy shivered.

'Daisy, you have a visitor,' said Foxy as she opened the door and stood aside.

'So, this is your room. It is pleasant, is it not? I trust you are comfortable here, Daisy?' questioned Eddy, pleasantly. Seeing who her visitor was, Daisy shrank in stature and backed into a corner of the room. She was quietly reading a magazine when Foxy opened the door, now she was a quivering wreck. The last person she needed, or thought about seeing, was evil Eddy.

'Leave us,' barked Eddy to Foxy.

'I am not allowed to leave you alone with a patient,' quivered Foxy.

'Do as you are told, or you leave here.'

Glancing uneasily at Daisy, Foxy left the room leaving the door ajar. Standing outside in the hallway, she listened to every word.

'So, my pretty. I have a treat for you. A different medicine. I've given it to Matron.' Eddy was exuding a menace that made her cold; his eyes were hard and intent on her, as if reading her mind. 'You will take it. If you don't, your father will be sacked from the pottery.'

'I won't take it. I'm in my right mind; I shouldn't even be in here.'

'Yes, Matron tells me you are acting like a normal young lady; well, I can't have that. I want you mad, too mad to be released, and mad you shall become. Understand what I say.' He stepped towards her. 'Take the new medicine.' He then stormed out of the room, slamming the door behind him and giving Foxy a cold stare.

Coming back into the room, she found Daisy a quivering wreck crouched on the floor in the corner of the room.

'Oh, my pet. Come on, into bed and rest.'

'He wants me to be mad, Foxy. The way he treats me, I am beginning to feel it will be easier to be mad. What shall I do?'

'Don't fret, now. We'll think of something.'

'Foxy, dear Foxy. I don't want you to lose your job here. If it wasn't for the constant threat to my family, I would have found some way of escape by now.'

'I don't know what the answer is, Daisy. That Mr Eddy is very frightening. He appears to have some hold over Matron, our hands are tied.'

Finally tucking Daisy under the covers, Foxy moved to the door, whispering, 'Sleep for a while until supper, my dear. I won't be far away.'

Relaxing a little, Daisy closed her eyes and was soon sleeping.

CHAPTER TWENTY

Mabel stood looking at her naked reflection in the full-length mirror in the bedroom at the Laurels. She was pleased with what she saw. At twenty-six years of age, she felt as though she were in her prime; neat natural blond hair, sparkling blue eyes, clear complexion and a buxom figure. Eddy enjoyed exploring her body and she responded likewise. Spending time with Eddy was always a surprise even though just lately he was becoming aggressive in his lovemaking. But, she thought, the slaps he gave her added to the excitement, so long as he didn't become uncontrollably aggressive. She felt sexy today and, dressing carefully in a grey serge skirt and cream lace blouse over her silk camisole and French knickers, Mabel hummed whilst pulling on her stockings and placed her dainty feet in her black button-up kid boots. This morning Eddy planned to visit and take her out for a drive in his carriage. For the first time since knowing him, they would be seen together in public which could be interesting. I do hope he's in a good mood, she thought to herself. Of late he has been very grumpy and aggressive. I don't know from one day to the next what his mood will be. Donning her navy blue coat and a rather fetching floppy velvet hat of the same colour, Mabel made her way downstairs where she placed a bright green scarf around her shoulders and picked up her reticule from the coat stand. She wanted to be noticed.

Still yawning, having been up since before dawn, the stable boy harnessed Riley, the bay mare to the covered carriage and led her out into the yard. Grey clouds darkened the early morning sky, but Eddy was undeterred, nothing would stop him from meeting up with Mabel today. He was encouraged by the gloomy weather. The plans he had for her could only be enhanced by rain; muddy ground hid foot and hoof prints. Climbing up onto the front of the carriage, Eddy ensured he was comfortable before urging Riley to walk on towards the Laurels and Mabel. As Riley jogged along, several times Eddy patted his jacket pocket which held his hip flask.

'Mabel is becoming too much of a nuisance, always nagging me to leave Amy and go off somewhere with her,' muttered Eddy to Riley, as the mare clopped along the main road. Two days previously he had ridden out to the Furze Pools alone to check out the suitability of taking Mabel there. The area he had in mind appeared secluded and quiet. Only rabbits and squirrels would be aware of their presence.

As he closed in on the cottage, Eddy became increasingly excited, 'Mabel won't know what's hit her,' he muttered. Turning off the main road, he spurred Riley on up the dusty track, gorse bushes growing on both sides almost obscuring their way, and causing fine scratch marks to appear on the black carriage paint. Can't be helped, thought Eddy. 'Some minion back home will paint over it, isn't that what we employ those yokels for?' Cantering onwards he continued talking to his four-legged companion. 'She certainly is a liability. Last time I visited she demanded more money to keep quiet.' His voice rising, he continued, 'I won't be blackmailed. She has to go.' On the other side of the largest of the gorse bushes Josie Day, hearing a voice rising above the sound of hooves and carriage wheels, stopped looking for the wild violets she picked to sell on doorsteps and, still stooped, she edged closer to the hedge. That be that nasty man from the big 'ouse, she thought to herself. Wonder whom he be talking 'bout. I can't stand him and I'll be able to use what I 'eard one day. Useful 'tis that I know.

As Eddy eventually reached the cottage, thunder rumbled in the distance, unsettling the young mare as he tied her to the gate post. Standing on the cottage threshold and hearing the carriage wheels approaching, Mabel stepped out, turned and locked the door then put the key in its usual hiding place above the lintel. Striding up the path, she smiled at Eddy, who grimaced back as he jumped down from his seat on the carriage.

'Hello, my love,' she said to him, smiling. 'I am so pleased to see you; I just hope this thunder doesn't come to anything. I'd hate anything to spoil our picnic.'

'Yea,' replied Eddy grumpily, 'it would be too bad. Now, get in the carriage.' He helped her up as she lifted her skirt, showing dainty ankles.

'You sound unhappy, Eddy, is everything all right?' she asked him quizzically.

'Everything is fine, woman, now get in and sit down. Get settled, I want to be going.'

Climbing in after her and picking up the reins, Eddy spurred Riley forwards and up the lane.

'Where are we going?' whispered Mabel, slightly apprehensive as to Eddy's mood.

'To the Furzey pools.'

'Oh, I have heard of them but have never been. What are they?'

'Quarries that were dug for clay years ago and are now filled with water. The very fine clay in the water shows the light in different ways. Sometimes the pools are green, sometimes bright blue.'

'Sounds so romantic, Eddy.'

'Shut up, your chattering is getting on my nerves. Just keep quiet, will you. People will hear us.'

'But I thought that is what you wanted, people to see us together,' whispered Mabel. 'Why have you changed so, Eddy, you are acting as if you are fed up with me?'

'Since you ask, I am fed up with you, with your snivelling, grovelling for more money, pushing me to leave my wife. Huh, that will never happen, I know where my bread is buttered.'

'Oh, Eddy, why then are you taking me out here, after all I mean to you, all you mean to me. I just don't understand.

'You'll understand this,' growled Eddy raising his hand whilst steadying the reins with the other, turned and hit her across the face. His signet ring caught her cheek and drew blood.

Removing a small lacy handkerchief from her reticule, Mabel pressed it to her cheek. There'll be a scar there, she thought to herself. I'm beginning to feel scared, why is he treating me like this? Her nose was bleeding slightly and her head ached.

'Eddy,' she whined, 'that hurt.' Mabel decided to jump down from the carriage, and run away before he hit her again. Reaching over him and struggling to grab the reigns, Eddy, realising what she had in mind, roughly pushed her back away from him.

'Shut up, we're here.' His manner left Mabel in no doubt as to his mood. Looking at his angry face she knew she would have to be very careful how she acted. It was time to soothe him and take control of the situation.

As Eddy drew Riley to a halt, Mabel, calming down slightly, looked around her at the scenery. Set in a deep bowl, the green pool, formerly a quarry was surrounded by acres of heath, woodland and gorse with sandy paths winding their way around the pool. The supernatural light reflected the shapes of the trees and the nearby Purbeck hills.

'This is a beautiful place, Eddy,' breathed Mabel. 'So peaceful.' Turning to look at him, she continued in a tremulous voice, 'It's a pity about the weather. The thunder and lightning are getting closer.'

Facing her, his eyes showing the hatred he felt for her, he replied in a brutish voice, 'What I see is a woman who is getting on my nerves. If you don't shut up I'll have to hit you again, only next time it will hurt even more.' As Eddy spoke, a clap of thunder rumbled above the hills and large drops of rain splattered onto the roof of the carriage.

Removing the hip flask from his pocket he passed it to her. 'Drink this, it'll help ease the pain.'

Feeling frightened again, and needing to placate him, she took the cap off the silver flask and drank deeply of the contents. As the bitter liquid slid down her throat, she gasped and croaked, 'Whatever is this? It tastes terrible.'

Eddy turned towards her and grimaced. 'Poison, my love, just poison. You'll die soon.'

Mabel put a hand to her throat, then suddenly shuddered, twitched, and slid off the carriage, banging her head on the step as she fell heavily to the ground. Quickly dismounting, Eddy ran round to the other side of the carriage, and, ensuring Riley would stand still by tying her to a branch of a silver birch, he looked down at Mabel. She lay on the sandy path twitching, her face contorted with a rictus grin, her lips moving uncontrollably. Her unseeing glazed eyes stared up at Eddy as he knelt beside her. Taking her hand in his, he held her tightly as she continued to writhe and twitch. Suddenly, as the sky darkened, a streak of lightning split the air followed by a thunderous roar as the storm that had threatened in the distance now arrived at the Furze pool. Riley whinnied and struggled against the reins holding her and her hooves scraped the ground. Large hail stones hit Eddy on his bare head and bounced off the by now dead body of the nurse who lay on the ground beside him. The wind whipped up the sand from the path, sticking to Mabel's face and clothes and stinging Eddy's eyes.

'I must get her out of here,' he mumbled, 'before anyone comes along. The poison Matron gave me has worked its magic.'

Looking around, he glanced upon a large sandstone boulder. Just the job, he thought, as he walked over, picked it up and, removing the silk scarf from around her neck, he deftly placed the boulder in the fold of the scarf and then tied it tightly around the woman's waist. Rain almost blinding him as the storm continued its noisy progress all around him; Eddy stood and, holding Mabel by the elbows dragged her towards the edge of the Pool, then letting go, kicked her with force. Her body rolled over the edge of the quarry and into the aquamarine water. He stood carefully on a hillock of grass and watched her body sink down into the depths. Returning to his carriage he noticed her reticule lay on the seat. He picked it up and undid the metal clasp. Inside were just her handkerchief and a few coins.

'Nothing to connect her with me, there,' he said as he threw it a distance into the heath. He untied an agitated Riley who was still unsettled and unsure of the thunder and lightning and the rain which now fell like a massive curtain around her.

Jumping up onto the front board of the carriage, and bouncing onto the seat he cheerfully slapped the reins, called to Riley to, 'Giddy up,' who, unused to the terrain, slithered slightly and Eddy rode away from the murder scene laughing; 'easy!!'

CHAPTER TWENTY-ONE

Sitting next to the window and admiring the spectacular views, Tom was listening to the history the ticket collector sitting opposite him was explaining:

'The White Pass and Yukon Route that we're travelling on is a symbol of triumph over challenge. The railroad was considered an impossible task but it was literally blasted through mountains in only twenty-six months. Tens of thousands of men with picks and shovels and four hundred and fifty tons of explosives overcame harsh climate and challenging geography to create this railroad. The builders faced huge obstacles, including weather, terrain, distance and competition from other companies. At times the snow was ten feet high, but work still continued.'

Passing through a forest of dense woodland, Tom noticed a black bear clinging on to the branches of a birch tree. He gave an involuntary shudder; it was the first time he'd seen a bear since his accident. Remembering not to stare at the bear eye-to-eye this time, turning back, he concentrated on what the ticket collector was saying: 'The railroad cost ten million dollars to build. Nearly all the work between Skagway and the Summit was through solid rock. Black powder was used for blasting. The mountainsides were so steep the men needed to be suspended by ropes to prevent them falling off while cutting the grade. Thirty-five men lost their lives. We're just coming up to Trail of '98; you can quite clearly see the trail. Of course, not many use it now.'

Caleb turned to Tom and smiled. 'Do you remember, that, my friend?

'Not a lot, some memories are vague, others clear. I'm grateful to you, Caleb, for your patience.'

'On the other side of the train you'll soon see Dead Horse Gulch, where three thousand pack animals died through neglect or overloading. Must go now, and check out me passengers' announced the ticket collector as he rose from his seat and passed through the train.'

The rest of the trip was enjoyed in silence, Caleb amazed that they were not far from the route they took by foot and the hazards they encountered; Tom trying hard to remember the events. Both men finally relaxed, and sat back enjoying the passing scenery; the mountains, waterfalls and wildlife. Although summer, there was still a lot of snow around on the top of the mountains. Nearing Skagway, as the steam train reduced speed, Tom noticed the cemetery, in particular a tombstone standing out from the others. It was the grave of Jefferson (Soapy) Smith who had died in '98. Tom tried to think where he had heard that name before. Caleb put him wise and reminded him of the story. Before Tom could reply he couldn't remember it, they arrived at Skagway station and disembarked.

The editor of the *Skagway News* was sympathetic as he passed Tom the newspaper he had found amongst a pile of back copies. 'It was big news at the time. I can give you Mrs Wilmott's address and directions to the Baptist Church. If you came in on the railroad, you'll have passed the cemetery.'

'Thank you, sir,' croaked Tom. He was finding it difficult to take this in; his dearest brother Will had died.

'Caleb, it wasn't supposed to be like this. I had expected to find Will alive and well, and either still in Skagway, or having returned home.'

'It sure is a shock. What you need is a stiff drink, let's repair to the nearest saloon, Tom, and I'll stand you a couple of whiskeys.'

Sitting at a dirty table, on dirty, wobbly chairs which rested on an even dirtier floor, the two friends drank deeply from their grubby glasses, the bottle of expensive whiskey between them. They had to shout at each other over the noise coming from the men gambling, the piano playing and girls shrieking as they danced the cancan.

'Nothing changes here, Tom, it's the same everywhere, the noise, dirt and stench.'

'Finding out that my brother died a hero's death does nothing to ease my pain. After all I have been through, travelling to the ends of the earth to find Will, for it to end like this seems unbelievable.'

Ma Parson's brothel in Fish Street was built, as were the majority of buildings in Skagway, of wood. Tubs of flowers stood either side of the bright red front door. Lace curtains hung at the windows.

'This house seems respectable,' observed Tom as he and Caleb stood on the boardwalk looking up at the front of The Trout Rooming House. 'Doesn't look like a house of ill repute at all. If my father is the man you described knowing what I told you about him before I lost my mind, I would imagine him having palpitations when he learned that Will boarded in a brothel.'

'Well, come along, my friend. We need to collect Will's belongings,' said Caleb kindly, as he pulled the brass handle hanging next to the door. A few moments later, they were ushered inside by a middle-aged woman dressed smartly in a dark blue velvet dress, decorated with a lace jabot at the throat. Her grey hair was piled in tendrils on top of her head and decorated with a couple of blue feathers. The hallway was lit by kerosene lamps, which spread elongated shadows of the three people onto the walls. Considering the profession of Mrs Parsons, there were no other people to be seen, the only sound coming from the hiss of the wicks in the lamps.

'Hello, gentlemen, what can I do for you?' said Michele cordially and looking at them expectantly.

'I'm Thomas Thorpe, Will's brother. I understand he was staying here when he was killed. The editor of the Skagway News pointed us to you. I wonder if you still have his belongings?'

'Oh, yes, I do. I must just sit down, I had no idea Will had a brother. When did you get here? Have you come straight from England? How long did you travel? Now, I have so many questions, please, come with me into the parlour.'

Michele led the two friends into a dimly lit comfortably furnished room. Sitting at the piano, and looking through the sheets of music, a beautiful girl turned at their entry. Looking enquiringly at them, she stood up to reveal a fine lawn wrap tied with a ribbon around her waist. It appeared she wore nothing underneath. Caleb took a deep breath, but before he could disgrace himself by whistling his appreciation, Tom nudged him in the ribs.

'Rosie, this is Will Thorpe's brother, Thomas, and this is?'

'Oh, I'm Caleb. A friend.'

Hearing Will's name seemed to be too much for Rosie: she turned pale and not looking at either man, ran from the room sobbing.

'Rosie loved Will, they became quite close. I didn't approve of their relationship, but he paid well. He was a great guy, a perfect gentleman. We were devastated at his death. The whole town hailed him a hero; it was the talk of the town for a long while. Are you here in Skagway just to collect his belongings, Thomas?' asked Michelle as she poured three generous shots of brandy and handed them around.

'I came to the Yukon to look for him, as we hadn't heard from him for a while.' Tom then related all he remembered having happened to him since leaving Dorset, Caleb filling in lost details. Having heard the whole story, nodding silently, Michele rang a small hand bell and a heavy velvet curtain parted to reveal a Negro, his shiny brown skin and dark eyes in contrast to Michele's pale skin. 'Dobey, please go and get the bag from the cupboard under the stairs belonging to Will Thorpe. These gentlemen have come for it.' Bowing low, as Dobey left the room, Michele explained he was the house bodyguard.

'He's dumb, can't speak, but he packs a decent punch if anyone starts trouble. I found him wandering the streets and getting himself into trouble by fighting. He was originally an escaped slave, from a sugar plantation in the Deep South. Don't know where I'd be without him. Now, before you gentlemen leave here, may I offer you an evening you won't forget, on the house?'

Tom stood, cap in hand, looking at the gravestone bearing the details of Will's brave death. The irony of Will being buried next to 'Soapy' Smith was not lost on Tom. Looking through his brother's belongings, he discovered Will's diary, his travel journal, which he decided he would read on the journey home, and a bundle of photographs.

'Caleb, I feel sure I will know more about my family when I read Will's writings, it should jog my memory.'

Tom didn't feel the soft rain summer fall on to his uncovered bowed head. The Baptist minister explained that the townsfolk had paid for the stone and Mrs Wilmott and her daughter faithfully put fresh flowers on the grave every week. Upon being advised of his heir's demise, Lord Thorpe diligently paid the funeral bills, and wrote to those who helped bury Will. Tom felt humbled. He was even more eager to get back to Thorpe Matravers and his family. Having received news of one son's death and maybe details of their second son's demise as well, they must be suffering dreadfully. Choking back tears, he joined Caleb and set off towards the riverboats.

CHAPTER TWENTY-TWO

The freezing late February snow swirled around the men working alongside the railway track. Clay extracted from a quarry the other side of Poole Harbour was transported by tug to the railway line and transferred to railway trucks, as well as was coal, where a small train took it to a pottery siding. The little engine at its head emitted puffs of steam and, mingling with the dust, clung over everything, turning the snow and ice dirty rust colour. A shire horse snorted as he waited patiently to take the trucks from the train to the pottery. This was the last haul; the horse would soon be set loose to run free in the field next to the track, with his mate, after a hard day's work. If it felt cold at the pottery works, it was even colder down by the harbour, where the men who loaded and unloaded the clay, coal and pipes worked. Once the clay arrived at the pottery, the men placed it in the storeroom ready for the next day. Tomorrow, the whole process would be reversed, but then, instead of clay and coal for the gigantic furnaces, the finished pipes would be loaded and unloaded. These processes were worked six days a week, giving the workers Sunday off. The clay was used to make pottery pipes used in building works and until recently proved to be a successful business.

'You ready, then, Fred? I want me supper.' Alfie was eager to get home; the hooter had gone at least a minute ago. The men having finished the last loading were dressed in warm coats, scarves and caps.

'Oh 'ar, I be comin',' exclaimed Alfie, as the two men walked away from the building, doffing their caps at Mr Eddy. He looked at them with a snarl on his face. He despised the workers, lazy and smelly, all of them. The pottery employed over seventy workers of all trades from moulders to those who fired the massive kilns. Many of the workers had been with the company for decades; the Thorpe family were generous with the workers' wages, though some said, sarcastically, that they could afford to be. Though wealthy, they were well respected. All, that is, except Mr Eddy. He was further despised since the news about Mr Thomas arrived at the factory. With Mr Thomas now dead, despised Eddy appeared to be in full charge. Their lives would be more difficult than ever. Mr Thomas was strict with his workers, but fair. He needed to be strict as he had to consider the safety of everyone under his control. Now, Eddy didn't appear to care at all about safety, all he wanted was the work load doubled, to make more money.

As Fred and Alfie joined other tired, cold men for the walk home, they all anticipated their coming meal. This was the late shift, these men working from six in the morning until seven at night. The hours were long and the work hard, some men working outside in all weathers, but jobs in Dorset were scarce, they must take whatever they could. Getting out of bed these days was difficult, frost formed patterns on the inside windows of their cottages, and didn't thaw all day.

'Mr Eddy be in a foul mood today,' stated Sid Cox, wrapping his scarf tighter around his neck. 'Don't know why. After all, he 'as a good life livin' up the big 'ouse.'

'Aye,' agreed George Edmonds. He lived at number twelve The Terrace, next door to Alfie at number eleven. The families were proud of their homes and The Terrace, which fronted the main road through the village, was always tidy. George, being a keen gardener wanted to check his vegetables. Even though it was snowing and dark when he arrived home, he took an oil lamp down to his plot to check out his leeks under the snow. He knew that Cherry, his wife, would have his supper keeping warm on top of a pan of boiling water on the stove.

'He's taken a real dislike to Bert that I do know,' exclaimed Fred. He lived at number five and often chatted to Bert about his sow, over the fence.

'Twere a pleasure to go to work once. Now, 'tis n't so great. So sad Mr Tom and Mr Will have both died. They was both good blokes, toffs though they were. Now we got that bastard bossing us around,' reflected Fred.

'Well, I go up 'yure, see ya tomorra,' hailed Sid as he walked towards Miller Lane.

Sid lived with his wife, children and parents-in-law above the village shop which his mother-in-law ran. His father-in-law was an invalid, having endured an accident in the pottery. He'd worked as a stoker and tripped, falling heavily and burning his legs badly. Sid liked George, and the two men enjoyed gossiping about the comings and goings in the pottery. Reaching The Terrace, the chaps bade each other goodnight, and, each opening their front gates, walked into their homes aware of the aroma of hot food.

Bert was checking the temperatures on the kilns when Mr Eddy approached him. As the shift was changing, workers were coming and going all around them. The pottery boiler needed to be kept firing to enable the stationary steam engine to power the machines which produced the pipes.

'My office, now!' Eddy shouted to Bert above the noise.

Bert stood inside the small room and looked around. Wooden filing cabinets were stacked around the walls, and a battered desk piled dangerously high with ledgers stood in the middle. A portrait of Queen Victoria hung on the wall.

The rug on the grubby floor had seen better days. It was so different from when Mr Tom worked from this office, he always ensured it was clean and tidy and kept up-to-date with the paperwork. Bert anticipated anxiously what Eddy wanted with him. Since Daisy left to work as a governess, the manager picked on him ceaselessly. There was also the worry of keeping Ivy out of Eddy's way until she started her nurses training. Bert anticipated he and Jane would feel uncomfortable having the baby living in the big house and he was right. Jane in particular was finding it hard working there, knowing the baby was her grandchild and there was nothing she could do about it. Jane also missed having Daisy around for company in the evenings when he needed to stay at work.

'Production is down. I told you last week I want output to double and it hasn't. I want to know why. Find out the problem and do something about it. By Friday.' Eddy squared up to Bert, held him by the lapels, spat in his face then released him. A nasty smell of whisky and cigar smoke, combined with halitosis emanated from Eddy, making Bert almost, but not quite, gag.

Bert shrugged off the humiliating act as he left the pottery. He knew why production was down; it was Eddy and his attitude to the workers. He was drinking heavily, paperwork was piling up, and bills hadn't been paid. The women, not feeling safe when he was near, went out of their way to avoid him. But he'd have a word with those few workers he knew weren't pulling their weight one hundred per cent. Production was down, not up, admittedly, and they would all have to work harder. The conditions they all worked in were harsh and Bert felt sure that nothing would change whilst Eddy was in charge.

Passing the field, Bert whistled. The two heavy horses lumbered up to him, nudging his pockets for their evening carrots. These beasts accepted him unconditionally, not like the beast at the big house, chuckled Bert.

CHAPTER TWENTY-THREE

Caleb Howard relaxed as the scenery flashed past the window of the first class LSWR railway carriage. Since leaving Waterloo station, they were relieved to have the carriage to themselves, which was unusual, as there were only two other passenger carriages, all three carriages being coupled behind the brake van, with the rear guard's van at the tail end. Caleb was fascinated by how small steam railway locomotives were compared to the Canadian locos; he found the railway journey had been an interesting one, never having travelled on a British steam train before. Although the trains were different, the scenery they passed was similar to that of Canada. Most of the line passed through open countryside with small towns dotted here and there where workers and farmers sought rural landscapes that were within easy reach of a railway station. Cows, sheep and crops dominated the fields on both sides of the line. Trees were in full leaf and the greenness of the countryside was impressive. The two friends were fast approaching the final hour of their journey. Since leaving Skagway, apart from the stay in New York, their feet hadn't touched the ground. Caleb paid for everything, naturally, as Tom had no idea if he had any money, the bank details lost to him. Tired, he laid his head back on the white starched headrest. The ticket collector having been around, ensured they were comfortable.

In R. H. Macy and Co in New York, they purchased new clothes, also paid for by Caleb, and both of them looked smart and respectable in their new suits, ties, leather shoes and straw boaters. Tom patted his top pocket, where Daisy's handkerchief rested. Although at the time he didn't know why he kept it, obviously for some sentimental reason, he was now thankful. Despite Caleb relating what he knew about her, he couldn't quite remember all the details of her face and figure, but some memories were becoming clear. He could now remember the harvest supper where he first met her, and a picture of the school was on his mind. A turquoise dress featured in a lot of his dreams, but he couldn't, as yet, remember why.

'How are you feeling now, Tom?' asked Caleb. He was concerned that his dear friend may be ill. He was still finding difficulty remembering some things. Other times he repeated conversations.

'My head still aches, I long to breathe in some Dorset air. After the smells we endured, the sweet air of Thorpe Matravers will be a treat. I hope that Ma and Pa won't be too shocked at seeing me. I left a handsome young man and am returning a wreck. I also have an Athabascan Indian wife. I wonder how they will take the news.'

'Ha, that I can't guess at, my friend,' snorted Caleb. 'I'd like to be there when you tell them the news.'

'It will be great to see Amy again; you'll like her, Caleb, she'll be very understanding. Though I'm sure she has a husband, I can't bring him to mind. I can remember she has a gentle dog, called Florence. Funny how I remember some things, and not others.'

'I'm sure I will like Amy, if she is your sister, she must be a great lady. Not far now, I imagine. We've travelled a fair way in the past weeks.'

'It was really good to visit Clyde and Emily Harwell in New York. Their laid-back hospitality certainly helped us on our journeys.'

'They sure did,' agreed his friend.

'Caleb, did I mention the follies that I built with my own bare hands?'

'Indeed. Only about twenty times. How about we go to the dining car and find us a whisky and some lunch?'

The days following the birth having been difficult, Daisy couldn't understand why she had been incarcerated in Melbury Hall. Escaping had been her obsession, and now she made it, she had escaped and was back where she belonged. It was so easy to slip past Foxy and casually walk around the garden until she found a wooden door in the wall open. Walking through had been unbelievably easy; the stupid trustee having left the door wide open. So intense was her need to escape she was wearing only a cambric dress and canvas slippers. Her feet became sore from the sharp gravel digging her soles. None of this discomfort bothered Daisy as she fled and ran along the Stoke Road towards home and safety. As she ran, she felt Tom's presence very close to her; 'he's on the train, I know he is. He's on the train,' she chanted, her breath becoming more laboured as she fled. The drugs they forced her to take slowed her body.

There was no sign of anyone from her family in the house in the Terrace. Not one of them visited her at the Hall. She just couldn't understand it. The medication had had an effect; she knew that she wasn't in her right mind. Making her way out of the back door, she slowly walked down the path. The place where she found most comfort was still there. 'It's so unfair! Just because Tom's dead, and I can't live without him, they put me away in that awful place,' she wailed as she reached her destination.

Daisy was crying. Keeping a secret was a painful business. Deep, heart-wrenching sobs racked her body as she curled up in the armchair in the old railway carriage. Her surroundings reminded her of her dear granny and grandpa, now dead, but who used to live here. The aroma of the violet toilet water granny once used still clung to the cushions and curtains. The carriage sat at the bottom of the garden, surrounded by the chickens that pecked and scratched the bare earth. She felt that she couldn't take any more. Nobody was around to hear her despair, except for the chickens.

Slowly rising from the chair, Daisy stepped off the doorstep, leaving the door open to allow the hens to peck around inside. She noticed nothing as she made her way past the washing hanging on the line and the pigsty, through the back door, across the scullery and up the narrow stairs to her bedroom. Bending down, she pulled out the cardboard box from under her bed and blew the dust off the top. Taking off the lid, she released the turquoise dress from its covering of tissue paper. 'This is beautiful,' she whispered as she held it to her face. The silk caressed her cheek and she noticed that it still smelled of honeysuckle. She'd expected it to smell musty; the dried flowers in amongst the tissue paper ensured the dress retained a pleasant aroma. Holding the garment in her hands, she now knew what she had to do. Having decided she quickly took off the fustian garment they forced to wear and stepped into the silk dress. It took her a while to fasten the tiny pearl buttons on the front of the bodice. The dress fit her perfectly. The fabric whispered as it flowed around her legs. It curved into the small of her back like a second skin, flaring out over her hips.

Keeping the canvas shoes on her feet, Daisy flew down the stairs, out of the front door, through the gate and onto the road verge. She knew the times of the trains and realised there wasn't much time before the London train reached the Halt. She ran like the wind. She was going to meet Tom, she'd promised to wave to him from the crossing gates. She'd go one better than wave. He was bringing her a fur coat back from Alaska, he'd promised.

Stan and Ada's house was situated right next to the platform at Thorpe Matravers halt. Stan, the crossing keeper was just closing the gates to traffic, prior to the London to Wareham train speeding through. He then turned around and slowly ambled back to the tiny ticket office. As soon as the train was through, he would go back and open the gates again. Not much passed along the lane that the railway tracks crossed; just a few farm carts and the carriages belonging to the gentry at the big house.

'A cup of tea is just what I need,' mumbled Stan to himself.

Standing in her kitchen and looking out of her window, Ada saw a flash of turquoise dash past at speed. 'Funny,' she mumbled to herself. 'That looked just like Daisy Evans. She should slow down 'afore she 'as an accident.'

CHAPTER TWENTY-FOUR

As the last bend of the journey came into sight, Tom and Caleb swallowed the last of their whisky, having enjoyed a lunch of steak followed by a jelly pudding.

'The motto for the County of Dorset is "Who's afeard"' quoted Tom as he speared a potato.

'Well, that sure is the right motto for you, my friend. After what you have been through, I reckon that motto should be reserved for you alone. Your bravery amazes me.'

'Well, I was certainly a feared of that bear in Canada, as my scars show. I think some people are embarrassed when they look at me, others are interested to hear what happened,' said Tom as both men stood up prior to leaving the dining saloon. 'I wonder how my family will...'

Tom didn't finish what he was going to say; as they walked down between the tables, the carriage suddenly shuddered and the wheels screeched as the train slithered along the line. Tom lost his balance, and falling against Caleb, both men dropped to their knees, Tom painfully hitting his head on the opposite seat. Steam hissed through the open top part of the windows. Glasses flew off the nearby shelves and wine bottles clanked as they slid sideways. A metal ashtray fell onto the floor with a clatter sending cigarette ends and cigar butts in all directions. As

Caleb helped Tom to his feet, there came the sound of someone screaming and men shouting.

'Wonder what's happened?' queried the steward as he hauled himself back off the floor where he'd fallen behind the bar.

With an ominous feeling, Tom limped to the carriage door, pulled down the leather strap to release the window and looked out. Seeing a young woman wearing a turquoise silk dress running down the track, alongside the train, he uttered, 'Daisy! My Daisy!' Opening the carriage door, Tom jumped down from the train onto the tracks. The pain from his head and damaged hip took his breath away for a moment, but he stood still until it eased. He could no longer see the woman dressed in turquoise, but he had a feeling he knew where she was headed. As he slowly lolloped down the track, he was aware of a strange sensation; he knew who he was. He knew who Daisy was! It was all coming back to him. It must have been the bang on his head when the train suddenly stopped; it was all becoming clear. Daisy was the girl he loved; she was the love of his life. How could he have forgotten her? The memory of his having given her the turquoise silk dress upon his departure to Alaska was now clear, but why was she running away, down the track? He set out to find her.

Moving slowly along the side of the track, Tom noticed a gap in the wooden fencing. Drawing closer, he could see a scrap of turquoise fabric attached to a loose nail. Daisy must have gone that way and caught her dress. 'She is in a fearful hurry,' said Tom to himself. Climbing through the gap in the fencing with difficulty, Tom winced in pain. His hip and his arm were searing with the effort of using them, but he knew he must carry on. Daisy could be seen in the distance, still running like the wind, towards the Bottomless Pond. She then disappeared from sight. Tom halted as he heard a splash.

Following Tom's abrupt departure, Caleb shut the carriage door and retreated back to the compartment. Looking out of the window he saw Tom limping down the line after Daisy. 'Better keep a low profile. Don't want Tom to be fined, or whatever it is they do in this country if you jump from a train,' muttered Caleb to himself.

The train guard was walking down to the engine driver and shouting something Caleb couldn't hear. Eventually, finding nothing of consequence, he blew his whistle, waved his green flag and climbed on board. The train hissed smoke into the damp air and they were off again. Within minutes they arrived at Wareham station, where Caleb alighted. It didn't take long for him to find a porter, who collected his and Tom's luggage from the guard's compartment, located a hansom cab and installed Caleb and the luggage safely inside.

Tipping the porter, he thanked him, then turning to the cab driver he said, 'Do you know the way to Thorpe Matravers Park? I need to go to the home of Lord and Lady Thorpe?'

'Oh, ar, I can take you there. You be sounding like an American, that right?'

'Actually, I'm Canadian, from Vancouver.'

'What be you doing 'ere then, me 'and some?' asked the driver kindly, as he whipped the horse into a trot.

Caleb realised he needed to be careful what he said. The first people to know Tom was back and not dead as folk believed, should be his family. 'Oh, just visiting the family.' Caleb looked about him; the heathland was beautiful, dark brown shrub land brightened up by bright yellow bushes. He could see two ponds in the distance. There were a few fir trees, dotted amongst the bushes.

In the hope of changing the subject, he asked, 'What are these bushes with the bright yellow flowers called?'

'That be gorse, sir. Grows real prolific in these parts.'

'It's unusual, but I love the scenery.'

'Did you know either of the sons? They both went to Alaska, so I 'eard, and didn't come back.'

'Yes, I knew....' Caleb didn't finish the sentence; a man carrying a girl in a turquoise dress appeared from nowhere and hailed the cab. Pulling on the reins, the driver halted the hansom.

Running past Ada in her station house, there was just one thought in Daisy's mind; to see Tom. Her beloved Tom. He was coming to find her, but he wasn't on the train. She asked Stan and he was adamant: 'No, my lovely. He can't be on the train, he be dead. You know that.'

'She looked just like a ghost was after her,' Stan had said to Ada that evening. 'I should have done something to stop her from running down the track. Why was she asking for Tom? I assumed she meant Master Tom from the big house.'

'She ran past me like the wind, Stan. There was nothing you could have done. Don't know why she was looking fer him, though. Sounds a bit fishy to me, but don't you go blaming yerself.' Stan knew he would never get over the fact he hadn't stopped Daisy, it would be on his conscience for the rest of his life.

Tears ran down Daisy's face as she ran down the tracks. Everyone kept telling her Tom was dead. Even Stan, and he wouldn't tell a lie. Just behind her she heard mocking laughter making her wail out loud. She kept running, through the gap in the wooden railway fencing, across the heath towards the ponds. She felt lightheaded since escaping from Melbury Hall; how easy it had been to get away from that place. She couldn't take any more of those drugs and she couldn't take any more of Eddy sneering at her. Every time he came to her room she screamed, and been sedated again. The needles the doctor stuck in her arm were frighteningly large. Then when she woke up again, they would force her to swallow medicine. People in that house showed such cruelty to her. Except Foxy. She was nice. As she reached Bottomless Pond, she heard it again, the mocking laughter, just behind her, or was it inside her? Was it a magpie's laugh or a seagull's cry. It could be the call of the curlew, wheeling and soaring in the sky. Where was the laughter coming from? Stopping on the edge of the pond, and turning around, she looked back the way she had run. There, away in the distance, was a man, limping towards her.

'Tom! No, it's a ghost,' Daisy screamed as her foot slipped and she went down into the deep, deep pond. Hearing Daisy scream made Tom's blood run cold; if only he could run faster, his disability was a real burden. Reaching the pond five painful minutes later, he looked down, and there, floating on the top of the water, was Daisy. The full skirt of her turquoise dress billowed out around her and her beautiful hair was tangled in the weeds. In her right hand she held a sprig of honeysuckle; both hands were showing just above the water, as in supplication; as if this was what she wanted. With her eyes closed and her mouth gently parted in a slight smile she appeared peaceful. Looking back on that moment in the following days, Tom would be reminded of the picture of Ophelia, painted by the Pre-Raphaelite artist, John Everett Millais.

Without hesitation, he jumped in, the icy cold water taking his breath away. Putting his arms around his beloved girl, and treading water, he gently carried her to the edge of the pond, where he placed her on the bank. Heaving himself up, with a supreme effort, he made it on to the bank himself. His clothes soaking wet, he shivered. Bending down, he picked Daisy up and carried her, as best as he could, a few yards to the road. His hip was paining him, but that was nothing compared to the pain he felt on realising that his dear beloved, his dear Daisy, was dead, drowned. If only he had been a few minutes sooner. He bowed his head, nuzzling Daisy's neck. He could smell honeysuckle, the sweetness reminding him of the times they spent together in the hermitage. As tears streamed down his face, looking up, he thought he saw a carriage coming towards him from the direction of Wareham.

CHAPTER TWENTY-FIVE

'Sir, madam, I have to speak to you. Something has happened,' announced Hibbs as he entered the drawing room. He looked pale and shaken. Matilda and Harry were taking afternoon tea, Matilda in the act of pouring a second cup of Earl Grey for Harry.

'Mr Hibbs! What? What's wrong?' asked Harry.

'There's nothing wrong. But it's such a shock. It's such a shock.'

Matilda stood, swaying slightly, prepared for another announcement of bad news. How much more can this family take? She fleetingly wondered as she waited for Mr Hibbs to speak.

'I don't know how to tell you this, but…'

'Come on, man, out with it.' Harry was becoming impatient with the butler's prevarication.

'Mr Hibbs, what is it?' Matilda was now running out of patience. The butler was behaving very strangely indeed and appeared to be crying. Neither Harry nor Matilda knew if the old man was crying tears of joy or sorrow.

'I know they said he was dead, but…'

Matilda glanced behind Mr Hibbs and saw someone standing in the doorway. She fainted, falling to the floor, mercifully missing the small table on which stood her prized glass decorative perfume bottles. It was Harry who spoke his name. 'Tom. Is it really you?' he said, turning as white as a ghost.

When Matilda came to, Harry having administered the smelling salts he found in her bag, he gently and lovingly wiped the perspiration from her forehead with her dainty handkerchief. Her beloved son was sitting on the sofa next to her, her husband on the other side of Tom. It was a very wet, shivering, Tom; he hadn't had chance to change his clothes for dry ones.

'I'm sorry it was such a surprise,' he said. 'I was going to write, but I was afraid you wouldn't believe it. You could have thought it was some joker playing a trick on you. I met some strange characters in Alaska.'

Mother and son held each other in a long embrace. Then he turned and took his father's hand in his own. As he turned, Matilda gasped with shock at seeing the side of his face. The scars that ran deep across the left side of his face and down his neck looked like pale tracks against the rest of his suntanned skin. His left ear lobe was missing. His face, he knew, was a frightening sight. Although his sight and hearing were damaged, he learnt over the past year to turn his head towards the speaker so that he could make out what they were saying.

'You gave us all a shock,' sniffed his father. 'We thought you were a ghost come to haunt us.'

'I know, Papa. But once I knew who I really was, I couldn't wait to come home.'

Mr Hibbs had retreated back downstairs to see if Mr Howard was comfortable, the two men having placed Daisy's body on the settle in the servant's hall, neither knowing where to lay her. Caleb relayed the tale of Daisy's drowning to Mr Hibbs, who had been visibly shocked when he opened the front door to their knocking. Jane, fortunately, deciding to walk to Wareham to buy some silks for her mistress, was due to come back at any time. Mr

Hibbs would break the sad news upon her return. He also sent a message to Bert, asking him to hurry to the Park. Another message was sent to Mr Eddy at the pottery. Secretly, Mr Hibbs wouldn't be surprised if he was at the public house over the road, rather than where he should be, supervising the workers. Rumour was Mr Eddy was frequently worse for wear with alcohol. Miss Amy was out riding and wasn't expected to return for a while.

He then returned with four glasses of water on a tray alongside the brandy decanter, which he placed on a small table next to his Lordship, before retreating back downstairs, leaving the master and mistress to enjoy the return of Master Tom.

'But… we had a letter.' Harry was perplexed. 'From a North West Mounted Police official telling us you had been killed by a bear. How could they have made such a mistake?'

'Caleb was under the impression I had been killed, so he contacted the police, who had no option but to write to you. I was saved by an Indian. I will relate everything that has happened in time. I suffered amnesia, but my memory is slowly returning.'

'Take your time, son. We have plenty of time to hear your story,' said Harry. He still couldn't believe that his son was home. He heard many wild tales in the court room, but no situation could ever compete with this one.

'Where is Daisy?' enquired Tom, miserably. 'She drowned in Bottomless Pond, which is why I am wet; I jumped in to save her. I don't know if she fell in, or deliberately jumped. She caused the train we were travelling in to stop suddenly. She was running along the tracks near the Halt.' Tom was turning very pale, and he felt nauseous. It was all becoming too much; his memory returning, seeing Daisy and feeling full of hope, then finding her drowned. He now realised that it was Daisy who was the love of his life. Grace was his wife, he knew, but Daisy held a special place in his heart.

'Daisy? Why are you asking after Daisy?' enquired Matilda, feebly. 'I don't understand. Why did she drown? Why did you jump in to save her?'

'Daisy was encouraged to enter a home for the mentally deranged, Tom. It's a long story, and one you need not trouble yourself with.' Harry was beginning to feel uneasy. Had Tom been involved with Daisy? It was beginning to look like it.

'A mental institution? But why? What happened?' Tom had so many questions that needed answers. Harry was determined to play the situation down; Matilda, Amy, Jane and Bert were under the impression that Daisy was a governess to a family in the north of England. To reveal the truth would mean they would realise he had lied to them all. There were too many skeletons in the family cupboard now, he would need to be careful what his loved ones were told; there were reputations to uphold. He thought that Daisy was safe in Melbury Hall and well looked after. Now, it seemed that she wasn't cared for, otherwise, how else could she have escaped; there were going to be some questions to be answered.

'Harry, what is that you said? I was under the impression Daisy was a governess. Now, it appears she was in a mental institution.' Matilda, visibly upset again, enquired of her husband.

Harry stood up abruptly and faced both his wife and son. 'There appears to be a great deal of happenings to be cleared up. But firstly, I would suggest that Tom changes out of those wet togs. I'll ring for Hibbs.' Harry was using his magistrate's voice, which made Matilda flinch slightly, as he walked to the mantelpiece and pulled the bell.

Jane strolled along the road leading out of Wareham, enjoying the afternoon sunshine. She was often pleased when her mistress sent her to the town for small shopping expeditions. As she chose the silks she chatted to her friend, Martha, who happened to be in shop at the same time. Martha was experiencing difficulty deciding which shawl suited her best, and Jane's advice had been sound; 'The blue wool one. It matches your eyes.'

As she walked Jane looked back on her life. 'If only everything was as simple as choosing colours for shawls and silks,' she mused. The past year had been very difficult; Daisy's news of her pregnancy, her stay with Nanny, the birth and now Daisy working as a governess in the north. Only last night she had said to Bert, 'I wonder why we don't get letters from Daisy, Bert?'

'Maybe she be too busy to write, my dear. Her employers may not allow her much spare time.'

'I suppose so, but I do miss her. I miss Ivy too, but at least we get letters from her telling us about her nursing training.'

'The 'ouse do seem quieter,' replied Bert.

'I feel so sad every time I see Nanny with Rose. After all, she is our granddaughter. They hardly ever let me see her.'

Jane's reflections came to an abrupt end, as a police constable riding his bicycle very nearly knocked her over. 'Mind 'ow yer go, missus,' he shouted as he pedalled as fast as his stout legs would carry him, towards Thorpe Matravers.

In the pottery, Bert watched as two men stacked clay pots in a wooden crate, prior to dispatch by the cart horse to the harbour. He enjoyed his work when Mr Eddy was out of the way, but he realised the peace would eventually be shattered upon the return of the drunkard. The workers were all amazed at the way his horse knew the way to the pottery and Thorpe Park with a virtually unconscious master in the saddle.

Eddy was definitely the worse for wear having spent the past two hours in the Horseshoe Inn. The landlord from his local, opposite the pottery, last week barred him for fighting with a stranger who just happened to accidently spill beer on Eddy's jacket sleeve. So now he must ride his horse to the outskirts of Wareham to slake his thirst. He knew he would have to go back to work at the pottery soon, but one more whisky would settle him for the return journey. He was constantly on tenterhooks these days in case the body of the woman he had killed had been discovered. Even if she was found, nothing could point to him in any case, but the guilt of his actions was causing him to drink heavily.

Amy cantered Artemis along the towpath of the River Frome, which was, for once, empty of walkers and sightseers. The afternoon sun turned the slow flowing river on which swans and ducks floated, into a sparkling haven. As she pulled on the reins to slow her horse, she spotted a kingfisher sitting on a branch. Swiftly, it was gone, and then it reappeared with a tiny eel in its beak. How beautiful, thought Amy, you don't see that every day. Reaching the quay, she turned Artemis towards the Park and galloped home.

The staff were attempting to find out all the news from Master Tom's friend, Mr Caleb. He was sitting at the kitchen table nursing a cup of tea, made for him by Aggy, one of the kitchen maids. The poor man felt he was under interrogation by Cook, considering the questions she was asking him. She had sat down abruptly when she saw Daisy's lifeless body being carried into the servants' hall. 'What a shock; that beautiful girl, drowned. Such a tragedy.

What a waste of a young life,' she wailed. 'Master Tom, back from the dead too, it's altogether too much!'

'One life gone and one found. 'Tis a miracle,' sobbed Aggy.

'Now, my girl, you watch your tongue,' admonished Cook. 'Get back to preparing those vegetables, we've still got a dinner to get for the family. They will need good food to give them strength, and there are two more men, so be sure to do enough.'

'I need to go and see Tom,' said Caleb, as he stood up, pushing the chair behind him. 'Can you show me the way, please?'

'John, show Mr Howard to the drawing room, and don't talk to him.' Cook was often stern with the staff; they needed to be kept in their place. Madam was looking for a new housekeeper, the last one having left due to Mr Eddy's constant attentions. The female staff were constantly on the lookout for him, he could be quite dangerous, the way he prowled the corridors looking to catch a housemaid off her guard.

'Constable Waterman, sir,' announced Mr Hibbs as he held the door open for the policeman.

'Thank you, Mr Hibbs. Leave us alone to speak with the constable, when I ring for you, show him Daisy's body.'

'Very good, your lordship.' Slightly bowing his head, he shut the door and retreated down the back staircase to the kitchen, where he faced Cook. 'Tell all the staff, including those outside, to gather here in five minutes.' Moving into the servants' sitting room, he walked over to the settle where Daisy's body lay, and looked down at her. 'Poor lass,' he said.

James Hibbs knew much more than any other member of staff about the goings on in the house; even more than Jane was aware of. He knew where they put Daisy for the past few months; he knew that it was her baby upstairs, and he also knew who the father was. But, being the man that he was, he would tell no one of these things. His loyalty was to his master and mistress, Master Tom and Miss Amy. They were always good to him during his thirty years of employment. He had served them, firstly as a footman, then working his way up to butler. It had been hard work, but secure employment. Now, he needed to address the staff.

'As you are all aware by now, Mr Tom has returned from Alaska. He was inadvertently declared dead. He suffered from amnesia, but was brought back to health by Mr Caleb Howard. We must all thank God for his safe return.' Mr Hibbs paused slightly, for effect, before continuing; 'Sadly the body of Daisy Evans is resting in the sitting room next door. She has drowned in a tragic accident. Her father has been summoned from the pottery, and, hopefully, Jane is on her way back from Wareham. No one is to breathe a word to either of them, before I have had a chance to talk to them.'

'Aggy, stop snivelling,' interrupted Cook.

'Not a word of anything that happens in this house is to be breathed outside of these four walls. We need to continue, as we have always done, to respect the family's privacy. Anyone who disobeys these instructions will be dismissed, without a reference,' continued Mr Hibbs. 'The constable has arrived and is with the family now. Miss Amy and Mr Eddy are back, so see to their horses,' the butler added, dourly, looking at the stable lads. 'Now, go about your duties.'

Having dismissed the staff, Mr Hibbs and Cook sat at the table silently supping tea, whilst they waited for the drawing room bell, and for Bert and Jane to arrive.

Constable Waterman stood in the drawing room facing the family and Caleb. Eddy and Amy were as stunned as her parents at the sight of Tom. When she saw him, Amy wrapped her arms around her dear brother and cried, not just at the fact that he was alive and back, but at the sight of his facial injuries.

'My dear, darling Tom,' she sniffed. 'It's quite unbelievable. I do love you so. You must tell us all that has happened to you.'

'I will, all in good time, but you need to know about Daisy,' explained Tom. At the sound of Daisy's name, Eddy's head suddenly shot up. After reluctantly greeting Tom, he suddenly fell into a drunken stupor in a chair near the window. Now, he was alert and wondering what Tom was about to say; what about Daisy Evans? Despite the fact he was worse the wear from whisky, his senses were slowly returning. Surely Tom had no idea where she was. As far as he was concerned, she was safely ensconced in Melbury Hall. Matron would have informed him of any problems. So, what was going on?

As soon as he received the message, Bert left the pottery and, seeing Jane in the distance ahead of him, called to her. She paused in her walking, turned and saw her husband sprinting towards her. Pausing to catch his breath, he explained that he had been called up to the big house. 'I wonder what they want,' he panted. 'It sounded urgent.'

'A constable on a bicycle passed me ten minutes ago, riding in the direction of the Park. It looks like something is afoot.'

CHAPTER TWENTY-SIX

Daisy Evans was buried in the graveyard of St. Mary's church, just a few yards from her grandparents' grave. The constable having given evidence to the fact that he believed Daisy accidently slipped into Bottomless Pond ensured that she would be given a Christian burial. Despite the fact her mind was been unbalanced at the time, it had definitely been a tragic accident. The mourners included Lady Matilda, Amy and Tom, much to the astonishment of the villagers. Not only had Master Tom returned from the dead, but rumour had it that he had been in love with Daisy when he left for Alaska. It was also rumoured that he was the father of the baby adopted by Amy and Eddy, and that Daisy was the mother. She hadn't, as people were led to believe, become a governess in the north of England, but been sent to the local 'loonie bin' following the birth of the baby. Harry and Matilda tried to cover up the facts surrounding these events, but eventually rumours abounded, as they did in villages. Thorpe Matravers in Dorset was no exception; the villagers thrived on rumour, as was the case for centuries. It was as common place as was the folklore. The fact that Daisy drowned in Bottomless Pond, which legend declared was dug by fairies was not lost on some folk. The fairies, they believed, brought Tom back to the Park, and it was upon seeing him that Daisy ran to the pond and slipped.

'The fairies can only be seen by and help those whose Christian faith is weak as their powers are limited to such as want faith,' quoted Annie Weeks who lived in a scruffy, untidy hut on the common. Her herb remedies, which she sold, were often used for common ailments. Some people were afraid of her, and gave her a wide berth; others claimed she was a witch.

During the funeral service, Tom kept his head held high, not a spark of emotion showing on his face. The villagers, at first, were curious about the scars on his face and neck and some, embarrassingly, stared. His injured leg was extremely painful, due, possibly, to his dip in the pond, but more probably, because of the stress and unhappiness at Daisy's death. In the church and at the graveside, Bert also showed very little emotion, in contrast to his wife and only daughter now, Ivy, both of whom wept copiously. Ivy was given a short leave from her training to go home for her sister's funeral. The Evans family were dismayed at the amount of lies the family had told them, such as Daisy having been a governess, when in fact she was incarcerated in Melbury Hall.

One evening, as they stood in the scullery where Jane was stacking dishes, Bert mentioned to Jane that maybe, when the period of mourning for Daisy was over, they should perhaps move to another town. 'It would be a fresh start, Jane,' he said, as he sympathetically placed his arms around her shoulders and hugged her tightly. 'The villagers are thriving on rumours. The trouble is, Jane, most of what they say is true.'

'All accept the fatherhood of Rose. They haven't yet found out that evil Eddy raped our beautiful daughter twice and made her pregnant.

'I can never forgive him for that. Now, Ivy, make your mother a cuppa, there's a good lass.' Bert walked to the back door, put his cap on his head, and, after speaking to his pig, headed for the ale house, where he could down a few beers with his mates.

'I wish I had known the truth, Mother,' said Ivy, blandly as she placed two cups on that table. 'I could have helped Daisy. We may have our differences, and she could be incredibly bossy at times, but I loved her.' Ivy reached for her handkerchief and blew her nose, which was already painfully red.

'We believed it was all for the best, Ivy. You were young and desperately wanted to follow in the footsteps of the Lady with the Lamp. We didn't want any scandal to interrupt your ambitions.'

'Well, as father said, perhaps you should move. Make a fresh start. But what will you do? Where will you go?'

'God will tell us, Ivy. God will guide us.'

The atmosphere at dinner around the dining table in the Thorpe house was heavy; none of the family felt in the least bit cheerful. Harry sat at the top end of the table, as was the custom, with Matilda at the other end. Amy sat at her father's right, Caleb at his hostess's right and Tom next to Amy. Eddy was absent, and no one cared enough to enquire as to his whereabouts.

'Mr Howard, this must be a trial for you,' observed Harry, between mouthfuls of roast lamb. 'I can only apologise on behalf of the family, but it has been an extremely difficult time for us all.'

'I understand completely, sir.' Caleb lifted the cut glass goblet and sipped the delicious red wine. He appreciated Lord Harry's cellar. 'I am only too pleased to be here, and I hope I am of help to you, Tom.'

'My dear friend,' replied Tom. 'I don't know how I would have coped without you.' He had been shocked and astounded when he heard all the news about Eddy attacking

Daisy, and the subsequent events. He was aware of the rumours too, that the child was his. If the villagers cared to work out the dates, they would have realised that he went to Alaska long before Rose's conception. It pained him beyond measure to think that his dear beloved was subjected to unspeakable assaults by his own brother-in-law and then to be hidden away in Nanny's cottage to have Eddy's baby. Poor girl, then to have the indignity of being sent to Melbury Hall, not only by Eddy, but by his father's action too. Baby Rose was lovely, and he was pleased his sister had a child to love, but she was Daisy's child, conceived in anger and pain and handed over because of Eddy's selfishness. At times his anger at Eddy and his father threatened to overwhelm him; the steadying influence of Caleb was the only thing that kept him from releasing his anger on those concerned.

'I need to cull a few stags and hinds that are overtaking the Park, Mr Howard,' announced Harry. 'Would you care to accompany myself and Tom tomorrow morning? Having tried to save my son in Alaska, I guess you must be used to handling a gun.'

'I would be honoured, sir. What say you, Tom?'

'Of course. If you don't mind, Mama and Amy?'

Matilda and Amy both agreed they should go out. A day in the Park would benefit the men. 'We'll bring lunch out to you,' smiled Amy. 'I'll inform the kitchen, and we'll come in the shooting brake.'

Tom was yet to inform his family of his marriage. Not only did he have a wife, but an Athabascan Indian wife at that. He would have to find the right time to break the news. He would ask Amy to support him. Thinking of Grace, he suddenly realised he missed her. He also missed her way of life; it was so simple. Although he enjoyed the luxury of Thorpe House and the servants, he was beginning to realise that he needed the simplicity of Alaska and the wildness of the prairies, the magnificence of the mountains, the variation of the weather and the uniqueness of the Indian lifestyle. He wasn't too sure whether he was legally married to Grace according to British law. His father would be able to look into the legality, but first, he needed to break the news.

CHAPTER TWENTY-SEVEN

Bending over the whitethorn bush, Grace retched and retched. The morning sickness she was experiencing was draining her reserves. Her throat felt raw and her stomach painfully empty. She would have to look for some mint leaves to make the tea that would help alleviate her symptoms. The band were preparing once again, the move to winter camp, she needed all the strength she could muster. Her pregnancy was no surprise. She and Bear always enjoyed making love together in their large sleeping bag. She wondered who this baby would look like; white-skinned like Bear or dark-skinned like herself? One thing was certain, the baby would be brought up as an Athabascan Indian, of that she had no doubt. Bear certainly took the band into his heart and his life was now part Indian despite the fact that he was so far away in England. He would want his child to be brought up by her and her family, especially if he never returned. Grace was confident her family would look after them both.

'I will make you the tea,' announced Winnie Longhair, making Grace jump; she hadn't heard her sister approach. Winnie was observant when it came to the women and pregnancy. She was excited at the thought of helping Grace along the way.

'Thank you, Winnie.' Grace was trying her hardest to be brave, as an Athabascan Indian woman should be, but thinking about her dear Bear Man was breaking down her reserves. Their brief marriage was a happy one, and now he was so far away and unaware of the coming child. His memory returning was due in part to Caleb, Bear's friend.

'Do you think my Bear Man will return?' she asked as the two women sat in the warmth of their tepee. Grace moved back into the family home after Bear left to travel to England. As Grey Eagle's sister, he was obliged to look after her as was their custom. He was pleased to do so, as was Winnie. The two months since Bears departure were busy. The group returned from Dawson City content in the knowledge that they bartered enough goods to see them through the winter. Some of the Canadian dollars paid for canned food. The Indians were gradually being introduced to non-Indian ways, which, Grey Eagle had said, was inevitable. Carrying on the traditions was important, but so too, was the health and well-being of the band, and if that meant buying goods, then so be it.

'I do not know whether to be happy or sad that he knows who he is,' she continued philosophically. 'It must be good for him to return to his real family, but I need him here. I think there is a special girl back there. I found an embroidered handkerchief in his pocket after he was attacked by the bear. I guessed a girl once gave it to him, but he did not remember anything.'

'Did he know you are to have his baby before he left?'

'No. I did not know myself then. Our baby will be born at springtime. I am so happy about this baby. It will be a boy, I am sure.'

'Maybe he return then. Maybe he come back to you.'

'Yes, Winnie, maybe he will.

CHAPTER TWENTY-EIGHT

In a fiery finale to the season, the trees and hedges were bringing a whole new palette of colour to Thorpe Park. Amongst them, the broad leaves of the acer foliage glowed gold with bright red tints. The buttery yellow of the hornbeam featured orange overtones in the neatly clipped hedges surrounding the driveways. In contrast, the red berries of the hawthorn glowed red; the white flowers of summer giving way to their new autumn colouring.

Sitting on a wooden bench on the terrace on the west side of the house, Eddy smiled. No one had missed that slut Mabel. So far he had got away with her murder. He thought back to that day at Furze Pool, remembering how she had sunk from view and how amusing it had been that her green scarf matched the colour of the water as she went down. 'Perfect!' he grinned.

Tom and Amy reined in their horses as they approached the first of the follies in the Park a few days later. Artemis and Aurora both enjoyed the hour's gallop which took them from their stables, across the heath and now, back to the Park. Dismounting first, Tom helped Amy down from Artemis, leaving the horses to roam freely and munch what grass was left from summer. Tom was delighted to be reunited with Aurora and was touched that the stable lads had still exercised her every day.

'I need to talk to you, Amy,' confided Tom, as they strolled around the different shapes and sizes of the follies. 'I'm going to tell you about something that happened whilst I was with the Athabascan Indians.'

'Why are you telling me, Tom?' queried Amy.

'Because, as my sister, I may need your support when I tell the same thing to Mama and Papa. I hope you will understand and not judge me too much.'

'Fire away, Tom. What you tell me can't be too bad when you consider what you have been through, both over there and here. It has been a dreadful time for us all, but having you back is just short of a miracle.'

'I'm married.'

'You are what?' Amy asked, thinking Tom was joking.

'I'm married,' he patiently explained. 'To an Athabascan Indian woman called Grace. She is the sister of Grey Eagle, the chief of the band. Do you remember me mentioning him when I related my story to you all?'

'Yes, I do, so tell me, what is she like?'

'She is beautiful. Small, dark-skinned and her black hair reaches down her back to her waist. She is clever and funny and is ten years older than me. She has a fascinating face and a comely figure. At first, when Grey offered her to me, I felt obliged to take her in gratitude for what they did for me. But then I came to realise that I loved her. I still do, love her, that is.'

'Did you love Daisy, too?'

'Yes, I did. But that was a different kind of love. Looking back, I loved Daisy in the way a young man loves a young girl. It was all so innocent. When I left she was a virgin, and I promised myself to her. We were to be married when I returned.'

'You knew that Papa would disapprove. It would have been very difficult for both of you, being from different classes.'

'I realised that. I was besotted with her, she was like a puppy at times, bouncy and excited, and despite the fact she worked in the school. We went out quite a lot, in secret. I think that Eddy followed us sometimes. Did he ever say anything to you?'

'Once. When he confessed he was Rose's father. I must admit, I took little notice of him following you both at the time. The attacks were a far more important matter.'

'I am so sorry Daisy suffered so much and then died. We will never know if she accidently slipped into the pond, or whether she jumped. I still feel enormous guilt. Her mind must have been disturbed, and seeing me could have scared her into jumping. If I hadn't gone to find Will and left her, tragedy could have been averted.'

'Darling brother, don't torture yourself over Daisy. It was tragic, yes. And Eddy has a lot to answer for. I believe that is why he is constantly drunk; the guilt is having an effect on him.'

'Papa has cancelled all wine and alcoholic drinks from being delivered to the house. Eddy must be buying the stuff himself.'

'I don't really care, Tom. Our marriage has never been happy. I've banished him to the east wing of the house. What he gets up to is no longer my concern. My only regret is that Rose will grow up possibly knowing that her father is a drunkard and a rapist.'

'So sad, Amy.' Tom stopped walking and ushered his sister into the hermitage. 'Daisy and I would meet in here. It's so secluded, we could be alone. It was here that I gave her the turquoise dress she was wearing when she drowned. She still smelled of the honeysuckle she had placed in the dress box. She was clutching the flowers in her hand, just like Ophelia when I pulled her out.'

'Don't dwell, Tom. Move on. Tell me more about your wife. Grace, did you say?'

'Yes. I do love her, but in a different way. A mature way. A grown up way. My time in Canada and Alaska was a voyage of discovery in a sense.'

'Tell me more.'

'I have discovered who I really am since regaining my memory. The old Tom was wealthy, spendthrift, carefree, concerned about follies and local history and in love with a local girl. The new Tom is mature, a married man. A man who has learned the value of nature, of learning how to live on no money whatsoever. The Indians I lived with showed me how to live such a simple life. It was magical.' Tom paused, swallowed the emotion he was feeling and carried on; 'They hunted and trapped moose and buffalo and other animals, and then used every part of the beast in their everyday life. They lit huge fires and sat around them smoking the pipe in the evenings, telling tales and legends. They celebrate events with hundreds of relatives who build large camps and hunt together.'

'Will you go back, Tom? Do you want to go back?' Amy knew she needed to ask her brother this question, yet she was apprehensive. She was used to his company again.

'I have to return at some time, it's only fair that I find Grace and tell her of my decisions. I must tell Mater and Pater first, about Grace I mean. I will need to judge their reaction.'

Amy paused, looking around the moss covered walls of the hermitage before asking, 'Will you bring your wife here, to live with us?'

'A difficult question, Amy. Will she come back? Will she be accepted? If we have children, they will be of mixed race and they will be heirs to the Thorpe family estate and all that involves. The cultural difference will be huge. Grace may be shunned by society and the villagers. I wouldn't want her to be subjected to that pain and hurt.'

'What is Caleb going to do, do you know?'

'He feels responsible for me, in a funny sort of way. He is happy to go along with me, whatever I decide. He is rich, has no responsibilities until his father pushes him into returning to Vancouver and the family business. He has been an amazing friend to me as well as good company.'

'Papa likes him. I overheard him offering Caleb a job as gamekeeper, old Rex having become quite infirm with arthritis.'

'What did Caleb say?'

'He would consider it, but you were his priority. What a treasure he is.' Amy shivered and pulled her riding jacket closer to her body. 'It's turning chilly, Tom, I want to get back home to the fire and afternoon tea.'

'Amy, yes, but before we go, now that you know about Grace, will you support me when I talk to the parents?'

'Of course I will, brother dear. Now, come on, let's find the horses and get back.'

Lord Harry was angry. Angrier than he had been for a long while; not even the past events concerning Eddy's violence towards Daisy and her subsequent death had had such an effect on his emotions as what he just heard. Tom stood facing him in the dressing room where Hibbs was helping him into his dinner jacket. Following his ride and chat with Amy, Tom decided to take the bull by the horns and confront his father that evening.

'I can't believe it. Are you telling me the truth, son?' shouted Harry.

The butler gave a dignified cough; 'Shall I leave, your lordship?'

'No!' snapped Harry. 'Stay and listen to what this son of mine is telling me. Married... humph.' Harry turned his back on Tom; he needed time to control his emotions. He felt angry, yes. Not just because his son had married without them knowing about it, but to an Indian woman.

'Father, you have to understand. I completely lost my memory. I hadn't a clue who I was.' Tom was feeling angry himself, now. 'The Indians cared for me, brought me back to life. The bear attack was horrendous. Put yourself in my place. What would you have done?'

'That's beside the point,' Harry shouted coldly. He was beginning to feel out of his depth with the situation. Much as he loved Tom and was pleased to have him back, the implications of this marriage were huge. Feeling Hibbs standing behind him brushing his jacket with the clothes brush, he turned so swiftly, that poor Hibbs dropped the brush. 'Stop titivating, man.' It was so unusual for his master to act in this way that Hibbs' countenance changed; his face flushed a deep pink, and then ebbed away, leaving him pale and shaking.

'Perhaps you had better leave us, Mr Hibbs,' Tom said gently to his faithful servant. The butler appeared to have aged considerably in the past twelve months. The difficulties the family were going through were obviously affecting the servants, too. They were affecting the whole household. 'Please go down to the kitchen and tell Cook dinner will be delayed.'

'Very good, Master Tom,' he replied gloomily before softly closing the door behind him.

'Do you realise the implications of this, Tom?' Harry enquired impatiently. 'Ancestrally, the blood line will include a non-white line. I assume this woman is dark-skinned?'

'She is, Papa. She is beautiful and dignified. I love her very much.'

'I shall look into the legal implications of this marriage. Do you have any paperwork? A marriage certificate?'

'No. It was an Athabascan Indian ceremony during their annual clan meetings. It was part of their culture that weddings were conducted at that time. Father, they believe in the importance of community, they have responsibility to their peoples. They have taught me sharing and survival lessons that have been passed along since before memory. I can't just dismiss all of that.'

'Heathens! Well, I shall look into it all very carefully. I don't suppose they can even read and write?'

'They are very cultured. I just followed their native ways and customs. They don't use, or indeed, need, paperwork. I was honoured to take Grace as my wife.'

'Well, if the marriage is legal, we'll arrange an annulment. It can be sorted, after all, I am a magistrate, and I should be able to do something.'

'No, Father. No annulment. Whether I am legally married or not, I love my wife.'

'I don't know what your mother will say.'

'I expect she will be far more understanding and loving than you are when I tell her.' Tom enunciated each syllable with great care. He guessed his father would be upset, but he hadn't been prepared for such anger. 'I am going down to tell her straight away.'

Harry watched as his son strode confidently to the door, which he opened and passed through, leaving it open. Father followed son down the stairs to the drawing room and the women. His face set, Harry walked over to the chiffonier and selected a cigar from the ornate silver box that stood there. Then he settled himself down in his high-backed leather armchair and ignored them all.

'Shall you go back to Alaska, Tom?' enquired Matilda gently as the family were arranged around the fireplace in the drawing room. The mantelpiece held a variety of Christmas cards and invitations, dark green holly weighed down with red berries surrounded the large gilt mirror. Tom decided, wisely, and his father had agreed, to tell his mother the news after dinner. Hibbs was recovered from the earlier upset with his master and after he served the coffee he retired for the night. In the kitchen he explained all to Cook as they sat in the pantry drinking their cocoa. 'The family are falling apart, Cook. I'm looking forward to my retirement. Only yesterday I received a letter from my brother and his wife offering me a home in their cottage in Somerset. Wearne is a quiet hamlet; I could easily settle there and be happy.'

'Well, James, you must do what you feel is right. This 'ouse 'ain't the same, I know. They 'ardly touched their dinner tonight and I made a good sherry trifle.'

'Mr Caleb enjoyed his dinner tonight, Zena,' James said soothingly. Occasionally, like tonight, the two called each other by their Christian names. They would never do so in front of the servants.

'Lovely man, that Mr Caleb. Wonder what will 'appen?'

'Mr Tom may go back to Alaska. I can't imagine his lordship accepting a native in the house as his daughter-in-law.'

'Well, whatever 'appens, James, I shall support the family, they been real good to me.'

'Yes, Mama, I will return to Alaska,' Tom answered, sitting next to her on the sofa. He gently took hold of her hand, which was cold. 'Are you warm enough? It's quite chilly tonight.'

'Shall I fetch you a wrap, Lady Matilda?' enquired Caleb, who was standing at the drinks table, ready to pour brandies if necessary. He could see how upset everyone was. Tom was his dear friend, and he had his full support, but in the short time he lived in the house, he realised a fondness for everyone. Well, except Eddy, but then, he hardly saw anything of him, thankfully.

'No, but thank you, Caleb. I am fine. Just sad, I don't want to lose Tom again.' Matilda looked at the man who was now so much part of their lives. She was so grateful he cared for Tom. He was the first Canadian she had met, and was entranced by his manners and thoughtfulness.

'I must go back, Mama. It is only fair on Grace, that I go and explain the circumstances. She needs to know who I really am,' explained Tom. 'I won't go until next spring. It will be too difficult travelling during the winter, with the rough seas and heavy snow.'

'So we shall have you here for Christmas,' smiled Amy, sitting quietly sipping her coffee. 'What about you, Caleb? Will you stay here, or will you go?'

'I will decide after Christmas, if you will have me for a few months longer.'

'Of course you must stay,' soothed Matilda. 'We would love to share Christmas with you.'

'I look forward to experiencing an English Christmas, 'twill be a joy.'

'That's settled then,' agreed Amy. 'After all, it may be the last Christmas Tom spends with us.'

'Herrumph…' coughed Harry.

That night as he sat in his dressing gown next to the bed where Matilda sat propped up on her pillows, he asked: 'Where have I gone wrong, 'Tilda?'

'What do you mean by gone wrong, Harry dear?'

'Tom. How did such a pleasant, well-mannered young man turn into the angry man I spoke to this evening? He is so adamant that he will return to that native woman he supposedly married.'

'Harry, you were very angry yourself, no wonder Tom retaliated.'

'Our lives have been torn apart! What will people think? After all, as a magistrate I have a reputation to keep.'

'You really must calm yourself, dear. It will all settle down. Tom may change his mind and stay here,' sniffed Matilda, who was beginning to feel emotional. Harry shouting at her was unsettling.

'He must realise his responsibilities. We need him here. The family needs him, the estate needs him. The pottery is making a small profit; I'm pleased to say Eddy appears to be pulling his weight at last. Tom needs to be here!'

Amy and Caleb had decided to ride out to Studland early the next morning. The wind was bitterly cold, but the sky was a clear blue with a few fluffy clouds hanging high. As they reached the shore and cantered the horses through the swirling foam, their manes flowed wildly in the wind.

'Gee, this is so exhilarating,' shouted Caleb.

'Come on, we'll gallop to the heath. I'll show you the Agglestone.'

'The Aggle. What?'

'Follow me, it's not far.'

Having dismounted, Caleb stood looking at the stone in awe. The way the huge boulder was balanced upon small stones appeared to defeat gravity.

'Agglestone Rock is also known as the Devil's Anvil,' explained Amy. 'It weighs, if my memory serves me right, about four hundred tons.'

Caleb was intrigued. 'How on earth did it get here?' he asked, rubbing his hands down the sandstone.

'Legend has it that the devil threw the rock from the Needles on the Isle of Wight with the intention of hitting either Corfe Castle, Bindon Abbey or Salisbury Cathedral.'

'Wow, amazing.'

'Aggle is an old Dorset word meaning, wobble.'

'You sure know a lot of legends and history, Amy. It is a great place to live, this Dorset of yours.'

'It could be yours, too, Caleb, if you stay. I can introduce you to some very eligible young ladies. It's not been much fun since you arrived, won't you stay?' Amy crossed her ankles and leaned against the shelter of the stone, away from the wind as she spoke. Her pretty face was slightly marred by the dark circles under her eyes. The past weeks had been mingled with anger at Eddy, sadness for Daisy and the fact that Jane and Bert were moving away to Wimborne, where they accepted positions in a large house. But, on the bright side, there was her sweet little daughter, Rose. Tom was back, but she didn't think he would be in Thorpe for long.

'I will be going back to Vancouver, Amy. My family need me. I am so grateful for your family's hospitality. I will have a lot to tell my parents. You know, I have been away for almost two years. It really is time I returned.'

'We will miss you. You have been such a help to Tom, our gratitude to you will be difficult to express.' Amy let the tears she needed to shed flow down her cheeks. 'Do you think Tom is going back to Alaska, Caleb?' she sniffed.

'Yes, I think he will. If he decides to go, we can travel back together.'

Two days into the New Year, Harry summoned Tom into his study. Glancing around, Tom noticed the stags' heads and antlers newly hung on the walls. 'Did your new gamekeeper put them up, Papa?' enquired Tom. 'Are they the heads of the stags you and Caleb caught when you culled back in the autumn?

'They are indeed. Don't you think they look fine?'

'Marvellous, Father. Caleb tells me he's going home to Vancouver in the spring. His father needs him and his mother is unwell.'

'I offered him a home and job here, he is just the sort of man I need around the Park. He's confident and companionable, he's been extremely helpful and he gets on with everyone. Amy offered to introduce him to some eligible young ladies if he stays. He could make a good marriage.'

'Not like me, then,' murmured Tom, but he knew his father had heard him. Not only had his marriage disappointed his father, but Tom had been unable, due to his injuries, to be of much use to him. He started by working in the pottery at first, but clashes with Eddy proved to be too stressful. Although still drinking heavily, his brother-in-law had pulled himself together and the pottery was showing a healthy profit of late. Tom filled his time writing a journal, describing his adventures and was proving to be cathartic; also it helped Tom come to terms with the fact that he needed to make the biggest decision of his life. Should he stay in Alaska, or should he bring Grace back?

'I've asked you in here, to tell you my findings regarding this so-called marriage of yours,' declared Harry.

'What are they?' enquired Tom apprehensively.

'It has taken a while for me to ascertain the lawfulness of a marriage between you and that Grace woman.' Harry's research was extensive; it had taken a great deal of paperwork passing hands across the Atlantic. Once, he travelled to London to meet up with an old friend of his from school, who was an eminent lawyer in the Temple. Now he faced his son with his findings.

'Miscegenation is the name used to describe an inter-racial marriage. It appears there is no such law forbidding such an alliance in Alaska. It applies to some states in America, but not where you were.'

'Well, Papa, thank you for going to all that trouble, but it makes not the slightest bit of difference. As far as I am concerned, I am married to Grace, whether legally or not.' Tom stood up as straight as he could, considering his injuries. He had visited a consultant surgeon in London, who carefully examined him. His findings were that Tom was well cared for; the doctor could find no fault in the way the Indians used their treatments. In fact, he had admired their use of herbs and bark and skins. But, he explained to his patient, there was little he could do to improve Tom's condition. The skin on his face and neck would always be puckered, his arm would always remain bent, and his limp, he felt, would become more painful in cold, wet weather. All the diagnoses had been just as Tom had expected, he told Caleb on their journey home. The two of them decided to spend the week before the consultation enjoying a holiday in the capital. It enabled Caleb to sightsee; they went to see Buckingham Palace; visited the British Museum, The Science Museum and various art galleries. In the evenings they enjoyed the variety of theatres on offer and watched some of the latest productions, including *Lady Audley's Secret* and *In Town,* a musical comedy.

'If that is your opinion, Tom, then there is nothing more to be said. Your mother and sister will be heartbroken if you return to Alaska. A heathen woman will never fit into this family and village. Besides, we have a reputation to uphold. I can imagine what our friends will say when we bring an Indian woman to dinner. We will be the laughing stock of the county!' stated Harry haughtily.

'Will you accept Grace as your daughter-in-law if I return with her?' Tom felt he knew the answer to that question as he asked it.

'No!' replied his father emphatically.

'So be it, then,' declared Tom as he left the room.

CHAPTER TWENTY-NINE

The wind and pounding rain was carrying away chunks of soil. The relentless storm chewed away part of the muddy bank along the Yukon River. The woman standing on the edge of the bank moved slowly away as it crumbled; it was becoming too dangerous for her to stand there anymore. Although it was summer, the freezing rain drops bashed into her eyelids as she turned her head, knocking the fur-edged hood of her caribou skin parka away. Her silky black hair was neatly tied into a plait which hung down her back. On her feet she wore mutluks and her trousers were tailored from the lightest moose skin and embroidered with blue and green beads. Grace walked up the steep incline away from the now fast flowing river. The next paddle steamer wouldn't be coming around the bend of the river for at least three days. She knew off by heart the days on which she could listen out for the shrill hooting as the boat captain pulled the rope of the whistle, warning of their imminent arrival. The summer season started with warm weather and soft cool breezes, but the storm then raged for two days, ending the pleasant atmosphere. Upon reaching the top of the incline, Grace turned and looked back. The dark waters swirled over the boulders strewn along the opposite bank of the river. She finally, slowly and anxiously, made her way back to the camp. The peoples of her band were already started on packing up their belongings. In a few days they were to move to another camp; the fishing here was ended and they were going to be following the buffalo. When they reached the plains the buffalo roamed, young boys would dress in coyote and wolf skins as a disguise and force the cattle to stampede. Then, at full gallop, the animals would fall from the weight of the herd pressing behind them, breaking their legs and rendering them immobile. The cliff itself at about a thousand feet long, and at its highest point dropping ninety feet into the valley below, would be unseen by the herd, due to very poor eyesight. The bone deposits will be thirty-nine feet deep. After falling off the cliff, the carcasses are processed. The camp at the foot of the cliffs can provide the people with everything they need to process a buffalo carcass, including fresh water. The majority of the carcasses were used for a variety of purposes, from tools made from the bone, to the hide used to make dwellings and clothing. The importance of the site goes beyond just providing food and supplies. After a successful hunt, the wealth of food ensures the Athabascan bands enjoy leisure time and pursue artistic and spiritual interests, thereby increasing the cultural complexity of the society. Such an important event was not to be missed, but Grace was anxious not to miss Tom if he was coming back as he had promised.

'Was he not on the steamer?' enquired Winnie, as she stepped out of her tepee to meet her sister-in-law.

'No. Next boat will be three days now. If this storm eases.'

'Grey has promised me he won't move until the next steamer has called into Dawson.'

'I know my Bear will come, the spirits have told me so. But waiting is not good for me, it affects my milk, will turn it sour.' Saying this, Grace moved into the tent and drew close to the fire, removing her wet clothes as she did so. On the far side, the baby propped up in the papoose that was made of birch bark, spruce root and moose hide, gurgled as he looked at his mother. His dark hair shone in the firelight

221

as he waved his fists at her. He had just started to realise that he had a voice and often squealed, sometimes jumping at the sound he himself made, causing anyone watching him to laugh.

'Baby Yakez, how lovely to see you,' crooned his mother as she untied the strings of the papoose, picked him up and carried him to a roughly hewn chair. 'Are you hungry, little one?' Unbuttoning her shirt, she placed the baby to her swollen breast, where he hungrily and noisily drank from her large brown nipple. 'Oh, if only your daddy could see you, but he doesn't even know you exist.' Grace held back her tears, it wasn't easy being brave.

On Monday the second of July, 1900, Thomas Thorpe leant on the rail of the paddle steamer *Alaskan Princess* as she steamed around the wide bend of the Yukon River, a few miles from Dawson City. As the whistle blew he wondered, as he had so many times since arriving in Alaska, how he was to find Grace and her band. He decided he would hire a strong horse and set out for the wilderness and search, feeling certain he could remember important landmarks. Or perhaps he could hire an Indian tracker, there were bound to be some of those in Dawson; he would make enquiries at the North West Mounted Police fort. They were helpful when he last came here. Wherever the buffalo herded, the band would not be far away. He longed to find them and to be with his wife again. He remembered how his father had reacted to his leaving and the harsh words that passed between them. Once again, he told Tom his wife was not welcome. He remembered his mother's tears and his sister's entreaty to take care, the words she used almost the same as those she said the first time he left for Alaska. Before, he had left Daisy with promises that he would return and marry her. Now, he was sad that Daisy was dead, and he was returning this time to his Indian wife.

The journey had been uneventful, staying with Caleb and his family for three days, in Vancouver before continuing his journey, Mr and Mrs Howard overwhelming in their hospitality and it was sad parting from his dear friend. But, as Caleb quoted; 'onwards and upwards, friend.'

The morning sun shone brightly in a cloudless Canadian sky as Grace stood, yet again on the bank of the Yukon River, this time she carried Yakez in the carrier on her back. The baby's name meant 'heaven', and if only her man could be on that steamer, then, heaven it would be. The storms of the past few days passed over, turning the trees to an even brighter emerald green and emphasising the songs of the birds as they twittered amongst the leaves. Listening intently, she heard the whistle from the steamer and the noise of the paddles as they turned; it was the same sound she heard twice a week. Grey gave her time to go and see the steamer, but he warned her they would leave without her if she didn't return as soon as the steamer passed the dock. As the hull of the steamer came into sight, she saw a man standing at the bow rail. Was it Bear? Could it be Bear?

Tom couldn't believe his eyes. Standing on the bank of the river was the most beautiful Indian woman he had ever seen – Grace, his dear Grace, come to meet him. As the steamer made its slow way towards the wooden dock, the woman ran alongside, keeping pace, with her child bobbing up and down. The sound of Yakez Thomas Thorpe's laughter reached his father, as Tom clambered over the rails, jumped down and not waiting for the gangplank to be put down, ran to his beloved. Holding out her arms wide to embrace him as he ran towards her, Grace had one thought in her mind; 'heaven'.

INSPIRATION

Having been born and brought up in Dorset, I wanted to use descriptions of the beauty of the countryside in this, my first novel. Set in 1898, the story required me to research the way people lived and worked, rich and poor side by side. I checked archive material from various publications with regards to the farming ways and attitudes of the 'Gentry' and the workers.

Several years ago I was privileged to travel to Alaska with my husband. I was struck by the stunning scenery and a train trip to the Yukon set my imagination aflame. The research, again, was wonderful and some of stories I perused led to me forming characters, some cruel and some humorous.